SOMEONE
LIKE HER

SOMEONE LIKE HER

A K2 Team Novel

Sandra Owens

Published by Montlake Romance, Seattle

www.apub.com

Amazon, the Amazon logo, and Montlake Romance are trademarks of Amazon. com, Inc., or its affiliates.

ISBN-13: 9781477820902
ISBN-10: 1477820906

Cover design by Kerrie Robertson

Library of Congress Control Number: 2014913508

Printed in the United States of America

This book is dedicated to the man who has learned to tolerate burnt dinners and being ignored when I'm on deadline: my husband, Jim, who also happens to be my very own hero.

CHAPTER ONE

———— ❧ ————

The house appeared normal—the yard nicely maintained, no rusted cars up on blocks, no beer cans scattered on the grass. Maria Kincaid was prepared to drive away if anything seemed suspicious, but the pretty pink flowers in the window boxes calmed her unease. Her pulse raced as she tapped her fingers on the steering wheel with a mix of trepidation and excitement.

"Here goes nothing," she murmured as she exited her car, dropping the keys in the pocket of her slacks.

It was the end of April and already the afternoon temperature registered in the low nineties, a typical Florida spring day. Heat blasted off the sidewalk, and the silk blouse she'd chosen to wear was already sticking to her skin by the time she reached the door. The choice might have been a mistake, but this visit could turn out to be one of the most important of her life, and she'd wanted to make a good impression.

She put her finger on the doorbell but hesitated. Was this something she really wanted to do? If the man who lived here turned out to be the one, how would it change her life? What if she didn't like him? She was pretty happy with the way things were now, so why go and mess it all up?

Her purse—heavy because of the law book she'd forgotten to take out—slid off her shoulder, and she shifted it to her other side.

Well, she could stand there all day debating the wisdom of ringing the doorbell of a man she'd never met, but if she didn't do it, she'd never know. The decision made, she put her finger back on the bell just as the door flew open and a teenage girl barreled into her.

"Whoa." Maria grabbed the girl's shoulders, stopping her.

"Help me," she said, her eyes wild and unseeing as she tried to escape Maria's grasp. The girl's shirt was torn, and there was a purple bruise blooming on her face.

"What's going on here?" Maria squinted, trying to see past the girl, but the interior of the house was dark, not a sliver of light showing through the tightly closed blinds. Yet the hairs on her arms stood on end at the sense of being watched.

"He tried to . . . he was going to . . ." The teen burst into tears.

"Who?" Maria gently touched the swollen skin. "Did your father do this to you?" What in God's name had she walked into?

"He's not my dad. Please, miss, let me go."

"Who the hell are you?"

At the accented words, Maria looked up to see a large man outlined by the light shining in through the open door. The sun beat down on her, and a waterfall of sweat flowed down her back. Whether it was the stifling heat or a rush of fear that made her light-headed, she didn't know.

She did know danger when faced with it, though, and she pushed the teen behind her. "Run!" The girl didn't have to be told twice, taking off like a racehorse out of the starting gate.

Maria turned to do some running herself when the man's hand wrapped around her wrist and pulled her inside. Unless this stranger beat him to it, Logan was going to kill her on grounds of stupidity, and he would be entirely justified. She'd spent a large portion of her childhood fending off the unwanted advances of men, and she unleashed every dirty fighting trick her brother had taught her on the man trying to hold her down.

———— ✺ ————

Middle-of-the-night phone calls weren't unusual. Long accustomed to awakening at odd hours to all sorts of noises, Jake alertly reached for the receiver at the same time he eyed the clock. Had the operation gone wrong?

"Buchanan here."

"Jake?"

Maria's voice was the last one he expected. Just hearing it sent his heart into overdrive. He sat up, as if by doing so he could get closer to her. "What's wrong?"

She laughed. "Why do you immediately assume something's wrong?"

One hundred and ninety-three miles between them did nothing to conceal the brittle note of her laughter. "It's two in the morning for one thing. You should be sleeping. Don't you have an early class?"

Silence.

"Dammit, talk to me."

"I'm in trouble, Jake." Her voice cracked on his name.

For her, he would step in front of a bullet, but she wasn't his to protect. She was so far off-limits he might as well be wanting the moon.

He forced the words through his teeth that had to be said. "Then you should be calling your brother, not me."

"I . . . I can't talk to Logan right now. I just can't. Please, you have to come." The words were punctuated by a sob.

Jackson Kennedy Buchanan, in an attempt to be as honorable as his namesakes, opened his mouth to say no, not happening. "Are you home?" He pulled the phone from his ear and glared as if it were responsible for the decidedly inadvisable question. She'd probably had a fight with a boyfriend and needed a shoulder to cry on.

Maria Kincaid—top-of-her-class law student at Florida State University and weeks from graduating—didn't get in trouble. Maria Kincaid, the woman her brother had put off-limits by threat of death. The boss didn't want his sister anywhere near a man known as Romeo to his SEAL buddies.

"No, I'm at a motel. I can't go back to my apartment." She hiccupped.

Jake flipped on his bedside lamp, squinting when the light hit his eyes. He stood and walked to the window. "Why not?"

"Jake, honey, come back to bed."

The woman crooking her finger at him let the sheet fall down to her waist. Rose . . . no, Rosie, leaned over to the nightstand and picked up a condom, then waved it at him with a come-hither smile on her face.

He strode into the bathroom and closed the door. "Why can't you go home, Maria?"

"I'll explain when you get here."

Although he hadn't agreed, they both knew he would go to her. "I can't just take off without informing your brother."

"I know, but you have to promise you won't tell him you're coming here."

Did she have any idea the position she was putting him in? Of course she did, so whatever the problem, it wasn't good. He weighed the consequences of hiding this from Kincaid against an image of Maria alone and in trouble. The decision took less than a second.

"I promise." A heavy sigh followed his words. He might as well accept he'd be dead meat when the boss found out.

"I'm at the Bluebird Motel on Highway 27, south of I-10, room four." She hung up.

Jake was strong. He'd been a SEAL and was now second in command at K2 Special Services, a company his former commander, Logan Kincaid, had started. As K2 accepted black op assignments from the government, sometimes Jake felt like he was still in the military. Along with Kincaid and the others on their team, he still held to SEAL training methods. Before Maria's call, however, he hadn't known he was strong enough to crush a phone with his bare hand.

He let the pieces drop onto the bathroom floor, went to his closet, and pulled out the always-packed duffel bag. It would take a little over two hours to reach her if he broke all the speed laws—which he would.

After quickly dressing, he went to the bed and patted Rosie's bottom. "Time for you to go home, babe. Up and at 'em."

As soon as he crossed over the I-10 bridge leading out of Pensacola, Jake pulled his backup cell out of his pocket and made the dreaded call. "Yo, boss," he said when Kincaid picked up.

"Is there a problem with the mission?" Like him, Logan Kincaid answered his phone as alert as though it were high noon.

"No, everything's proceeding as planned in that respect." Delta Team was deep in Somalia; their objective was to rescue a tycoon and his wife hijacked by Somalian pirates when their sailboat had been blown off course in a storm.

Jake swallowed hard and prepared to lie to the man he respected above all others. "Thing is, boss, I need some personal time. Don't ask me to explain, because I can't. I'd tell you if I could, but it's not my story to tell. There's just something important I need to do . . . that I *have* to do. I know this is coming out of left field, and it's not

5

good timing. I've never asked anything like this before and wouldn't now if there was any other way. It's important, boss."

Shit, he was rambling. He never rambled. Shutting up was the best option.

A long pause. "Is it your mother?"

"No, Mom's fine. Just trust me on this, Logan."

"I always trust you, *Jake*, but you don't sound like yourself. I'm concerned."

You should be. He clamped his lips together. That he'd used Kincaid's first name—something he never did—was a mistake. Kincaid never called him by his first name, either. New ground there. "I'll call Turner to let him know I'll be gone for a few days. He's up to speed on the operation."

"At least tell me where you're going."

"I'll touch base later." Pretending he didn't hear the question, Jake clicked off. There was only one person in Tallahassee of interest to Kincaid. If Jake told him that was where he was headed, the boss would be hot on his tail.

No matter what the trouble turned out to be, Kincaid was going to be royally pissed when he found out Jake was the one Maria had called. And he would find out. Nothing stayed secret from the boss for long, and by now, his antennae were assuredly twitching.

What are you getting me into, Maria?

Thank God Jake agreed to come.

Maria pulled the sliver of glass out of her arm and pressed a square of gauze over the trickle of blood. How had she gotten into this mess?

She snorted. Wrong question. *Why* was more like it. Damn her and her curiosity. Why did she have to know everything?

Hadn't some long-dead poet once claimed ignorance was bliss? She should've listened.

Holding her arm under the faucet, she let cold water wash over it, and then patted it dry. After pouring peroxide over the wound, she dried it again before applying a Band-Aid. The bottle of Advil was next, and she shook out two—thought about whether it was enough—and added one more.

Maria rummaged through the bag of supplies she'd hurriedly grabbed at Wal-Mart and found the liquid foundation. The cut lip she couldn't do anything about, but maybe she could hide the bruise emerging on her face. One glance at it and Jake would want to kill someone.

The very reason she hadn't called Logan. At least Jake would only contemplate murder. Her brother would commit one. Not to mention the fact that he wouldn't understand why she'd gone searching for a father she'd never met. That one of the men in Lovey Dovey's stud book, Hernando Fortunada, lived near Tallahassee had seemed an omen and was impossible to resist investigating.

Three of her mother's johns during the year Maria had been conceived had Spanish names. Using her knack for digging up information, she had found current addresses for two of them: Hernando Fortunada and Miguel Garcia who was now living in San Diego. For Jauquine Cruz, she'd found a death certificate. She'd rather liked that name.

She prayed Fortunada wasn't her father because, if so, daddy was a rapist. At least that was the conclusion she'd come to after barely managing to escape from the man. Had he raped Lovey Dovey? Maria gave a snort at that ridiculous thought. Her mother had spread her legs for any man with five dollars in his pocket.

And who in her right mind legally changed her name to Lovey Dovey, anyway? Much less insisted her two children call her by the ridiculous name? Visions of grandeur had filled Lovey Dovey's head after watching a movie about the famous stripper, Gypsy Rose Lee. She'd pranced around for months—a feathery pink boa wrapped around her neck—telling anyone who would listen that she was going to be a bigger name than Gypsy Rose Lee.

"Hollywood's gonna come calling, just you wait and see," she'd often bragged to Logan and Maria.

"Like they're going to want a two-bit, drunk whore," her brother had once whispered.

Maria had been too young at the time to understand what her mother did for a living. All she knew was she didn't like the tequila bottle always in Lovey Dovey's hand because her mama turned mean when she drank from it.

Worse were the men Lovey Dovey brought home. Even as a young child, Maria didn't like the way they looked at her with a strange light in their eyes. It wasn't until she was older that she understood the only thing standing between her and her mother's johns was Logan.

Couldn't get worse, could it? A whore for a mother and a rapist for a father. Her hysterical laugh echoed off the bathroom walls, and she put her hands over her ears. She was seriously losing it. *Please hurry, Jake.*

The torn clothes had to go. She peeled them off and put on the jeans and long-sleeve T-shirt she'd bought. Thankfully, she had forgotten to take her credit card out of her pocket when she'd stopped for gas before going to Fortunada's house.

There had been an awkward moment at the store when she'd handed it to the cashier. The girl had eyed her torn, bloodstained blouse and bruised face, and Maria had been sure she was going to be asked for her driver's license. As Fortunada had her purse and wallet, that wouldn't have been possible to produce.

"I had a fight with my boyfriend. No problem, I dumped the jerk." She'd glanced around. "I'd really like to get out of here, though, before he comes looking for me." Turned out the girl could relate and had taken pity on her.

The foundation she'd bought covered most of the bruising but did nothing to hide the swelling. She grabbed the brush out of the plastic bag. After covering as much of her face as possible with her hair, she studied the results in the cracked mirror.

A mirthless chuckle escaped. She had the appearance of a furry animal—a raggedy black sheepdog maybe. Oh well, it'd have to do. After emptying the shopping bag, she pulled the price tag off the small tote and put the toiletries in it. Wadding up the clothes she'd removed, she stuffed them into the plastic bag and put it in the garbage can. Now that she had done her best to hide the evidence of her stupidity, all she had left to do was wait for Jake.

She turned to leave the not-too-clean bathroom, and her gaze fell on the discarded clothes. Could they be evidence the cops could use against Fortunada? Crap. As much as she never wanted to touch them again, she decided she should hold on to them.

She carried the tote and the plastic bag with the bloody clothes to the dresser and set them next to her car keys. Thank God she was in the habit of dropping those into her pocket. She surveyed the room. The Bluebird Motel was no five star, that was for sure—hell, it couldn't even claim two. Now what? If she had her law books, she could at least study for her exams while she waited. A check through all the drawers produced nothing to read, not even a Bible.

With the tips of her fingers, Maria lifted the once-white-but-now-yellowed bedspread. A large stain marred the left side of the sheet. Who knew what had been done on the thing? There were probably bedbugs just waiting to attack. She leaned down and peered at the corners of the mattress but didn't see any. Didn't mean they weren't there.

It would be another hour or more before Jake arrived. A nap would be nice, but she hesitated to get into the nasty bed. Yet, hadn't she grown up in a house that would make this room seem like the Ritz-Carlton?

"No offense, Ritz, just saying it like it is," she muttered.

She pulled off the cover and threw it on the floor. Deciding she didn't want anything slithering over her in the dark, she left the lamp on. Careful not to touch the stain, she crawled onto the right side of the mattress.

Bedbugs be damned, she was exhausted.

CHAPTER TWO

The man chased her, the heavy tread of his boots pounding the pavement, growing louder as he caught up with her. Maria tried to run faster, but her legs refused to cooperate. Oh God, he was right behind her. He reached for her and grabbed her hair.

She screamed and shot out of the bed, gasping for air. Frantically searching her surroundings, she saw nothing familiar.

Where the hell was she?

The pounding continued.

"Dammit, Maria. Open the fucking door."

Jake.

Thank God. She rushed to the door, tripping over the cover she'd thrown on the floor.

"Stop your banging, I'm coming." The noise mercifully ceased.

"Unlock the damn door," he said, much quieter.

Untangling herself from the offending spread, she stumbled toward the safety of his voice. The lock and chain were barely open before he pushed his way in and took her in his arms. Unable to resist Jake's strong, fierce hold on her, Maria pressed into his embrace and tried to catch her breath. Maybe she should've called her brother, but she was glad she'd called Jake. So very, very glad.

He rested his chin on the top of her head, and she felt his chest rise and fall as though he too craved air. "Christ, you scared the hell out of me, woman. I was about ready to kick the door down. Why were you screaming? Why are you hiding out in a motel room?"

Where to begin? Wriggling away, she stumbled back, although it was the last thing she wanted to do. If she could spend eternity in his arms—no questions needing answers—she would fall to her knees in gratitude. But he hadn't traveled two hundred miles to be put off.

The cover she'd removed from the bed rested on the floor between them. She stared at it, half expecting the thing to undulate like some kind of giant anaconda, proving the nightmare was real.

"What happened to you?" He brushed back her hair and gently touched the bruise. "Jesus, Maria, who did this? You better start explaining, or I'm going to call your brother. You should've called him in the first place. Talk."

His tone sounded so cold and forbidding when she'd thought he would show up and . . . what? Cuddle her? Carry her home with him—no explanations needed? *Stupid, stupid Maria. So naive.* She just never learned.

"Tell me what's going on, or I'm getting in my car and returning to my warm bed . . ." Something she couldn't decipher glimmered in his eyes as he paused, his gaze focusing on her. ". . . where a lady eagerly awaits me."

Maria didn't believe him. He wouldn't leave her like this. Not that she doubted there'd been a woman in his bed. There always was. She quashed the hurt, although why she cared was a mystery. Jake was what he was, and he hadn't earned the nickname Romeo from his teammates for no reason. All that really mattered was that he had come when she'd called, and she somehow knew he always would.

"Start talking." There wasn't a sliver of tolerance in his voice.

She glanced around the dingy room. There were no chairs to be seen, and she couldn't imagine them snuggling on the bed while she told him about her quest for *Daddy dearest*.

"Can we go somewhere else? This room gives me the creeps. Besides, I'm hungry." When stressed, food comforted her, and she really was starving. Her last meal had been lunch the day before.

Jake gestured at the tote and plastic bag on the dresser. "Is this it?"

She nodded.

He picked them up along with her keys, wrapped his hand around her elbow, and escorted her out the door. "Where's your car?"

"Sally's over there behind the dumpster."

"Why doesn't it surprise me you named your car?" His lips thinned as he took in how she'd tried to hide the Mustang behind the dumpster. "Just how deep have you stepped in it, Maria?"

"I don't know." At his raised brow, she admitted to what she feared. "Maybe up to my eyeballs, I just don't know."

His gaze swept across the parking lot. "I don't see anyone suspicious lurking about. We'll leave your car here for now, at least until I know what I'm dealing with." He prodded her toward his Challenger.

Maria glanced over her shoulder at her beloved Mustang and sent up a little prayer that no one would steal it.

Expecting a grilling as soon as the doors closed, she found Jake's silence unnerving as he drove away from the motel. Tension rolled off him in waves. The all-night diner he pulled up to was only a few streets over from the motel. How he knew it was there was anyone's guess. But then, he always seemed to know things others didn't. When she started to open her door, he put his hand on her arm.

"Wait." He stared into the rearview mirror for a minute. "Seems safe enough. Don't get out until I'm at your side."

Yes, safe. Jake would make certain of it. Maybe she should have tried to handle this herself, but at least she could admit she was out of her element. There were things she was good at, but creeping into dark basements the way women did in scary movies wasn't one of them. She didn't know how to investigate this on her own.

Maria dreaded having to explain why she had asked him to come. Poor little girl, looking for a daddy who'd obviously never tried to find her—although to give him credit, he probably didn't know she existed. With all her being, she hoped Fortunada wasn't him. Either way, he'd stolen her fantasy that all she had to do was announce herself and her father would welcome her with open arms, and most important, he'd be nothing like Lovey Dovey.

Positioning himself behind her, Jake followed Maria into the diner. The place was empty except for one man in a business suit at the counter. Jake led them to a table away from the window and sat facing the door. She slid into the booth across from him.

The waitress sauntered over, slapped a food-stained menu down, and poured two cups of coffee before turning her attention to Jake.

"Morning, honey, what can I get ya?"

He glanced at the woman's name tag. "Surprise me, Terri."

"If only. As for breakfast, big boy like you, you look like a steak and eggs kind of man."

"How 'bout that? We've only just met and already you know me so well." He flashed a grin that would have curled Maria's toes if he'd meant it for her.

A dreamy smile appeared on Terri's face.

Maria rolled her eyes. "I'd like a chili dog, loaded. Fries and a chocolate shake."

The waitress tore her gaze away from Jake. "For breakfast?" Before Maria could answer, Terri's eyes narrowed. "He do that to your face?"

Maria put her hand over the bruise. She shook her head. "No. No, it wasn't him. I was . . . I was in a car accident."

Terri's obvious relief that the handsome devil sitting in her diner wasn't a woman beater was almost funny. Or it would have been if Maria had been up to laughing. She didn't blame Terri for eyeing him like he was a piece of candy she wanted to devour. He was a handsome, hazel-eyed devil. The only thing marring his face was a shrap-metal scar along his right cheek near his ear. She'd always thought it gave him character, that without it he would be too perfect.

"I see your ordeal, whatever it is, hasn't affected your appetite," he said after Terri left.

"You know I eat junk food when I'm upset."

"And when you're happy, sad, and all the emotions in between."

True. Next to Logan and their foster mother, Mrs. Jankowski, he knew her better than anyone else. Not even her one boyfriend had understood her the way Jake did. There had been a time when she'd thought he liked her as more than a friend. But if he had, he hadn't acted on it. She'd had a suspicion—still did—that her brother had warned him away.

"Time to talk, Maria."

She supposed it was, but couldn't stop a sigh from escaping. "I found a book—"

"More coffee, honey?"

"Yes, please," Jake said.

Terri shoved a milk shake in front of Maria. While the waitress tried to make small talk with Jake, Maria busied herself removing the paper from the straw. Forgetting about her cut lip, she tried to suck the shake through the straw and winced.

Once they were alone again, Jake shrugged. "Sorry. I'm not trying to encourage her."

No, he wasn't. He just couldn't help being a chick magnet. "Didn't say you were."

He leaned back and closed his eyes for a moment. His head lowered and he leveled an intense gaze on her. "I have a feeling we're going to be interrupted all through breakfast. We'll put a hold on the conversation we need to have for now."

A reprieve. "Okay."

All too soon, he'd paid the bill and ushered her out to his car. Ten minutes later, he pulled into a mall parking lot and parked at the far edge, under the shade of a tree. After turning off the engine, he shifted to face her. "Spill."

No putting it off any longer. She touched her swollen face. "A man by the name of Hernando Fortunada did this, but I'm not sure what I interrupted. If I had to guess, I'd say he was about to rape a teenage girl."

Jake didn't trust himself to speak, and instead, focused his attention on the fingers clinching the steering wheel. His knuckles had turned white from the force of his grip. From the moment he'd seen the bruise on her face and the cut lip, he'd been on the edge of violence. He itched to get his hands on the bastard who'd dared to hurt her. And now, she was telling him she'd been a witness to an attempted rape and the man beat her up for stopping it?

That certainly explained her not wanting to call the boss. One glimpse of his sister's face and Kincaid would've gone on a rampage. And she thought she could hide this from her brother? Her only chance of that would be if she moved to another planet.

As calmly and tenderly as he could manage, he said, "How the hell did you get involved in something like this?"

She jerked back against the car door. Well hell, he might as well have slapped her. Around her, he just didn't act right. He scrubbed at his face. "Sorry, that came out wrong. Start from the beginning . . . please."

Her eyes filled with tears. God help him, but he wanted to pull her onto his lap and hold her, somehow take away the hurt. The first time he'd met her, he had actually stuttered when her brother introduced them. A first for Romeo.

She'd been nineteen, a college student—a girl, for Christ's sake. He didn't touch girls, liked his women grown up, something he reminded himself every time he saw her. No longer a girl, she was twenty-four and so stunning he had trouble breathing normally around her.

Long hair so black it almost shimmered ink-blue; dark brown, cat-shaped eyes—bedroom eyes—and full lips that begged to be kissed to forever and back. Instead, he took her hand, the most he would allow himself to touch. It was ice cold even though the early Florida morning was already warm. She gripped him as if he were her lifeline. He shouldn't like that so much.

In an effort to put a wall between them, he'd purposely told her there had been a woman in his bed. Although true, he wasn't sure there was a barrier he could erect to keep Maria out, simply because he didn't want to.

"Well? I'm waiting." The only thing he really wanted to know was where to find Hernando Fortunada.

She darted a glance at him before focusing on their joined hands. "You want to hear it from the beginning? That would be the day I was conceived by an unknown man, but I'll skip ahead. After

Lovey Dovey died, Mrs. Jankowski helped me pack up her stuff. A few things worth salvaging we gave to Goodwill, but most of it we threw away. But there was one box she said I should keep and go through some day. I finally did that a few months ago." She paused and turned her face to the window.

He stayed quiet, giving her time to compose herself. Every problem Maria and her brother faced seemed to be tangled up somehow with their mother. Jake had never met the woman, she'd died before he and Kincaid had left the SEALs.

Maria had once told him Mrs. Jankowski was the only reason her brother wasn't in prison and she wasn't a whore like Lovey Dovey. It was impossible to comprehend a woman like their biological mother. Jake himself couldn't wish for a better mom, one who was everything a mother should be.

"I'm guessing you found something that led you to this point?"

Maria nodded. "I found her stud book."

Huh? "You'd better explain that."

"This is so embarrassing." Her head fell back on the seat and she closed her eyes. "I found a book she'd kept the year I would have been conceived. Across the front . . . you know those little gold stick-on letters you can buy?"

"Yeah, I know what you mean."

"On the front in gold it said *Stud Book*. She kept a record of the names of the men she'd been with, and she rated them with stars. Their looks, their proficiency in bed, and the . . . the size of their penis. Stars . . . they got stars with five being the best."

Good God Almighty. Jake tried to imagine his mom doing something like that and almost laughed at the absurdity of it. Just managing to smother his ill-advised humor, he tried to think of what to say. This was far from amusing to Maria. Was "I'm sorry" appropriate? Maybe, "interesting mother you had"?

"I don't know what to say." That seemed safe enough.

"Yeah, not Mommy of the Year material, was she?" Maria slipped her hand out of his and wrapped her arms around her waist.

That was when he noticed the red stain on her sleeve. "Dammit, Maria." He grabbed her hand again and pushed the sleeve of the T-shirt up her arm. Dried blood crusted the edges of a bandage just above her elbow.

Brown, sad eyes peered hopelessly up at him. "I'm sorry," she whispered.

He kissed her.

CHAPTER THREE

She kissed him back.

Maria's chilled hand slipped around the back of his neck, bringing Jake to his senses, and he pushed her away. What had made him forget she was off-limits? When he thought about it later—and he thought about it a lot—he couldn't pinpoint the moment he forgot she was off-limits.

Was it the blood? The sad eyes? The small voice? He was almost willing to chance ruining his friendship with Kincaid, but she was hurting, and he was taking advantage of her.

He attempted to make a joke of his misstep. "Sorry. I was aiming for your arm but missed the mark. You know, kiss it and make it better."

"Whatever. It was just a stupid kiss. Nothing to get all weird about."

Her eyes shuttered, became blank. The boss could do that, too, Jake thought. Must be something they learned growing up in their house of horrors.

"Wait here," he said as he exited the car.

At the back of the Challenger, he grabbed the first aid kit from the trunk. His lips tingled, and he put a finger on them. It had been wrong to kiss her, and even though he should regret it, he didn't.

Her warm, soft mouth had been everything—and more—that he'd imagined for years now.

The trick would be not kissing her again. Because he desperately wanted to, especially now that he knew how incredibly good she tasted. Spicy and sweet—a little like a chili dog and a milk shake. He grinned as he closed the trunk.

Once he got her Band-Aid changed, he tossed the kit onto the back seat. "So, you found your mother's book. How did that get you to what happened last night?"

"Will you hold my hand again?"

Touching her was as dangerous as stepping his way through a minefield, but apparently he thrived on danger because he laced his fingers through hers. Oh yeah, he was in serious trouble.

She blew out a weary-sounding breath. "As soon as I realized what the book was, I stuffed it away in a drawer. But I couldn't stop thinking about it. What if my father's name was in there?"

"Considering your mother's . . . um, activities, I would think there could be a lot of possibilities," he said, hoping she wouldn't take offense.

That earned him a little snort. "Now there's an understatement if I've ever heard one. I hadn't given much thought to who my father might be before. I mean, there were so many possibilities, why bother? But then I had this book that might have his name in it. It was like being a kid and dying to open a present under the Christmas tree, one you can't stop shaking and poking at." She gave a mirthless laugh. "Not that I know what that's like either."

The woman was breaking his heart. "So you got the book back out?"

"I tried to ignore it. I even threw it in the garbage when I couldn't stop thinking about it. That same night, I got out of bed and dug it back out. I don't know if I can make you understand, but the only parent I have to define myself by is my mother, and she never loved me. Not that she loved Logan either, but at least she sometimes seemed to like him. I didn't even get that from her."

Soulful eyes peered up at him. "She might be dead, but I can still hear her. 'You're so stupid, Maria.' I heard that one over and over. 'I wish you'd never been born, Maria.' That one was her favorite."

Jesus. The way her voice had changed just then—sounding exactly like a vindictive, chain-smoking bitch—planted a clear picture in his mind of how it must have been for her as a little girl. He'd give a thousand dollars to unsee it. It was one thing to be aware of how Maria and the boss had grown up, but he'd never considered the hurt that lived in her.

"Your mother was the stupid one, Maria. You must know that."

"Must I?" She shrugged as if having a mother who hated her was of no importance. "So, to answer your question—"

"Question?" If he'd asked a question, he couldn't remember it. He couldn't get past the hurt little girl she'd once been . . . still was.

"Pay attention, Jake. I don't talk about my mother to just anyone."

Whoa. He didn't want to be special to her. Couldn't be even if he wanted. Not only had her brother threatened to do him bodily harm if he so much as looked at her wrong—*wrong* meaning with lust in his eyes—but he was Romeo. He didn't do permanent, and she was as special as they came. Maria deserved better than he could ever give her.

He stared out at the empty parking lot, unable to meet her eyes. "Go on. You were telling me about your mother's book."

A squirrel raced down the tree nearest them, followed seconds later by another one. A spring mating dance ensued between the two before they disappeared into the branches above him. Were they getting it on even as he sat in a now-stifling car with the one woman he could never have, no matter how much he wanted her? He turned on the car and rolled down both their windows.

"I just kept wondering, you know. If I could find my father, would he love me? Maybe not right away. I don't expect that, but later, if he had a chance to get to know me. So, I got the book out of the garbage and searched for men with Spanish names. I found three. Are you curious how many stars they got?"

Not even. He switched off the ignition. "Only if it's relevant to what happened." Did she realize she was seeking validation that she was loveable from a man she'd never met? What if she did find her father and he wanted nothing to do with her? What would that do to her?

"It's not, and I'm glad you don't want to know. Leave it to Lovey Dovey to keep records like that. I felt dirty just reading it. Anyway, you know if you put a computer in front of me, I can find anything."

That was an understatement. She'd been instrumental in hacking past firewalls and exposing the dummy companies behind the cult that had kidnapped her brother's wife. Like a bloodhound on the scent, Maria had found their compound location in the Ozarks, and sniffed out the leader's sordid background. Without her, the outcome might have been much different.

Considering it was one of her mother's johns she was searching for, it might be better if she wasn't so computer savvy. "So, you went to work tracking down father possibilities?"

"You know me so well, Jake. I love that about you."

He would have taken her words as a joke if her eyes hadn't turned wary. There had been a sort of longing in her tone—a wistfulness. She couldn't possibly mean she loved him. He'd long ago admitted that there was chemistry between them. The attraction he'd felt for her had turned to full-blown lust on the night of her twenty-first birthday party.

Kincaid had walked into the restaurant where they were meeting to celebrate, his wife on one arm, Maria on the other. The air had swished out of Jake's lungs. Maria had been away at school, and he had avoided her whenever she came home on breaks, and hadn't seen her in almost a year. The black-haired beauty on the arm of her brother hadn't been the girl he remembered. Somehow, in that time, she'd transformed into a woman, and a sexy-as-hell one at that.

He glanced at their hands where they rested on the console, hers browner than his, and rubbed his thumb over her skin. "Tell me the rest."

"Okay. There were three possibilities, and I found addresses for two of them. Turned out one, Hernando Fortunada, lived just north of here in Ridgeville. I didn't see any reason not to pay him a visit, and maybe I'd find a father who, when he knew I existed, would be proud to call me his daughter. I had this picture in my mind, you know. If he was my father, he would be glad to see me. If not, no harm done." She shuddered. "I couldn't have been more wrong."

It was only through sheer will that he didn't yell at her for going to a strange man's house alone. He pressed his lips together. If he opened his mouth, whatever words came out would no doubt cause her to close up like a damn clam.

"Fortunada, who I pray to God is not my father, did this when I interrupted whatever was going on with the girl. Problem is, he now knows who I am and where I live."

It hurt to breathe. She'd been in the grasp of a possible rapist, one who'd had his hands on her with the intention of shutting her up. Jake had never been so glad of his skills. He could protect her. His decision—instant and final—to not let her out of his sight until this Fortunada bastard was in jail or dead would have repercussions. Let Kincaid do his worst. Even if it meant getting fired for not delivering Maria into the safety of her brother's arms, Jake didn't care.

"I'm curious. Did you think you would take one look at him and say, yes, that's my daddy?"

She flinched. "You don't have to be sarcastic, but no, I didn't think that. I kinda hoped he would look like me, but I thought he wouldn't object to a DNA test once I explained who I was. Then once he knew I was his daughter, he would maybe love me."

Maybe love her? She asked for too little. He could no longer ignore how much she was hurting, not only from the wounds on her body, but deep in her soul. He wrapped his hand around that gloriously silky hair and gently tugged her head to his shoulder.

"I have to find him, Jake. If Fortunada's my father, then both my parents are trash and it's better to know that now so I can get on with my life. I just need to know," she whispered, turning her face into his shirt.

And he just wanted to kill someone. Her mother, her father. Didn't matter. "I need to know what we're up against, Chiquita Banana. How does he know who you are?" The kiss he planted on her forehead was pure impulse. She slipped her hand under his shirt, and his skin rippled, hot and wanting under her fingers. Any other woman, and he would have had her under him in the blink of an eye.

This one, though, wasn't for him. Calling on every damn control technique he'd learned since making it through each torturous day of SEAL training, he managed to keep his hands—along with other parts of his body—from claiming her.

Maria pressed her nose against Jake's shirt and breathed him in. It had been a long time since he'd called her by the pet name. Not since her twenty-first birthday had he called her Chiquita Banana, and she'd missed it. Missed him.

Their kiss had been tender and special. At least to her. She assumed to him, probably all in a day's work. She felt his stomach muscles tense under her fingers, and he pulled her hand away, gently pushing her back into her seat.

"I know this is hard, but you have to finish telling me."

She'd much rather he kiss her again.

It was hard because talking about it meant reliving it, a reminder of her stupidity. When she slipped her hand back into his, he let her. "I had my finger on the doorbell when the girl ran out of the house and crashed into me. I pushed her away and told her to run. When I turned to haul ass myself, he grabbed me and pulled me inside."

"Go on."

He spoke in his SEAL voice, the one she heard the guys use when they got serious about something. Likely, he would yell at her again when he heard the rest.

"We fought. He hit me in the face with his fist, so I kneed him in his balls." She could still see the fisted hand coming at her and had known she only had a slim chance of getting away. "Then I hit him on the head with my purse. It was the creep's bad luck that I forgot to take out one of my textbooks, and it dazed him. I ran out the door, jumped in my car and sped away. End of story."

"End of story?" Jake echoed, still in his take-no-shit SEAL voice. "Somehow, I doubt that."

"Well, there's one other little thing. The second time I hit him with my purse, he grabbed it and wouldn't let go. I had a choice of wrestling him for it or running. I ran. Now he has my wallet, so he knows my name and address."

With his free hand, Jake pinched the bridge of his nose. "Shit."

That about summed it up. "I'm sorry. I never dreamed something like this would happen."

"How did you get the cut on your arm?"

"There was a water glass on the coffee table, and when we were fighting it got broken. At one point he had me down on the floor and my arm got cut. That's when I kneed him."

Jake's eyes grew hard and as cold as the glaciers in Antarctica. He probably didn't know who he was more angry with, her or her attacker. Not that she blamed him. And he really wasn't going to like what she was going to say next.

"After we go to the police, I want to find the girl."

"Excuse me?"

If she hadn't already been used to Logan's intense scowls, she might have confessed her worst sins then and there. Was that look something they learned in SEAL school?

Jake gave her his fiercest glare, not sure which part of her statement to address first. Innocent brown eyes stared back at him—too innocent.

She arched a brow. "What? Why are you looking at me like that?"

The staccato sound of his fingers as they rapidly tapped on the steering wheel drew his attention. He stilled them and gave a shake of his head. "I'm almost afraid to know what's going through your mind right now when you say you want to find the girl, but we'll get to that in a minute. Are you telling me you haven't called the police?"

"No, I was waiting for you."

That didn't make sense. "I don't understand. You should've called them the minute you got a chance." Something flickered in her eyes. What was he missing? "Maria?"

"I can't breathe in here." She opened her door and got out.

At the front of his car, she leaned back against the grille. Her body folded in on itself—shoulders bent over—and a shudder passed through her.

"Why didn't you call the cops?" he asked, coming to stand in front of her.

Her answer was directed at the hands she held tightly clasped in front of her. "Because I'm afraid of them."

More senseless words. He waited for her to explain, but she remained silent. Everything he knew about her and the boss passed through his mind. If she was afraid of the police, it had to go back to their mother. Didn't everything?

"What did Lovey Dovey do?" Her eyes shot up to his. He'd hit his target. It didn't please him.

"I can't tell you," she whispered.

"You can and you will."

"Let it go, Jake."

He'd be damned if he would. "Why are you afraid of the police? I can be as stubborn as you, so you might as well tell me or we'll be here forever." It was hard to know if her sigh was one of surrender or annoyance.

"If I tell you, you can't tell Logan. If you do, he'll hunt the man down and kill him, then I'll be visiting my brother in prison." She half smiled. "And then Dani will hate me for it."

He matched her half smile with a full one. "I would never do anything to make Dani unhappy. Your secret's safe with me." He was digging his own grave by keeping Maria's confidences, but she seemed satisfied by his answer. She lifted her chin, and her eyes were as dark as the black clouds of a thunderstorm.

"When I was fifteen, Lovey Dovey was arrested for prostitution. Again." Her chuckle grated in his ears. "The cop who busted her turned out to be not such an honorable guy. She got him to agree to a trade. Her favors for him looking the other way."

Maria lowered her head again as though she could no longer meet Jake's eyes. "My mistake was to stop by at the wrong time. I was living with Mrs. Jankowski by then, but whenever Logan sent me money, I'd buy a few bags of groceries for my mother." She shrugged. "Any money Lovey Dovey got her hands on went to booze and cigarettes."

Jake didn't like where this seemed to be headed, but the door had been opened and as much as he wanted to slam it closed, she needed to tell her secret. "Go on."

Her fingers were laced together, and her thumbs spun furiously around each other. "He took one look at me and changed his mind about what would get Lovey Dovey out of trouble. Thankfully, Logan had taught me how to fight off a man."

"So, he didn't—"

"No, but not from lack of trying. My loving mother sat in a corner and watched. I think she might've even been turned on by it." She leaned her body forward and stared down at her feet. "So, that's why I don't like cops. I know most of them are good men, I really do, but what if there's another one like him?"

Jake came close to putting a dent in his hood with his fist. Well, he'd asked. He suddenly hated her mother with a fierceness he'd never felt before in his life for anyone.

"Maria." He gathered her into his arms and let his touch speak the words he couldn't find. She curled into him and he felt like he was holding a fragile kitten, but even that was deceiving. She'd fooled them all, even her brother. She'd put on a front, a magic act that had them believing she was untouched by the horrors of being Lovey Dovey's daughter. But the scars were there if one only looked deep enough.

"You're not going to tell Logan, are you?" she asked, her voice muffled by the press of his shoulder against her mouth.

He wanted to, wanted to shout his rage at her mother, the cop, even the boss. "Did you ever tell anyone?"

She shook her head. "Who was there to tell? The police?"

"Your brother would have been a good start, but I get why you think you couldn't. What's the cop's name?"

"Why, so you can kill him?"

"I won't, I'll just beat him to within an inch of his life." And then maybe kill him.

"I don't know his name. Never did, never wanted to."

That was just too damn bad. He walked to the passenger side and opened the door. "Let's go see the police. After that, we'll talk about why you want to find the girl."

CHAPTER FOUR

———— ❦ ————

Jake refused to let Detective Nolan take Maria into an interrogation room without him. He couldn't complain that Nolan was mistreating her. The man had been nothing but gentle with her. After the detective took photos of her face and arm, he had insisted on talking to Maria alone. She'd grabbed Jake's hand, panic in her eyes, and the cop had given Jake a look that said *go away*. Jake returned a look that said *not happening*.

So there he was, sitting in a room with army-gray paint peeling off the walls, listening to Maria once again explain how she'd been beaten up, and doing his best not to put a hole in the table with his fist. He'd almost done that when the detective had removed the clothes from the plastic bag and Maria's face had drained of color on seeing them.

"I didn't remember there being that much blood," she murmured.

When she finished and Nolan ran out of questions, Jake pulled out a business card, sliding it across the table. "It would be best if you found this bastard before I do. Keep me updated."

"Mr. Buchanan, I strongly advise you to return home and let the police do their job. Do not try to do it for us. You'll only end up getting hurt."

Jake couldn't help his snort. He snatched the card back from Nolan's hand and wrote a number on the back, then returned it. "I would suggest you note the name K2 Special Services on the front, then call the number on the back and ask who we are. Once you do, you'll understand why I respectfully decline your advice."

Nolan started to admonish Maria for not calling the police right away. Jake stood and cut him off. "If you need to reach us, my cell number's on the front of my card."

As they walked down the hallway, Jake called Jamie Turner, swore him to secrecy, and promised to fill him in later. But for now, he asked him to answer Detective Nolan's questions about K2 if he should call.

"Do you think the detective will be able to find the girl?" Maria asked as they exited the station.

"Maybe, given enough time. If he can get a search warrant, he might get lucky and find her name or a clue when they search Fortunada's house." Jake put his hand on her back and steered her toward his car.

"What do you mean if he can get a search warrant?" she asked as he pulled away from the station.

"And here I thought you were a student of the law. Unless they can find the girl, it's your word against his. They'll probably bring him in for questioning first. That is, if he's stupid enough to hang around. Did you mark his face, put scratches on his arms? That'll help."

"I don't know. I didn't stay long enough to check, but I'm sure I did. I need to go to my apartment."

Jake glanced at her. "Since he knows where you live, you do know you can't stay there."

"I have no desire to until I know he's behind bars. I need clothes and stuff, and we have to get Mouse. Then we have to go get Sally."

"Seriously, you have a mouse?"

She laughed. "No, a cat named Mouse."

What the hell was he supposed to do with her and a cat? But to hear her laugh was music to his ears. She'd been so sad since he'd arrived that it was killing him. He wanted to see the sparkle return to her eyes, see her happy again.

"The best thing you can do is get your cat and come back to Pensacola with me until they find this bastard."

"No, I can't. I have final exams that I can't miss."

It was worth a try. "Which way to your apartment?" As he followed her directions, he formed a plan in his mind. He also made a mental list of the places he could apply for a job when Kincaid fired him.

When they entered the complex, Jake made a slow lap around the building, but he didn't see anyone lurking about or sitting in a car watching her apartment.

"Mouse probably thinks I've abandoned him," she said when Jake parked in her space.

"Wait until I come around to your side before you get out." Not taking any chances, he slipped his gun out of the ankle holster. The complex seemed deserted, most of the residents—students— now in their classes, where Maria should have been safely sitting.

"How are you going to get in?" he asked.

"What do you mean?"

"Weren't your keys in your purse?"

She grinned and pulled them out of her pocket. "I never keep them in my purse. If it ever got snatched, at least I could get home in my car."

"Smart girl."

The grin faded. "Sometimes."

He felt like an ass for reminding her of how stupid she'd been. Had she really been all that foolish, though? She'd gone to the man's house in broad daylight, but who would have expected such an outcome? If nothing else, she was smart enough not to repeat her mistakes.

At the door to her apartment, Jake grabbed her arm and pushed himself in front of her. "Are you sure you closed it tight and locked it when you left?"

She tried to peek around his arm. "Positive, why?"

"It's not closed all the way, and there are scratches on the lock. Pick marks to be exact." Behind him, she grasped his waist, releasing a shuddering breath.

"Mouse," she whispered.

The word confused him for a second, but then he remembered the cat. Jake considered telling her to wait there, but then she'd be out of his sight when he searched her rooms. "Stay right behind me. In fact, put your hand on my belt so I know you're there. Don't talk, don't do anything but what I tell you."

When he felt her fingers grasp his belt, he pushed the door open and lifted his gun, resting the grip on the heel of his left palm. He stepped into the devastation of Maria's living room.

"Oh, God," she gasped.

He had shit for brains, should've predicted this, should've installed her someplace safe and come to her apartment alone. "Don't let go," he reminded her and walked into the kitchen. With his side pressed up against the wall and her behind him, he reached over and turned the knob of a door, pulling it open. A pantry, seemingly the only untouched space in her apartment. Strewn all over the kitchen were knives, forks, spoons, and dishes, many broken. This guy had been beyond pissed. Thank God Maria hadn't been home when Fortunada came calling.

"We have to find Mouse," she said, her voice trembling.

If the asshole had found her cat, Jake didn't want Maria to see the result. But he wasn't willing to leave her behind. He grunted

34

and set off down the hallway. Her bedroom door was ajar and the destruction there was the worst. Her bed had been sliced open, her dresser drawers upended, clothing ripped to shreds. She made a low keening sound, one that Jake feared he would hear in his nightmares. At least there was no mutilated cat.

"Mouse, here kitty, kitty. Come to mommy," she softly sang.

So fast that Jake almost shot it before he registered what was coming at them, a gray-and-white ball of fur flew out of the closet and straight at Maria. The drawn out *meooows* and *maaahhhs* were accompanied by hisses that Jake took to be a scolding from cat to woman. He didn't really blame the cat. The poor creature must have been scared out of at least three lives when the Devil decided to pay a call. Maria let go of Jake's belt to wrap her arms around her cat.

"Oh, sweetie, I'm so sorry. I should've come back and got you."

Did he really just hear her say that? He turned to tell her what he thought about her returning alone, knowing Fortunada had her address. Her face was buried in the cat's neck and the damn thing rested its paw on Maria's cheek, his green feline eyes locked lovingly on her as he chatted away. The reprimand died on Jake's lips.

"Stay here while I check the bathroom," he said and left them to their reunion. He made a full sweep of the one-bedroom apartment, and as he took in the destruction of all that she owned, his rage grew. This was a warning from Fortunada to Maria. Jake longed for just ten minutes with the man, no guns or knives, just bare fists.

He took out his cell and called Detective Nolan. When he finished reporting the break-in, he returned to the bedroom. Maria sat on the floor, her cat still cuddled in her arms.

Her gaze swept the room, then she looked up at him. "I can't live here, not even when this is over."

"No, I don't suppose you can," he said, sitting on the floor next to her. Without warning, Maria pressed against him and sobbed.

Jake tried hard not to notice the way her breasts bounced over his chest as she cried. It didn't work. He noticed. He was a very bad man.

Not good with crying women, never knowing what to say, he just held her until she quieted. "Better?" he asked.

"No."

"Yeah, stupid question. Detective Nolan's on the way. Why don't you see if you can scrounge up some clothes and whatever else you might need. As soon as we deal with the police, we'll get the hell out of here."

"The sooner, the better," she said and dumped the cat in his arms.

Jake entered into a staring contest with the creature while Maria dug through the scattered clothing, salvaging what she could. The cat's green eyes narrowed to slits as if he knew just where Jake's mind had been a few moments before.

"Good God, what's wrong with him?" Jake asked.

Maria glanced over her shoulder at Mouse, scrunched up in a corner of his carrier and yowling his displeasure at being inside a car. "He thinks he's going to the vet."

Jake glanced at her, a puzzled look on his face. "Why would he think that?"

"Because the only times he's in a car, that's where the car goes."

"Well tell him to stop."

"Mouse, stop."

Her cat increased the volume of his protest, and Jake gave her an eye roll. Maria lifted a hand to her lips to hide her smile, the first since she'd stepped into a living nightmare. How she would manage to deal with everything without Jake, she couldn't imagine. Along with all the other reasons she hadn't wanted to call her brother, his wife, Dani, was due to deliver their son any day now. Logan wouldn't have been at all happy to leave Dani's side.

"Do you know where we're going? We need to get Sally," Maria said.

"Yes, and we'll pick up your precious car on the way. That damn possessed cat's riding with you."

They were both almost yelling, trying to talk over Mouse's wails. "Cut him some slack, he's had a bad day what with the break-in and the car ride."

"No worse than mine and I'm not shrieking like one of the Devil's own minions."

Jake was starting to sound testy, like his patience was nearing its end. Well, she couldn't really blame him. He'd been dragged out of his bed—one where he claimed he had a woman—dealt with the stupidity of his boss's sister, and then sat with her while she told her story to the police, held her while she cried over her destroyed apartment, then dealt with the police again, and now had a crazed cat on his hands. Oh, and he'd lied to Logan because of her and that one probably bothered him more than even the cat.

"I'm sorry," she said.

The frown on his face dissolved, and he shook his head. "No, it's not you, it's me. I can't stop thinking about your breasts and it's pissing me off." His eyes did a rapid blinking thing. "Hell. Tell me I didn't just say that."

Maria tried to stop her grin, but failing, turned to stare out the window so he wouldn't see it. He was thinking about her breasts? Little shivers of pleasure danced their way from her heart to her toes.

"So, if you're not going to assure me that my mouth isn't saying things it shouldn't, then please accept my apology."

She really wished he wouldn't apologize as she liked him thinking about her, breasts or otherwise. "Whatever," she said, annoyed now.

"You know, I hate that word."

She glanced at him. His lips were pressed together, and he stared straight ahead. Just to mess with him, she said it again. "Whatever." Mouse followed up her response with an ear-piercing yowl.

"Jesus, I've died and gone straight to hell," he muttered.

"And your punishment is a pissy woman and her evil cat?"

His lips twitched, and his eyes crinkled at the corners. "Don't forget beautiful. A beautiful, *off-limits* pissy woman and her devil cat."

She could live with that. The *he thought her beautiful* part, anyway, but she was going to have to do something about the *off-limits* part of the equation, and she knew exactly where that one came from. Her brother was going to get a piece of her mind for putting his nose in her love life. When she got up the nerve to face him, that is.

They turned into the Bluebird Motel's parking lot, and there was her Mustang, just where she'd left it. Maria breathed a sigh of relief. No one had messed with Sally.

"Follow me," Jake said once they got her and Mouse moved to Sally. He'd even buckled her in as if she wasn't capable of doing it herself. His fussing over her was kind of cute, actually. She started to ask him where they were going, but he was already walking back to the Challenger.

About three miles down the road, he turned into a fast-food chicken place, rolled down his window, and pointed at a parking place before getting in line for the drive-thru. Maria backed her car into the slot to wait for him. She glanced at her watch. No wonder she was hungry; it was going on three.

After he paid and was given three paper sacks, he pulled out and motioned for her to follow him again. Mouse had quieted down when she'd turned off the car, but as soon as she started it, he let her know his opinion in no uncertain terms.

"I'm sorry, sweetie," she told him. "He stopped for food, so I'm sure we're almost there, and I promise we're not going to the vet." Mouse apparently didn't believe her.

Jake headed back in the direction of her apartment but then turned left a few blocks before it. They'd travelled about three miles when her phone rang. It was so unexpected that she shrieked and Mouse, obviously believing all the noise signified the end of the world, went into hyper-super-duper-I-can-be-louder-than-you mode.

Maria grabbed the cell off the passenger seat and looked at the ID. Jake. "What?"

"What the hell's going on? Why are you yelling and why does your cat sound like he's dying?"

She considered tossing the phone out the window. "I'm yelling because I feel like it, and my cat thinks he *is* dying. What do you want?"

"I wasn't sure if you still had your phone or if it was in your purse."

Couldn't he have waited until they got to wherever they were going to ask her that? "I left it on the seat of my car when . . ." she trailed off, not wanting to talk about going to Fortunada's house.

"Okay," he said, his voice turning softer, kinder. "I'm going to pull over in a few minutes, and I want you to park in front of me. We won't be stopped for long. I just want to make sure no one's following us."

"Where're we going, Jake?"

"Almost there," he said and hung up.

Why the mystery? And how did he know about this place? They were driving down a residential, tree-lined street, not a hotel or motel in sight. It was an older neighborhood but nicely maintained, the homes far apart and set well back from the road. When he pulled to the side of the road, she obediently stopped in front of him. She looked in her rearview mirror to see him doing the same as he watched the road behind them. Without doubt, he knew how to keep her safe and, right now, that was all that mattered.

Her phone rang again and, thinking it was Jake, she almost pushed the icon before she saw it was Logan. Crap. She stared at the ID until the ringing stopped, then checked her messages. Five from her brother, each one more demanding than the last. Double crap. If she didn't call him back by five, he was headed her way, he'd said on the last one.

Jake waited ten minutes and, apparently satisfied they weren't being followed, headed out again. He made a right turn, and halfway down the block, turned onto a long driveway and nosed up to the two-car garage, its door opening. He had a remote control for it? Was this his little hideaway where he brought women? All the way to Tallahassee? That didn't make sense, but nothing else did either.

It didn't escape her notice that it was only a few miles from her apartment. Her brother claimed the hair on the back of his neck stood up when something wasn't right, and for the first time, she understood what he meant. She smelled something rotten, and there wasn't a dead fish in sight.

CHAPTER FIVE

The boss didn't want his sister to know about this place, so he now had one more reason to kill Jake. Jake closed the garage door, then helped Maria unload her car. Inside, she sat the cat's carrier down and looked around. He could see the questions forming and tried to think of a plausible story.

"Jake, why do you have a garage door opener to this house?"

"Ah . . ."

She glared at him. "Don't even think of trying to lie. What is this place for?"

Kincaid planned ahead for everything, so why hadn't he thought of a cover story? "It's like this," he said, then closed his mouth. It was like what? Right now he thought he might prefer to be in Afghanistan, listening to sniper bullets whizz past his ears.

Okay, not really, but finding himself caught between brother and sister was almost as bad. One of them was going to fire him for going behind his back, and the other was looking up at him with dark, coffee-colored eyes he couldn't bring himself to lie to.

He set the paper sacks of chicken on the kitchen counter and leaned back against it. "Your brother got a little paranoid after Dani was kidnapped, and you know how he plans ahead for any situation. He wanted a safe house close to you." Jake shrugged. "If it was ever needed." Along with Kincaid, both he and Jamie Turner had access to this place, just in case.

She walked to the door of the living room and after a quick peek, turned back to him. "So why didn't he just let me live here?"

Now that was a dumb question. "Then it wouldn't have been a safe house, would it? Plus, it's too isolated. He was more comfortable knowing you were in an apartment complex with night security."

Fire shimmered in her eyes, and the desire to bed all that heat hit him hard. He moved to the table and sat, hopefully before she noticed the bulge in his jeans. A low growl sounded from the carrier at his feet, and Jake glanced down. The inappropriately named feline was giving his crotch the evil eye.

He was losing it. Nothing some food, a good night's sleep, and about two hundred miles between him and the temptation of Maria Kincaid wouldn't cure. Maybe.

"Have you both come and stayed here while you spied on me?"

He jerked his gaze to hers. "No, of course not."

Well, he hadn't, but the boss had once when she was in the middle of breaking up with the uptight boyfriend. Kincaid wasn't happy that the kid hadn't believed Maria when she'd told him it was over. An overnight stay and a few words with the ex-boyfriend had taken care of the problem, but Jake wasn't about to go there.

But it wasn't spying, so he wasn't lying, and, God help him, now he was rhyming. Any time he got near her, his brain short-circuited.

"Maria, bring those bags over here." At her rebellious look, he belatedly added, "Please."

She huffed an annoyed-sounding breath but did as he asked, plopping the sacks down in front of him. "What'd you get me?" she asked, taking a seat across from him.

"A chocolate shake, cheese fries, and wings. The kind where you need a fireman standing next to you before you can eat 'em."

Her pleased-with-him grin went straight to his heart, causing it to do disturbing cartwheels in his chest. She wasn't his, could never be, but the foolish thing refused to believe it. Turning his attention to the food, he chowed down on his grilled chicken breast, corn, and pinto beans while thoroughly enjoying watching her. No matter her troubles, she could eat with enthusiasm. Considering what and how much she ate, it was beyond him why she didn't weigh a ton.

Jake stilled when she licked her fingers after cleaning the bone of her last wing. It was the way she went about it—her eyes closed as if she were in ecstasy as her tongue lapped each finger—that had him straining against his jeans. *Jesus.* He stood, knocking over his chair, and headed for another room. Didn't matter which one as long as she wasn't in it.

"Logan left a message giving me until five to call him."

Well, that was as good as a bucket of ice water dumped over his head. Returning to the table, he picked up his chair and sat. He'd received similar messages from the boss. Kincaid's antennae were definitely twitching. "Yeah, he's left me several. Guess you'd better call him."

The smile that appeared on her face was one a woman used on a man when she wanted something, and he was pretty sure he knew just what. Although, if she kept looking at him like that, he'd probably agree to anything, a fact he fully intended to keep to himself.

"No."

Her eyes blinked. "No, what?"

"I'm not calling him first." Her surprised expression said he'd guessed right. "I'll listen to what you tell him so I don't say anything I shouldn't, but I won't lie to him so give him the truth."

"I don't know where my phone is."

Little liar. "No problem." He slid his cell across the table.

She stared at it for a few seconds, then chuckled. "It was worth a try. You know this is going to result in me being locked up for the rest of my life and you being killed for aiding and abetting me."

"I know." And even knowing it, he would do it all over again if she asked.

Her hair fell over her face as she lowered her head and punched in her brother's number. As he listened to her talk, Jake studied the woman who'd fascinated him for so long and tried to understand what it was about her that called to him so deeply.

Maybe it was just lust for a woman who was off-limits. It was the forbidden-fruit theory. That had to be it. If he could make love to her, he would get over it. Yeah, that was the problem, and one easily solved if she was agreeable, and he thought she was.

The big question, however, was whether he was willing to face the consequences. Kincaid really would kill him, at the very least fire him. It just might be worth it. Yet, this was Maria. He would be the lowest of men if he took her to bed. She deserved better than to be one of Romeo's numerous conquests.

Jake stared at the phone Maria held out to him.

"Logan wants to talk to you," she said, concern in her voice.

He thought he might rather handle a rattlesnake. Thankfully, she'd told Kincaid the truth about why she was at Fortunada's. Jake took the phone and steeled himself, inhaling a big breath.

"Yo, boss."

"Give me one good reason, Buchanan, why you didn't tell me the *something* you had to take care of was my sister."

So much for pleasantries. Not that Jake expected any, but the calmness in Kincaid's voice was deceiving. That was the thing about the boss, why they'd nicknamed him "Iceman" when he was their SEAL commander. The calmer the man got, the deadlier he got, and right now Jake was lined up in the Iceman's sights. Not a place anyone in their right mind wanted to be.

Jake glanced at Maria. She stared back with sympathy. Kincaid wasn't going to like his answer, but it was the truth. "Because she wouldn't tell me where she was unless I promised not to tell you, and she wouldn't tell me what was going on until I got here. Would you have preferred I refused to help her, left her to handle this on her own?"

There was a long pause. "My preference, *Romeo*, would be for you to be nowhere near Maria, but what's done is done. Put her in the car and bring her home. Now. Tonight."

Christ, he was really starting to hate his SEAL nickname. He held out his cell. "He wants you to come home."

She took the phone. "I'm not coming home, Logan. I have to deal with the classes I missed today, find someone who has notes I can borrow, and I have exams tomorrow I can't miss. Then there's—"

When she held the phone away from her ear, Jake could hear the heat in Kincaid's voice. Apparently, where his sister was concerned, the Iceman wasn't so calm.

"Are you finished with your tirade?" she asked, putting the cell back to her ear. "Guess not." She listened some more. "I'm not leaving school and that's final. Look, I know you're worried, but I'm at your safe house. Which you neglected to tell me about, but I'll grill you about that another time. If you want Jake to go back, fine, but he's doing a great job of protecting me, so I'm asking you to let him stay. Please, Logan. Wouldn't you feel better knowing I had a bodyguard?"

She winked at Jake. She'd always been able to wrap her brother around her little finger. Too bad he didn't have that ability with

Kincaid. Jake's gaze skimmed over Maria, over the black hair curling around her face and falling halfway down her back, the exotic eyes as dark as rich coffee, and the full lips he'd kissed for the first time.

Had that been only a few hours ago? He wanted to kiss her again. Longer, slower, taking his time to taste her sweet spiciness. He would wrap her hair around his fist and hold her close. He would . . .

Hell. He was becoming aroused again just thinking about kissing her. And other things. Living in her pocket and keeping his hands off her was going to be the very devil. He shifted on the hard kitchen chair and subtly reached down to adjust his jeans.

"You're mine for as long as I need you," Maria said cheerfully as she handed back his phone.

Even though he definitely should, he had absolutely no problem with that. "From your conversation, I guess you need to study for exams tomorrow. I'll leave you to it." If he didn't get away from her immediately, he might forget she was off-limits.

"Oh, I might have stretched the truth a little there, and I can get class notes from my friend Gina. What do you want to do tonight?"

Lay you down on a bed I know this house must have somewhere. Strip you naked and explore every part of you, lick every single inch of you. Then bury myself so deep inside you, you'll never want any man but me.

He managed a glare. It seemed the right thing to do. "You lied? Dammit, Maria. Apparently, you couldn't care less that your brother's gonna crucify me before all this is over."

"Pffft," she said with a dismissive wave of her hand.

Pffft? Would that be on his headstone? *Pffft. Here lies Jake Buchanan. He got stupid and fell for the wrong girl, and then her brother murdered him.*

The cat let out a plaintive meow. Jake knew exactly how the furry bastard felt.

Maria jumped up and came to the carrier, opening the door. She hugged Mouse, burying her nose in his fur. "Poor baby. You've had such a horrible day. Let's go check out the house and find a room you like."

Jake scowled at Maria's back as she walked out of the kitchen. His day hadn't been a bed of roses. He crushed the food wrappings, stuffed them back into the bag, and went looking for a trash can.

———— ❧ ————

Maria adjusted the ball cap Jake had bought her, along with a pair of sunglasses to disguise her features. She kept her eyes on the girls with brown hair. There were so many of them. Why couldn't her girl have been a redhead, or even better, have bright pink or purple hair?

"Anything?"

She sighed in frustration. "No."

He wasn't happy about sitting outside a high school and watching the students file in while she tried to find the girl who'd run away from Fortunada's house. They couldn't even be sure it was the right school, only that it was the closest one to where she'd last seen the girl. Maria had to find her, though; had to make sure she was okay. She also needed to know why the girl had been there. Had she been lured to the house for despicable reasons?

She had witnessed firsthand the life of a whore. If the girl was headed down that path, or being led in that direction, then someone needed to step in and do something about it. If it meant keeping a girl from ending up like Lovey Dovey, Maria wouldn't stop until she found her.

"Well, we gave it a try," Jake said when the last students hurried inside, the doors closing behind them. He started the car.

47

"School lets out at three thirty, so we need to be back a little before then."

His eyes squeezed shut. "I just knew you were going to say that."

She waited for him to open his eyes and then gave him a big smile. "And I knew you'd understand. Thank you."

He opened his mouth, closed it, shook his head, then made a laugh-snort sound. "I'm doomed," he said mysteriously.

"Poor Jake." She patted his hand. "I need to check in at school, let my professors know I'll miss a few classes. After that, can we stop at a grocery store?"

"If you're going to tell me you're making dinner tonight, then I'll know the apocalypse has arrived."

She thought that was funny. "No, you'll wake up tomorrow to the same old world. I need to get Mouse some food and cat litter. But speaking of dinner, what would you like for lunch?" His grin, forming at the pace of a snail, sent her heart into a fluttering frenzy. "What?"

"Speaking of dinner, what would I like for lunch?" His grin grew wider. "Only you, Maria."

She didn't get it, and shrugged. "Whatever."

"Yeah, whatever." He glanced in the rearview mirror, then turned the car toward Florida State, a smile still on his face.

During the next three hours, she scheduled a makeup exam; arranged to get class notes from Gina, who fortunately took almost all the same classes; and caught a few minutes with her professors during class breaks. All the while, Jake stood quietly by her side, ever alert, ever supportive.

Maria hadn't missed the way Gina's gaze had appreciatively roamed over Jake from head to toe when introduced to him. After promising her friend she'd call later that night to explain what was going on, Maria slipped her arm around Jake's and pulled him away before the word that was dancing on the tip of her tongue spilled out: *Mine.*

By the time she'd finished all her tasks it was after one. Way past time for lunch. "Come on, I'm starving," she said, grabbing Jake's hand and heading for his car.

His big hand engulfed hers, giving her a sense of safety, as if there were a wall around her that couldn't be penetrated by anything bad. Only one other man had made her feel protected and that had been Logan. But he was her brother and Jake was not.

Halfway through their lunch at a popular pizza joint near the college, Jake's phone rang. Maria listened to his end of the conversation as she finished off her double-cheese loaded pizza.

"Was that Detective Nolan?" she asked when he clicked off.

He took a bite of his spinach-and-goat-cheese pie. "Yeah, he had some info on Fortunada."

"Well?" she said when he hesitated. "And don't hold anything back."

"They still haven't found him, but the man has a long record." His gaze speared hers. "Especially for domestic violence."

Maria shuddered, wondering how many women he'd hurt the way he had hurt her. What if she hadn't been able to get away?

"He spent a year in jail for breaking the arm of a woman he lived with. He's also done time for breaking and entering, and car theft." Jake glanced down at his pizza, then pushed the remainder away before meeting her eyes again. "One of the women accused him of fondling her teenage daughter, then refused to testify against him. The girl denied anything happened. The cops think he threatened them, and they were too afraid to press charges."

Oh, God.

"Tells us he's far from a model citizen, but the disturbing thing is, he was picked up about six months ago for suspicious behavior. The police couldn't prove anything and had to let him go."

"And this suspicious behavior was?" The uncomfortable look on his face sent a warning that her fear for the girl was justified. *Oh, and please, God, don't let Fortunada be my daddy.*

"They picked him up outside the high school we were at this morning. A teacher reported seeing him watching the girls' softball team on three different days. He had a camera on him, but there was nothing on the memory stick so they couldn't hold him. After they got a warrant to search his house, they found pictures of some of the girls on the team. Nolan wants you to come in and look at them, see if your girl is one of them."

After a quick glance at her watch, Maria nodded. "We have time to squeeze in a quick stop by the station and still make it to the grocery store before it's time to be back at the high school."

"If the girl is in one of the photos, then we don't need to go back. We can let the cops take care of it."

As if she could leave the girl in the hands of people who could never understand a child being at the mercy of a predator. For years she'd lived in Lovey Dovey's house, hiding like Logan had taught her when her mother brought men home. Men who thought nothing of hurting an innocent little girl. It was impossible for her to walk away without knowing the girl was safe.

She shook her head knowing it was the last thing he wanted to see. "Sorry, no can do."

"Hell," he muttered with the resignation of one who'd expected her answer.

Maria just shrugged.

———— ❧ ————

Her girl hadn't been in Fortunada's photos, but Maria now worried about the four who were. Although Detective Nolan said he would pay a visit to each of them, Maria still watched for their faces as the students filed out of the school. Thirty minutes ticked by and as the stream of kids coming out slowed to a trickle, she was about to give up. As she turned to tell Jake they could leave, a girl walking with a gangly boy caught her eye.

"There she is." Maria grabbed Jake's arm. "What should I do?"

Jake turned the key in the car's ignition and backed out of the parking space. "Sit tight. We'll follow her until she's away from the school. We don't want some alert teacher calling the police."

"We can't lose her."

"I won't."

Maria breathed a sigh of relief when she saw the two halfway down the block. "How are we going to approach them? What if she tries to run? What if—"

"Hush and listen. I'll get us ahead of them, then we'll get out and walk toward them like we're just a couple out for a stroll. When we reach them, ask where Bradford Avenue is. I'll take it from there."

The plan worked and Maria, wearing her ball cap and sunglasses, stopped when they were alongside the girl. "Hey, is Bradford Avenue somewhere around here?"

The boy pointed to the left. "Yeah, just one street over."

Jake had positioned himself next to the girl. He wrapped his fingers around her upper arm. She narrowed her eyes and tried to pull away, but he held on.

"Easy. We're not here to hurt you. Maria, take off your hat and sunglasses."

"Hey, dude, let her go," the boy said, and stepped toward Jake.

Maria put herself between the kid and the girl. "Remember me?"

"I've never seen you before," she answered, her eyes wide and on Jake.

"Look at her, not me," he said, gesturing at Maria.

"What's going on here, Angie?" the boy asked.

"I don't know," Angie said, turning her gaze to Maria. "I've never seen . . . Oh, it's you."

"Yeah, it's me. Like my friend said, we're not here to hurt you, but we need to talk. I'm Maria Kincaid, and this is Jake Buchanan."

"Let go of me. I don't have anything to say."

The boy bounced on the balls of his feet, his wary gaze on Jake. "Angie?"

"You got a name, kid?" Jake asked.

"That's a stupid question, dude. Who doesn't have a name, and I'm not a kid."

"Then give me something else to call you. Make something up if you want."

Indecision crossed his face. He clearly wanted to protect Angie, but no doubt understood he wouldn't win a fight against Jake.

Maria placed her hand on his arm. "Angie's in trouble, and we can help her. Please, what's your name?"

"Why you wanna know?" he asked.

"Oh, for Christ's sake, his name's Eddie," Angie said. "Now that we've all been introduced, let me go. I got nothing to say."

"I think you do," Jake said. "We can do this the easy way, or I can call the cops. Who're looking for you, by the way."

Angie paled, turning an accusing eye on Maria. "You called them?"

Maria gently touched the bruise on Angie's cheek. "What did you tell your parents about how you got this?"

"She got up to pee in the middle of the night and smacked into her bedroom door," Eddie said. Maria raised an eyebrow, and he turned to Angie. "Isn't that what happened? That's what you said."

Angie's shoulders slumped as the fight went out of her. "No, that's not what happened." She gave Maria a pleading look. "Can we talk about this somewhere else? My mom might drive by, and I don't want her asking who you people are. There's a park on the next block. Eddie and I will meet you there."

Jake snorted. "And I'm the Easter Bunny. We'll walk with you."

To keep Eddie from trying to snatch Angie away and running, Maria positioned herself between them. Finally, she would find out why the girl at been in Hernando Fortunada's house.

CHAPTER SIX

———— ❦ ————

Jake stood next to Eddie, his gaze on Maria seated on the park bench next to Angie. "You her boyfriend?"

Eddie shuffled his feet. "Sorta."

How were you a sorta boyfriend? Either you were or you weren't. He supposed the girls thought the kid cute, but a haircut wouldn't be amiss.

"Why were you in that house, Angie?" Maria asked.

The girl clasped her hands so tightly her knuckles were white. Maria pried Angie's fingers apart and wrapped her hands around one of the girl's. "You can trust me."

"Whose house?" Eddie asked.

Angie raised her gaze to Eddie's. "Hernando's."

"Dammit, Angie, I told you not to talk to him. Did he do that to your face?" At Angie's nod, he turned to leave.

Jake caught his arm. "Where're you going?"

"To kill that bastard."

"No, you're not. Besides, he's not at his house, and no one's seen him for the past two days." Jake turned to Angie. "Let's start at the beginning. What's Fortunada to you?"

"My mom's boyfriend . . . I mean, he was her boyfriend. They broke up after he stole some money from her. Now she doesn't have enough to make the mortgage payment, and she can't stop crying because she's afraid we're going to lose our house."

Jake did the math. "So you went to see him to try and get the money back?"

Her eyes filled with misery, Angie nodded. "She's going to ground me for a month if she finds out. She told me to stay away from him. He was nice when they first started dating but at the end . . . well, he just got real mean. Now she's all worried and crying a lot, and I-I . . . You know, I just thought I could help."

Kids could be so stupid. She wasn't going to like what she was going to have to do, but that little revelation could wait until she finished her story. "What happened when you went to see him?"

Her shudder answered Jake's question, and he exchanged a glance with Maria. She'd seen firsthand how some men treated women and could guess what had gone on between Angie and Fortunada. A hardness he'd never seen before glinted in Maria's eyes and he could read her thoughts as if she spoke them aloud. She wasn't going to let this go until the man was dead or behind bars.

"What happened, Angie?" Maria asked.

Angie's gaze shifted to Eddie. "I think you should go home now."

"The hell I will. What did he do to you?"

"Easy," Jake said to the agitated boy. He put a hand on Eddie's shoulder. "It won't help her if you get crazy."

"I know. I'm okay." The kid swiped a hand through his hair. "But I'm not leaving."

"Look at me, Angie, and don't pay them any mind. Just look at me and tell me what happened," Maria said.

The girl took a deep breath and then trained her eyes on Maria. "He said he'd give me some money if I'd do things to him. I told him he was disgusting and it was no wonder my mom broke up with him. 'Who needed some old lady when I can have a fresh young thing like you,' he said and laughed. I realized I'd been stupid to go there and turned to leave. He grabbed me and was ripping off my shirt when you rang the doorbell. He let go and I ran out the door."

She shuddered again. "You saved me, and I wanted to thank you, but I was just too scared. I was worried about you, though. I'm so glad you're okay."

"I am," Maria said.

But she almost hadn't been. Jake glanced at Maria's cheek. She'd done a good job of covering her bruise with makeup. You could see it if you knew it was there, but Angie was too caught up in her problems to notice.

"What're we gonna do about this? The asshole needs to pay for hurting Angie," Eddie said.

"You need to leave Fortunada to the police." *And me.* Jake looked at Eddie and hardened his gaze. "You stay far away from the man. If you feel like you need to do something, then just be there for Angie and her mom."

Jake knelt in front of Angie. "You're going to have to tell your mom about this."

She gave a vigorous shake of her head. "She has enough to worry about already."

"Angie, I doubt he'll appear on your doorstep, but if he gets desperate . . ." He didn't want to scare her any more than she already was, but she needed to be warned. "You just never know what a desperate man will do. Your mother needs to know. Tomorrow, Maria and I will come by with Detective Nolan. You'll like him, I promise."

Angie slapped her hands over her face. "Oh, God."

While Maria comforted the girl, Jake nudged Eddie away and had a brief conversation with the kid before sending him and Angie home.

"Are they going to be safe? Shouldn't we have found out where she lives?" Maria asked, her gaze intent on the couple walking away. Eddie had his arm around Angie, and her head rested on his shoulder.

"Angie Davis, mother's name is Carol, 127 Marbury Avenue."

Maria blinked and turned wide eyes on him. He grinned and took her hand. "Come on, we'll follow 'em, make sure they stay safe."

———— ∞ ————

Maria sipped her wine as she watched Jake unwrap the cheese. She was helpless in the kitchen, but grating cheese was probably something she could do.

"Want me to do that?"

He sent a quick look of mock horror over his shoulder. "So you can slice your fingers on the grater? No thanks."

Because he was probably right, she didn't take offense. "I still don't understand why you'd rather have a boring piece of fish and broccoli than tacos."

"My body is my temple."

She couldn't deny his body was meant to be worshiped, but God forbid the day would come when she had to eat broccoli to stay in shape. Logan never ceased to scold her about her choice of food. That Jake would willingly cook two different meals and not insist she eat healthy did something funny to her heart.

Her gaze slid over his back, over the broad shoulders, down his spine to the trim waist, and below that to his lean hips. What would it feel like to slide her hands over his hard body, his taut butt? She marked the moment she decided, one way or another, she'd find out.

"Here you go," he said and put a plate on the table.

Three tacos and refried beans smothered in cheese appeared in front of her. Four tacos would've been better, but who was she to complain when she'd contributed nothing to their dinner?

He chose the chair next to her and when Mouse stood on hind legs, his paws on Jake's knee, his nose sniffing the air, Jake rolled his eyes. "Why's he bothering me and not you?"

"Cause you have fish."

He cut a sliver of the fish and tossed it across the kitchen. "Now go away, cat."

Mouse raced to the food, swallowed it in one bite, and in seconds was back with his paws on Jake's leg.

"Well that didn't work as planned," he grumbled.

Then Jake's hazel eyes focused on Maria as his fork, with a piece of fish on it came at her. She pressed her lips together and shook her head.

"It's just one bite. Come on, just a little taste." One side of his mouth curved in a sly grin, and he snatched her plate away. "If you want your tacos back, all you have to do is open your mouth."

The man knew just the right threat to use. Giving in with a sigh, she squeezed her eyes shut and opened her mouth.

"That wasn't so bad, was it?"

As much as she hated to admit it, the fish was pretty good. It tasted buttery and lemony. Nothing like the cheap, smelly catfish her mother used to fry . . . when she remembered she had children to feed. "It was okay, but I'm not eating any broccoli, so don't even try."

His amused chuckle didn't reassure her there would be no greens in her future. "I'll have you eating healthy yet."

Not if she had anything to say about it. She helped him clean up the kitchen, then excused herself to bathe. When she came out, he was on the sofa, his hair damp from a shower. Like her, he'd put on a pair of sweats and a T-shirt. His bare feet were propped on the coffee table, and Mouse was curled up on his lap, asleep.

"Looks like you've made a friend," she said, taking the other end of the couch.

He glanced down at her cat. "It wasn't my choice."

"You fed him fish. He'll love you forever now."

"Wish you'd told me that before I gave the furry demon any." His deceptively innocent eyes turned to her. "Want to talk about it?"

She didn't have to ask what he meant and no, she didn't want to talk about it. Not tonight. Maybe tomorrow she'd have her feelings sorted out. Or not. "Other than I pray Fortunada's not my biological father, what's there to say?"

"Even if you find out he is, it's no reflection on you."

Easy for him to say; he had June Cleaver for a mother. His father had probably been perfect, too. "Do you remember your dad?" she asked to change the subject. The wistful, fond smile that appeared on his face confirmed her guess.

"Just bits and pieces. Him giving me my first little-boy baseball glove and not yelling at me when I couldn't catch half the balls he tossed at me. I remember how he would carry me around on his shoulders and I'd feel like the king of the world. Things like that."

Of course, she was happy he'd been so lucky to have great parents, but she couldn't help feeling a little envious and resentful, too. Maybe it had been worse for him though, losing a perfect father at such a young age. When Lovey Dovey had died, all Maria had felt was relief.

It was just all so confusing. She'd worked hard to make something of herself, to be as different from her mother as possible. Now, she had the clues that might lead her to her father, and the yearning she'd long ago quashed to have a mom who loved her had returned.

Except this time, it was a dad she pictured affectionately smiling at her. God, her head was so screwed up.

"Where'd you go?"

She blinked, Jake's face coming into focus. "Huh?"

"You were a thousand miles away. Listen, I know you must feel overwhelmed by everything that's happened. Why don't you give yourself a night off, stop trying so hard to figure it out. Let it rest and maybe tomorrow it'll all be clearer."

Doubtful, but her brain was threatening to go into meltdown, so she'd try to put her thoughts aside for a while. The long, elegant fingers lazily stroking her cat's fur made her wish it was she those hands were caressing. That would help soothe her, for sure. His fingers slowly skimmed down Mouse's spine to his rear end and then back up. Mouse gave a loud purr, and Maria resisted joining him.

"Want to watch a movie or something?"

No, she wanted to lay her head on his lap and be the one he petted. "Sure. Want a glass of wine?"

"A beer for me, please."

She grabbed the remote and handed it to him. "Here, find a movie. No baseball."

"I only watch baseball when I want to fall asleep."

"You better not fall asleep." She went to the kitchen, poured a glass of wine, got a beer from the fridge, and returned. Jake was flicking through the channels, and she caught a glimpse of some kind of space movie. "Wait, what was that last one?"

He turned back to the channel. "Looks like *Alien*."

That movie should be able to divert her attention. She handed him his beer. "I've never seen it. Let's watch it."

"You like scary movies?"

"God, yes. But only if I'm watching them with someone, and I have to sit next to you so I can grab hold of you when the scary parts come on." His expression blanked and she thought he would refuse. Why didn't he want her sitting next to him?

Finally, he patted the space at his side. "Then I'm your man."

She liked the sound of that but wished he'd said it with a little more enthusiasm. Nestling against his side, she felt his body tense. Really? What was his problem?

The spaceship landed on a planet and she forgot everything but the movie. The astronauts were in a creepy cave with even creepier egg-shaped pods when Jake took her empty wineglass out of her hand and set it aside. She didn't remember drinking it. By the time goo-dripping aliens were popping out of people, Maria had her face pressed into Jake's chest, her hands gripping his shirt.

"Want me to turn it off?"

"No!" She had to know if somebody saved the cat.

He chuckled and his arm circled her shoulders, pulling her close. "Your eyes are closed, you're not even watching it."

"Am too." She opened one eye to prove she was, but quickly closed it when another astronaut's belly began to quiver.

By the time the movie ended, she'd practically crawled onto Jake's lap and he'd let her. Her one and only boyfriend had made fun of her for watching scary movies with her eyes closed. Jake had held her tight against him.

Maria opened her eyes and grinned. "She saved the cat."

His answering smile, the one she was coming to adore, lit his face. "And you scared yours so badly with your screams, he took off an hour ago."

"But you're still here."

"I am." His eyes searched hers, and hers answered the question in them with a yes.

Oh, God, yes. Please kiss me.

Their mouths met as if they were enacting a scene from a movie.

Slowly, so achingly slowly, his lips covered hers. She slid her hand around his neck, brushing her fingers through the bristle of his short hair, pleased when his skin quivered under her touch.

He'd kissed her yesterday, but that one had been borne of anger, his frustration with her getting the better of him. If a kiss could melt her bones, this one would. His lips lightly brushed over hers, his breath warming them. Jolts of electricity sparked through her when he nipped on her bottom lip, then captured it with his teeth.

When his tongue scraped across her teeth, she opened her mouth and his hand came to rest against her jaw as he explored her. His taste, flavored by the malt beer, made her drunk with desire.

Maria moaned, and he stilled. "Please." She would beg if necessary to keep him from stopping.

His mouth inched away and he leaned his forehead against hers. "No, we can't do this."

Jake never turned down sex freely offered. Why was he saying no to her? She placed her palm over his heart, felt it pounding. He wasn't unaffected.

"We can. I want you, and I think you feel the same."

He put his hands on her waist and lifted her to her feet. "Go to bed, Maria."

She searched his eyes but they shuttered, blocking his thoughts. "I don't understand."

"There's nothing to understand."

Jake turned off the TV and the lamp, leaned his back on the sofa, and tried to wipe from his mind the look of confusion and hurt on Maria's face as she left the room. *I want you, and I think you feel the same.* Damn straight he wanted her. He'd come close to taking her right there on the couch.

But he was Romeo. He loved 'em and left 'em. In the end, he would hurt her, something he'd never much worried about with other women. Of course, he'd always made sure the women he chose knew the rules, understood the game.

Maria didn't understand the game, and he would never want her to. She was different—special—meant for someone who had long term in mind. A man who would put a ring on her finger and honor his vows.

He didn't believe he had fidelity in him. A day would come when some tempting little thing would cross his path, and he'd go and royally screw everything up. If he ever hurt Maria like that, he'd shoot himself, saving Kincaid the trouble.

But, Jesus, she'd knocked the floor out from under him with that kiss.

From the time he'd kissed his first girl at age thirteen, he'd loved the feel of soft feminine lips on his, had made it his mission in life to kiss as many girls as possible. Then at sixteen, he'd lost his virginity to his twenty-three-year-old neighbor and never looked back. Though he now understood she was wrong to seduce a teenage boy, she'd taught him how to please a woman and he had very fond memories of her.

If someone asked him how many women he'd slept with, he couldn't begin to answer. He couldn't remember most of their names, though he'd always remember their faces as they came. Seeing their eyes dilate and darken, hearing their soft sighs and sometimes their screams, feeling the curves of their bodies as his hands explored them, it was what he lived for.

No, he wasn't the man for Maria.

A ball of fur landed on his lap and began to knead his stomach. Jake sighed. "Yeah, cat, I guess we guys have to stick together." He peered down at the creature. "You are a guy, right? Or have you been neutered? Maybe that's what somebody needs to do to me."

———— ❧ ————

Jake once again found himself standing next to Eddie as Detective Nolan questioned Angie and her mother. Nolan had agreed to hold the interview at the Davis house, his hope that it would put mother and daughter more at ease. Maria sat on the couch, her hand clasped in Angie's.

"When was the last time you saw him, Mrs. Davis?" the detective asked.

"I'm not sure exactly, about a month ago."

Jake studied the woman who'd been Fortunada's girlfriend. She was attractive, maybe in her midthirties. Her eyes, green like her daughter's, were red rimmed and swollen from crying. Even now, she had a handkerchief clutched tightly in her hand, dabbing at the tears falling down her cheeks.

Nolan handed her a mug shot. "Is this Hernando Fortunada?"

She glanced at it and gave it back. "That's him."

"Does he have a job?"

"He's a bartender at Missy's Place. At least, he was a month ago."

As Nolan questioned Angie about her visit to Fortunada's house, Eddie started bouncing on the balls of his feet, his hands curling into fists. Jake put his hand on the kid's shoulder and pushed him into the kitchen.

"You need to calm down, Eddie. Getting all agitated isn't helping anyone."

"I know, man, but I just get so pissed when she talks about what he tried to do to her."

"I understand, but she got away. What Angie needs now is for you to hold it together and be there for her."

"Man, I know that, but what I really wanna do is find the asshole and hurt him like he hurt Angie."

Jake caught the boy's gaze and held it. "Eddie, pay attention here. The man's dangerous. He's hurt people before. I'm an ex-SEAL, and even I would use caution where he's concerned. Let the police do their job." A small lie, that one. He'd have no problem tangling with Fortunada.

"No shit? You're a SEAL. Wow. Were you on the team that killed bin Laden?"

Jake suppressed a smile. The kid was a trip. "No, that was Team Six, but back to my point. The way you can help is to stick close to Angie and her mother. Like I said yesterday, it's possible Fortunada could show up if he gets desperate, maybe looking for a place to hide out. What if he does and they're here alone because you're out somewhere on a fruitless search for him?"

"Shouldn't I have a gun?"

Hell no. "You have a cell phone?"

Eddie's eyebrows met in the middle of his forehead. "Doesn't everybody?"

Well hell. He let his amusement go and laughed. "Yeah, you're right. You stick with your ladies and any sign of our man, you call the police, then me. Give me your cell."

Jake programed his number into Eddie's phone and handed it back. "Now, there's something else I need to know. Who holds the mortgage on this house?"

"Why?"

Jake had given this some thought and knew Maria would eventually ask the same question. "The Tango stole all of Angie's mother's money and now she can't make the mortgage payment. If I know Maria,"—and he was sure he did—"she'll probably want to help out." He would insist on contributing at least half.

"What's a Tango?"

Right. No SEAL lingo. "A bad guy. Can you find out?"

Eddie squared his shoulders, his stance one of the man he might grow into some day. "I already took care of that, dude. I had some money saved up, you know? Gave it to Angie this morning to give to her mom."

He was starting to like this boy. Jake exchanged a smile with the kid, giving him a manly slap on the shoulder. "Cool, dude." Had he really just said that? Jesus, he'd been sucked into a time warp.

Maria noted his return with a softening of her eyes as he escorted Eddie back into the room. *Stop looking at me like that, Maria.* Somehow, he had to put an end to this growing desire to make her his. When she turned those coffee-colored eyes on him in that warm way, he wanted to promise things he couldn't deliver.

Forever was not in his vocabulary.

CHAPTER SEVEN

——— ⌘ ———

Jake's gaze fell on Maria, then flicked away. He'd been quiet and distant all day, speaking only to answer a question. She'd given up trying to get him to talk. If this was how he was going to act for the duration of his time with her, then she hoped the police caught Fortunada soon.

The Davis living room was dark because of the drapes drawn over the windows. Jake stood off to the side, out of the small beam of light from the lamp, his face shadowed. She didn't need to look into his hazel eyes to recall the heat they'd held the night before when he'd kissed her. He wanted her, she was certain.

If she could choose who her heart wanted, it wouldn't have been Jake. He was exactly the kind of man she should avoid. But from the time she'd met him, he had fascinated her. Her teenage crush on him had blossomed into something more at her twenty-first birthday party. Logan's wife was a romance writer, and it had happened just like in one of Dani's stories.

She'd met Jake's gaze from across the room, and it was as if time had stopped. He'd taken a step toward her, but then he'd shifted his gaze to her brother and some kind of message had passed between them. From then on, Jake had avoided her as if she carried some kind of plague. She supposed she did, one named Logan.

When Jonathan had asked her out, she'd thought he was exactly the kind of man she should marry. Like her, he was going for a law degree and was goal oriented. Most importantly, he was as different as possible from the men her mother brought home. But she'd erred. It hadn't taken long for her to see he was too possessive and critical.

She loved colorful clothes, Jonathan didn't. It wasn't only her clothing that bugged him but also her eating habits, her cat, her love of horror movies—just about everything that made her Maria, actually. Then there was the sex. It hadn't lived up to her fantasies.

Looking back on it, she realized she'd hoped he would make her forget about Jake. Unfortunately, Jonathan had failed at that, too. She glanced at Jake and caught him staring at her. His gaze quickly shifted to the detective.

"If you think of anything else, Mrs. Davis, call me," Detective Nolan said, handing her his card.

Once outside, Maria stood close to Jake while they talked to the detective. Occasionally, she *accidently* brushed her arm against Jake's to gauge his reaction. Every time she touched him, he tensed. She suppressed a satisfied smile.

"I think if Maria and I drop in at Missy's Place, we'd be able to learn more than if you go there in cop mode, full of questions," Jake said.

Maria's ears perked up. When Carol had said that's where Fortunada worked, she'd decided—whether Jake agreed or not—they were going there.

Detective Nolan shook his head. "This is a police investigation, not a game for civilians."

As Maria opened her mouth to dispute that she thought anything about the situation was a game, Jake put his hand on her arm and gave it a slight squeeze. Message received, she waited to see what he would say.

"Did you call that number I gave you?" he asked the detective.

"Of course. And I was duly impressed, which was your intention. You might know how to kill a man three different ways with your little finger, but you're not an investigator, nor are you involved in this in any kind of official capacity."

"Tell that to her," Jake said, thrusting a thumb Maria's way. "You might also want to ask her what she'll do if you don't agree to let us check out Missy's Place."

When he winked at her, something warm and fuzzy fluttered in her stomach. How did he know her so well? That Jake understood she needed to do this maybe wasn't so surprising. That he knew she'd go no matter what Detective Nolan said was a bit alarming. How was she supposed to get away with anything if he was always two steps ahead of her?

The detective turned his attention to her and narrowed his eyes. "Is he saying you'll go there even if I order you not to?"

Refusing to be intimidated, Maria returned his stern look with a smile and nodded.

The man threw his hands up. "I give up. Call me if you learn anything."

Jake held the car door open for Maria. "Follow my lead." The smile she gave him was too sweetly innocent for his comfort.

"Stop worrying. Nothing's gonna happen to me as long as you're with me," she said.

He didn't like bringing her to where Fortunada worked—or had worked—but he'd known without asking that she was determined to do this. He doubted they would find the man behind the bar pouring drinks, which was the only reason he'd helped set this visit in motion. Glancing at the building, he was relieved it didn't appear to be some kind of biker bar or strip joint.

Maria slipped her arm through his, and he wished she would stop touching him. He also wished she'd worn something more conservative instead of the sheer, red silk blouse, the tight black jeans, and those *do me* shoes with the spiked heels and black straps.

It was impossible to keep his eyes off the red lace of her bra peeking out of the blouse, and her red-painted toenails. And why couldn't she have wound her hair into some kind of nun type of bun instead of letting it fall loose down her back?

She was so damn hot he didn't doubt he'd end up in a bar fight before the night was over. The first man to look at her wrong was toast. The tips of her fingers pressed into the skin of his arm. Seriously, she needed to stop touching him.

Jake escorted her into Missy's Place, his gaze sweeping the interior. It was nicer than he'd expected. An R&B band played on a small stage, and the tables were filled with well-dressed couples drinking wine and fancy drinks. He spotted two empty barstools and guided Maria to them.

"What can I getcha, beautiful?" the bartender asked, his gaze only on Maria.

A smile lit her face. "A chocolate martini, please."

Jake gritted his teeth and ordered a Glenlivet neat. The bartender might have some answers for them, so it wouldn't be wise to give him a bloody nose. This jealousy thing was not only uncomfortable, it was also unwelcome. He'd never felt it before and didn't like it one bit. If a woman he was out with saw a man she liked better, then she was free to go. There was always another waiting to take her place.

He turned a moody gaze on Maria. What was it about her that got under his skin? Putting aside the fact that she was gorgeous, he couldn't think of anything they had in common. He was a warrior; she the untouchable princess in the castle. She put food in her body that made him want to cringe. She loved the beach; he hated getting sand in his butt crack. She—

"What?"

He blinked. "What, what?"

"You're staring at me as if I'm some kind of weird puzzle."

She was a puzzle all right, but he doubted she'd appreciate him agreeing. "You really are beautiful."

Her eyes warmed. "Thank you."

It was the first thing he'd thought of to divert her attention, but now she'd gone all soft and doe-eyed on him. His finger seemed to have a mind of its own because it trailed a path down her cheek. Hell. Now he was touching her when he'd sworn it was hands-off where she was concerned.

"Here's your martini, gorgeous."

The bartender slid Jake's scotch to him, not taking his eyes off Maria. Smothering his urge to smash something, Jake considered how to bring up the subject of Fortunada.

"Is my Uncle Hernando working tonight?" Maria said.

Jake swung his gaze to Maria. He'd been right not to trust that sweet smile when he'd told her to follow his lead, but for openings, it was a good one. The man leaned on the counter, his face too damn close to Maria's.

"Hernando's your uncle?"

"Yeah," she said and leaned her head on Jake's shoulder. "I was hoping he was here tonight so I could introduce him to my husband. We're newlyweds and my uncle's never met Jake."

The man glanced at her ring finger, and Jake followed his gaze to see a band of diamonds circling her finger. Well hell, apparently he had a wife who planned ahead.

"Lucky man," the bartender said, giving Jake an envious nod.

"Don't I know it," Jake answered and then gave his *wife* a heated look.

Maria one-upped him when she turned mischievous eyes to him and said, "No, Tiger Toes, I'm the lucky one."

Tiger Toes? Jake could actually feel the grin slowly forming on his face. This would probably be a good time to take cover from the barrage of new sensations falling down on his head, but he ignored the warning and leaned toward Maria, fully intending to kiss her. Christ, she smelled good—earthy and spicy—the scent exotic like her.

"You two are giving me an overdose of sugar."

Maria reacted to the interruption by ignoring it, but Jake jerked his head back. What the hell was he thinking? That was the problem: he wasn't.

"Sorry, but sometimes she scrambles my brain." Too much information there and way too true. He tore his gaze away and shrugged. "Back to her question. Is her uncle working tonight?"

"No, man. Haven't seen Hernando for a few days. He was a no-show for his shift and I haven't heard a word from him since. He's got a paycheck coming, but I doubt the boss will turn it over since he left without so much as a good-bye."

"If I give you my cell number, would you call me if he shows up?" Maria asked. "It's been a few months since I've seen him. We stopped by his house a few times but haven't been able to catch him, and he's not answering his phone. I'm starting to worry."

Once again, the man turned a too-interested look on her, and again, Jake gritted his teeth.

The bartender grabbed a napkin and pen. "Sure. I'll be glad to call you."

Maria gave him a beautiful smile and rattled off Jake's number, then ordered jalapeno poppers and loaded potato skins.

Jake ordered a plate of fruit and cheese while wondering if he was a boring man.

They were halfway through their appetizers when Maria grabbed his arm. "I love this song. Come on, let's dance."

There were other couples dancing, most of them pressed tightly together. Jake reluctantly followed Maria onto the dance floor and placed his hand on her hip, keeping her an arm's distance away. But halfway through the song, she'd somehow inched closer and he gave up the fight.

He slipped his hand around her back, pulled her against him, and buried his nose in her hair. As they swayed to the slow beat of the music, something low and hungry settled deep in his groin. He pushed his leg between hers and she, his *wife*, practically straddled his knee. So much for his good intentions.

But he didn't care. Not now. Not tonight.

All he wanted was to feel Maria pressed hard against him, to hear her soft sigh when his thigh pushed between her legs. And oh yeah, she did sigh.

"Jake," she whispered.

"Maria."

He lowered his mouth to her ear and nibbled on the delicate lobe, felt the skin over her spine shiver under his hand. If he had a white flag, he'd wave it. He'd never surrendered any battle before, but this one he didn't resent.

For as long as it lasted, he'd go along for the ride. He might not know how to do *forever*, but he could love her like no other man until she wised up and sent him packing or he decided it was time to go.

His pulse kept to the beat of the music as her soft body coiled around his. He circled his arms around her, sliding his fingers into the back pockets of her jeans. She sighed again and rubbed against his hip. If she didn't stop doing that, he was going to throw her over his shoulder like some kind of barbarian and carry her back to his cave.

She looked up at him with those bedroom eyes—now almost black and shimmering with desire—and he lowered his mouth to hers. The couples around them faded, the music faded, and he was aware of nothing but Maria. With his hands still in her pockets, he caressed her ass with his fingers. His cock throbbed with the need to be buried inside her.

Another couple bumped them and Jake lifted his head, his surroundings coming back into focus. Damn, this was a first. He'd never before come this close to making love on a dance floor.

"Let's go home," she said.

Jake slipped his fingers around hers, led her back to the bar, and paid their tab. As words were beyond him, when they reached his car, he braced his palms on the door, caging her in. He lowered his mouth to hers and learned the answer to a question that had plagued him all day. Overnight, he'd convinced himself he'd exaggerated the memory of kissing her. He hadn't.

Her taste was different, though. Before, she'd tasted spicy and exotic, but now her mouth was chocolaty and sweet. She wrapped her arms around his neck and pressed her breasts against his chest.

"Get a room!"

Jake glanced behind him to see two men walking by and laughing. He turned back to Maria and leaned his forehead on hers. "It is good advice. Let's go."

"Okay." She put her palm on his cheek and gave him a quick kiss. "And don't start talking yourself out of what's going to happen when we get there."

She shouldn't have said that. It was as effective as jumping naked into the North Atlantic. There were a hundred good reasons for not sleeping together that he could spout off the top of his head without even trying.

"Maria—"

"Shut up, Jake. I mean it." She turned and yanked on the door handle. "Unlock the stupid door."

He reached into his pocket and clicked the remote. At the sound of the locks popping up, she slapped his hand away and opened the door herself, shutting it in his face once she was seated.

As he stared through the window at her, he debated his options. One: he could take her home and do what they both wanted. Two: he could take her home and then lock himself in his room, which neither of them wanted him to do. Three: he could call the boss and ask him to send Turner to guard her. Four: he could just shoot himself right now because he was going with number one.

Jake circled the car, slid into the driver's seat, and swiveled his body toward her. When she opened her mouth to speak, he crushed his mouth over hers. Whatever she wanted to say he didn't want to hear. No more cold-water words.

"Be quiet."

She grinned. "Okay."

Jake kissed her again, gently this time. "Let's go home."

Her warm smile banished his doubts about the direction they were headed. He wasn't sure he could let her go once he'd claimed her, and that should've concerned him. The thought of another man coming along and touching her when this thing between them cooled didn't settle well. Another first.

She would graduate in a week and be back in Pensacola. They could date—strangely enough, something he'd not done a lot of—and see how things went. Most of his hookups had been initiated at local watering holes, and he rarely saw the same woman more than three or four times. More than that and they started getting ideas.

Other than meeting for drinks and then falling into bed, he'd not put much effort into entertaining them. He wanted more with Maria than just falling into the sack a few times. There were movies he'd like to take her to, concerts, weekends away—maybe New Orleans. If he took her to Apalachicola, could he convince her to try oysters on the half shell? There was nothing on this earth better than chilled oysters with an ice-cold beer.

It would be an interesting challenge to work on her eating habits, get her turned on to eating healthy, or at least healthier. He didn't foresee her giving up all her junk food. Maybe he would try eating the things she liked once in a while. Not often, but . . .

Christ. He was already planning their life and they hadn't even spent their first night together. Where were all these thoughts coming from, anyway? It was entirely possible they'd spend one night together and that would be it. His lust for her would be sated and her fascination with him would fade.

He glanced at her to see she was watching him, and he slipped his hand into hers, bringing her fingers to his mouth and kissing them. "What are you thinking?" he asked.

Maria thought it best not to tell him she was nervous. Were they really going to do this? What if she didn't please him? He was used to women with experience, and other than the few times she'd slept with her ex-boyfriend, she had none. With Jonathan, it hadn't been particularly enjoyable. Once, she'd straddled him in an attempt to seduce him and he'd gotten angry, wanting to know where she'd learned her tricks.

It had been entirely the wrong thing to say. Lovey Dovey hadn't always been private with the men she brought home, and Maria knew all kinds of tricks, but from observation only. She'd never told Jonathan about her mother, instinctively knowing he would look at her differently. When he'd asked about her parents, she had told him they died too young for her to remember them.

So, she'd had no explanation for her knowledge of sexual acts and only answered that she had read about it somewhere, which caused him to question her taste in books. Since that would include her sister-in-law's hot romance novels—and there was no one on earth who could make her stop reading Dani's books—it had been the end of Jonathan.

"Hello? Where's your mind right now?"

Maria blinked and brought Jake back into focus. "I was thinking about Carol not having the money to pay her mortgage. I want to help." Well, she had been thinking that earlier. He'd put her hand on his thigh after kissing her fingers, and he gently squeezed it.

"Liar. That's not what you were thinking, but you own your thoughts and only need to share them if you want. As for the mortgage payment, Eddie took care of it."

"Seriously?"

"Yep, told me when I offered our help. He was rather proud of himself, so I didn't want to hurt his manly pride and insist."

"He's a nice kid. I'm glad he's there for Angie and her mom." And Jake had no idea how much it meant to her that he said she owned her thoughts. Jonathan would've hammered at her until she spilled, then would end up either mad or lecturing her.

She leaned her head back, closed her eyes, and blanked her mind to all but the feel of Jake's thigh under her hand. He had on a pair of slacks, the material soft and thin. His heat warmed her palm and she began caressing him with the tips of her fingers. A muscle twitched under her touch and she inched her way to the inside of his thigh.

He moved her hand closer to his knee. "Easy, Chiquita. You come much closer to the family jewels and I'm gonna wreck this car. As it is, I'm having a tough time not putting the pedal to the floor and getting us home ASAP."

Her apprehension returned. He seemed to really want her. What if she disappointed him? As the daughter of a whore, Maria Kincaid—of all women—should know how to please a man.

Too soon, he turned into the driveway. She considered asking if they could drive around for a while, but that would be cowardly and she'd only have longer to worry. She put her hand on the door handle, but he reached over and stopped her.

"Wait. I'll come around. But first, I need to do this."

He lowered his mouth to hers and kissed her. No tongue, no roaming hands, just a soft kiss that promised more. Not only did he open her door, but he slipped his arms under her knees and shoulders and carried her inside.

"I can walk."

His lips curved into a crooked grin. "I know."

As his mouth was glued to hers for most of the way to the house, it amazed her he didn't trip and land them both on their bottoms. With her help, they got the door unlocked, and once inside, he slammed it shut with his foot, then carried her straight into his bedroom.

He laid her on the bed, and Mouse jumped up and sat on her stomach.

"Oh no you don't, you fleabag," Jake said. He picked up the cat and put him in the hallway, closing the door. A loud protest sounded from the other side.

"He just wanted to say hi."

Jake's gaze roamed over her, starting at her feet and working his way up. "I plan to apply my tongue to various parts of your body, and I don't want to choke on cat hair."

"Oh."

"Yeah, oh."

She was fairly certain he was about to teach her how it should feel to be with a man. He prowled toward her—his eyes locked on hers—while unbuttoning his shirt. Her heartbeat notched up along with her intake of air. Her fingers fumbled with the top button of her blouse.

"Don't."

Was she doing something wrong already? She stilled, searching his eyes for censure. *Please, don't let him be like Jonathan.* He sat on the edge of the mattress, his shirt left on but unbuttoned. With his hands on either side of her head, he leaned down and nipped at her bottom lip.

He sat back and trailed a finger along the edge of her red lacey bra. "I'll undress you, Chiquita. It's all I've thought about doing all night."

"Oh, okay." With difficulty, she lifted her gaze from the expanse of his chest and its dusting of brown hair.

With a tilt of his head, he gave her a funny look. "You have done this before, haven't you? And I can't tell you how much I hope your answer is a yes."

Speech had moved into the realm of impossible, so she nodded.

"Thank God."

He scooted back and slipped off her heels, dropping them to the floor, then wrapped a hand around the back of her ankle while his thumb kneaded the bottom of her foot.

"I need to go shopping tomorrow." Where had that come from? Before she blurted out all her insecurities left over from Jonathan, she should slap some duct tape over her mouth.

The hand massaging her foot stopped. "I beg your pardon."

Oh, God. What was wrong with her? "I'm sorry. Forget it."

"I don't think so. Where's your mind right now?"

"Here?"

"I don't know, Maria. Are you?"

She pulled her feet away and scooted up, leaning back against the headboard. "I want to be here." She was ruining everything, but couldn't seem to stop.

He stood, kicked off his shoes, and came to the head of the bed. "Move up." He slipped in behind her, then pulled her back against him. "Now, talk."

It was an order from a man used to being obeyed, and she could put a stop to everything right now and never know what it might be like with him, or she could be honest and hope he was nothing like Jonathan.

She chose to be honest.

CHAPTER EIGHT

———— ❧ ————

Had she lied about doing this before? Was that why she looked away from him, not answering? If she was a virgin, he would cram his raging lust into an airtight box and send her to her room. Even though it might well kill him. If she was saving herself for a husband, he could respect that. Wouldn't like it, but he wasn't about to offer himself up for the role.

"I've only been intimate with one man. Jonathan."

That was the best thing she could've said, but what wasn't she saying? He circled his arms around her chest and breathed deeply, inhaling her scent. "And?" Her head fell back on his chest, resting there as if it was a natural thing for her to do. He liked it. Maybe too much.

"Yeah, there's an *and*. I never told him about my mother, about who she was and how I knew things I shouldn't. Whenever I thought he might like me to do something with him that I'd seen Lovey Dovey do . . . well, he didn't. It was like I disgusted him."

"He's an ass, Maria." Jake decided he was going to kill Jonathan. In the meantime, he still didn't understand her problem. "I'm not Jonathan. You can do anything you want with me, and I promise I'll still respect you in the morning."

She gave a little laugh and twisted in his embrace to face him. "I already know that, and that's not what I'm trying to tell you."

"Okay, what are you trying to say?"

Her chin lowered and her eyes focused on his chest. "There wasn't any pleasure for me, so I think maybe I'm immune to sex . . . you know, because of Lovey Dovey. And what if I don't please you? I don't want to disappoint you."

"You're joking, right? Look at me." When her eyelashes lifted, he said, "Christ, Chiquita, I've been hot for you all night, longer even." He put a finger under her chin and lifted her face. With his kiss, he showed her how much he desired her.

"Now listen," he said when he reluctantly pulled away. "I'm glad you told me. It makes a difference. So, here's the plan. I'll undress you at my leisure, play with you a little, and then you can show me what you think you've learned from that woman you call a mother. In return, I'll prove you aren't immune to sex. Okay?"

A smile slowly spread across her face. "Yeah."

His heart took a belly dive at the trust in her eyes. A part of him wished she wouldn't look at him like that. He should probably warn her not to fall in love with him. If he were a wiser man, he would send her back to her room with instructions to lock her door.

"Jake?"

He wasn't wise. "I'm here." He undid the first two buttons on her blouse and slid his hand inside the red lace bra that had tortured him all evening. With his thumb he flicked her nipple, then lightly pinched it.

"Oh, that feels good."

"This is just the beginning, Chiquita."

Her breast fit perfectly in his hand—her skin as soft as silk. He pushed her hair aside and pressed his lips against her neck, smiling when she grabbed his thighs. So, she feared she was immune to this? Not a chance. He'd barely started and already her fingers were digging into his legs.

He undid the rest of the buttons and pulled her blouse out of the jeans. "Up," he said, and slipped it off when she tipped forward. She leaned back onto him and he peered over her shoulder at his first glimpse of the red lace bra.

"Give me a minute while I catch my breath. You're beautiful, Maria."

She glanced down at her breasts. "Jonathan said they're too big."

"Like I said, Jonathan's an ass. I never want to hear you say his name again."

"Okay."

"Now where was I? Oh, yeah, I remember. I was about to do this." He trailed his fingers down the valley of her breasts, over her stomach and to her jeans, pleased when she gave a little shiver. With practiced ease, he unbuckled her belt and unsnapped the jeans.

So many times he'd done this, but never had he wanted a woman so badly as he did Maria. He ignored the warning bells going off in his head that he just might have left the safety of the shore and was diving headfirst into the deep blue sea without a lifeline.

She wasn't a one-night stand—a woman who understood the game—and he wouldn't treat her like one. For however long this thing between them lasted, he would be true to her.

He unzipped her jeans and exposed matching red lace panties. God have mercy. It would be a miracle if he lasted two minutes once he was inside her. Sliding his hand inside her panties, he cupped her mound and just held it there, letting her heat seep into his palm.

She pushed against his hand. "Jake, I need—"

"Hush. I know what you need." He slipped his fingers through her curls and into her folds. She was hot and wet, and he clamped down on his need to tear their clothes off and make love to her that very second.

At the moment, his needs didn't count. It was only about proving she wasn't immune to sex or to him. He pushed a finger into her sheath and found her clit with his thumb. With his other hand, he played with her breasts, tested their weight in his palm, flicked a fingernail over the nipples.

She raised her knees and pressed her feet to the mattress. Her breaths grew louder as she struggled for air. "Jake."

His name came out of her mouth as a rasp, as if she barely managed to speak it. In response, his cock pressed against the zipper of his slacks looking for a way out. It wanted her, and it wanted her immediately. He'd always been able to control himself, taking all the time he needed to get a woman ready, but with Maria he may as well have been a boy getting lucky for the first time.

"Jake, please."

"I know, baby, I know." Still circling her clit with his thumb, he slipped a second finger inside her sheath—now drenched with her cream—and she clamped her muscles around them. He lowered his mouth to her ear. "Let go, Chiquita. I'll catch you."

And she did.

Jake wrapped both arms around her chest, and sucked in air right along with Maria. What had just happened? When she came, so had he. Never had he done that before. Hell, he hadn't even unzipped his pants, hadn't touched himself. It had been amazing, and it scared the hell out of him.

He needed a time-out, needed to think about what he was getting into. What he couldn't do was give any hint she'd rocked his world to its very core, and now he needed some space to get his bearings back. Thanks to her idiot boyfriend, she would blame herself for doing something wrong.

"Still think you're immune to sex?"

She tilted her head back against his shoulder and gave him a big grin. "I think you've proven otherwise." Her smile slipped and her expression turned shy. "That was my first ever orgasm. Thank you."

If he were a peacock, he'd spread his tail and strut. "You're more than welcome, believe me, but you mean the first you've had with a man, right?"

She shook her head.

"Haven't you ever masturbated?" Didn't everyone?

Again, her head shook. "You have to understand, growing up with Lovey Dovey and everything with her revolving around sex . . . I don't know, I guess I just wanted to be as different from her as possible."

"And you are, but it isn't because you do or don't have sex, or even whether or not you pleasure yourself." He pulled her hair away from her neck, wrapped it around his hand, and tugged her head back. Eyes as warm as melted chocolate stared up at him.

He was in trouble all right, but he kissed her anyway.

Before this went any further, he'd best take that time-out and decide if the direction he was headed was where he wanted to go. "You know what?"

She twisted around and sat back on her heels. "What?"

His gaze strayed down to take in her magnificent breasts clothed in the lacey bra, on down over her trim waist, and then to the jeans, still unzipped and showing a hint of the red panties. He'd bet his retirement fund she tasted as good as she looked, and she was his for the taking. Nothing had ever stopped him before, so why was he hesitating?

"Do I know what?"

What the hell had he been going to say? He lifted his eyes to hers. "Let's go pig out on that ice cream you promised I'd like."

She scrunched her eyebrows together. "Now?"

"Since when have you turned down ice cream?"

"I did something wrong, didn't I? And now you—"

He put a finger over her lips. "Stop it. You did nothing wrong, Chiquita. You were amazing. We didn't have dinner and didn't finish our appetizers, and I'm just hungry. That's all."

Her expression said she didn't believe him. She should because she was, in fact, amazing. He just needed to get his world back in order, but he didn't know how to explain it to her.

"Come on, get up," he said, giving her a light slap on the ass. She reached for the blouse he'd tossed to the other side of the bed. "No, leave it off. I like you just the way you are."

That seemed to reassure her, and the light came back into her eyes. She scooted off the bed and held out her hand. "Ice cream it is, then."

"You go ahead. I'm just going to the bathroom, and I'll be right there."

After she disappeared down the hall, Jake banged his head against the headboard. There were a thousand reasons he had no business having her in his bed. But damn, he wanted her. He went into the bathroom and cleaned himself up, still marveling that he'd climaxed just from touching her and watching her come.

When he entered the kitchen, Maria sat at the table, one large bowl of ice cream in front of her. "Don't I get any?"

She held out a spoonful of ice cream. "We're sharing."

It would have been a good idea to let her put her blouse back on. He'd still not made a decision, and the red bra and all that exposed golden skin made it impossible to think. Taking a seat next to her, he opened his mouth when she aimed the spoon his way.

"All right, I concede that's really good." It'd been ages since he'd had ice cream.

"Can't go wrong with double chocolate fudge brownie."

"No, but I might OD on all the sugar." He obediently opened for her to feed him more.

She grinned. "If you do, I'll give you mouth to mouth."

"Will you now?"

"Oh, yeah, for sure." Her eyes strayed to his chest, and then she lifted her gaze to his. "My turn."

There was mischief in those eyes, and before Jake could wonder what she was up to she was sitting on his lap. She pushed his unbuttoned shirt aside, scooped up ice cream with her finger, and streaked his chest with chocolate. When she started licking it off, he accepted that he didn't have the willpower to resist her. Decision made, he joined in the fun.

He dipped his finger into the ice cream and smeared it over her lips. "You've had your turn, now it's mine." With a flick of his tongue over her bottom lip, he tasted her and chocolate. Groaning, he covered her mouth with his. She answered with a whimper and pressed her breasts against him, the lace of her bra scraping against his skin.

"You taste like sin," he said.

She lifted her head, a dreamy smile on her face. "And you kiss like an angel."

He laughed. He was as far from an angel as a man could get. "Just how many angels have you kissed to know that?"

"Just you," she answered, then added, "So far."

"Hey, I'm the only angel you need to be kissing."

She snorted. "I didn't say you *were* an angel, just that you kiss like one." Her gaze lowered to his neck. "Oops. I got chocolate on your collar."

"Then I'm going to have to punish you. I think I'll put you over my knees and spank you."

"You'll have to catch me first." She scrambled off his lap and raced to the other side of the table.

"With pleasure." Jake made a grab for her across the table. She shrieked and darted to the right. As he'd guessed the direction she would go, she ran right into him. He circled his arms around her and backed her against the wall.

"You're a bad girl. What do you have to say for yourself?"

"Just this." She wrapped her arms around his neck, pulled herself up his body, wound her legs around his waist, and pushed her groin against his erection.

"You can't possibly know how much I want you, Maria." He thrust his hips against her pelvis. Determined this time to have their clothes off and be deep inside her when he came, he slipped his hands under her bottom to carry her into the bedroom.

The door from the garage opened and Jamie Turner walked in. Maria's eyes widened just before she buried her face in Jake's neck.

"Shit," Jake murmured. He let go of her legs and, when her feet were planted on the floor, he whipped off his shirt, slipping it on her.

Stepping in front of her to block her from view, he glared at Turner. "Saint, what the hell are you doing here?"

Turner glared right back, his eyes sending a message that Jake was scum. "The boss sent me, and now I understand why."

Maria peeked around Jake. "Hi, Jamie. As you can see, we weren't expecting you, and when I see my brother he's dead meat." With her chin up, she marched out of the kitchen. "God, this is so embarrassing," she muttered as she left.

"Just what are your intentions, *Romeo*? Maria's not a woman you can toy with."

"Fuck. I know." Jake swiped a hand through his hair. He felt like a teenager caught making out by his parents. To keep from standing there like a guilty child, he picked up the ice cream bowl and busied himself at the sink washing it.

"And not just because she's Kincaid's sister," Saint said. "She's special, not your kind of woman."

Jake spun, clanging the bowl against the counter. "You think I don't know that?"

Saint shrugged. "I thought you did."

"What're you going to tell the boss?"

"For now, nothing unless he asks a direct question. I won't lie to him for you, though."

As if that was a surprise. Saint didn't lie for anyone. He also didn't cuss, drink, or sleep with every woman who crossed his path, thus his nickname. Kincaid probably wouldn't blink twice if it was Saint panting after Maria.

"And I'd never ask you to, but the boss seems to forget Maria's an adult, free to make her own decisions. I'm not forcing her to do anything she doesn't want, and I'm not out to hurt her."

Saint turned a chair around and straddled it. "That may be, but in the end you will. Unless . . ."

Unless Maria was the one woman he'd give up his lifestyle for. Jake remained silent, refusing to take the bait. He never promised something he couldn't deliver. A contemplative light Jake didn't care for appeared in Saint's eyes.

"You know, I've seen the way you look at her. It's different from how you look at other women. Maybe it's time you grew up, Jake. Stopped chasing skirts and settle down with a good woman." He glanced at the doorway through which Maria had disappeared. "Someone like her."

Who the hell did Saint think he was, Jake's confessor? "I'm tired of this conversation. There's an empty bedroom, last door on the right."

"First, I need you to bring me up to date on where everything stands."

"Tomorrow." Jake headed to his room, stopping at Maria's closed door. He considered knocking and asking if she was all right, but what was there to say? She was once again off-limits, and it was probably for the best. Saint was right. Eventually, he would hurt her.

He showered, something he'd planned for them to do together. Cleaning the sticky chocolate off her body was a chore he'd looked forward to. As the water streamed over him, he closed his eyes and imagined Maria standing in front of him and what he'd do. He'd yet to see her naked, but from what he had seen of her, a picture formed clearly in his mind.

As the fantasy developed, Jake slipped his hand around his erection and pretended it was her soft fingers holding him tightly and milking him. "Maria," he rasped as he came. His body jerked with a violence he'd never before experienced. Christ. If she could do this to him without even being next to him, what would it be like to have the real her?

He leaned his forehead on the wall, his breath harsh to his ears. Unbelievable. He'd climaxed twice tonight, and neither time had it been how he'd wanted. To be wrapped in her slick heat, to hold her close and watch her come, that was what he wanted more than he'd ever wanted anything.

Still, he didn't know what to do about it. Saint's words rang in his ears.

Someone like her.

CHAPTER NINE

———— ✿ ————

The smell of coffee floated down the hall, and Maria eyed her bedroom door. All she had to do was open it and walk out—just pretend nothing embarrassing had happened the night before.

She'd tried several times to contact Logan to give him a piece of her mind, but he wasn't answering his phone. He had to know why she was calling, and he was a coward for refusing to talk to her. It was past time he stopped trying to control her life. Her brother was just too used to protecting her and didn't know how to let go. She got it, she did. He'd spent most of his life taking care of her. But enough was enough.

A knock sounded on her door. "Maria, you up?" Jamie said.

"Be right there." As the sound of his footsteps faded, she inhaled a deep breath and left the sanctuary of her room. As she walked down the hall, her heartbeat picked up speed at seeing Jake. She'd tossed and turned all night thinking about him. God, the things he'd made her feel. He'd certainly proven she wasn't immune to sex, at least when it was with him.

She wanted Jamie gone so she and Jake could pick up where they'd left off. There was so much more he had to teach her, and she couldn't wait to start. To think she'd gone twenty-four years believing there was no pleasure in sex. But sex was what Lovey Dovey had, and Maria had seen no pleasure on her mother's face when she brought her men home or after they left.

It wasn't just sex with Jake, and she finally understood what making love meant. She wanted more. Lots more. Maria walked into the kitchen with a smile on her face, a smile intended for Jake.

The only man in the room was Jamie. Her smile wavered. "Jake's not up yet?" Even as she asked the question, she knew he was gone, could feel his absence.

Pity flashed in Jamie's eyes. "Ah, he left early this morning for Pensacola. The boss's orders."

"So he couldn't even say good-bye?"

"It was the crack of dawn, Maria. He didn't want to wake you."

"Rat bastard."

"Jake said—"

"Him, too, but I was referring to my brother. I'm twenty-four years old. I don't need Logan interfering in my life."

"Sit down."

She eyed the door, wanting nothing more than to lock herself in her room and have a good cry.

"Come on, sit. I'm a good listener, and you can burn my ears off while calling the two of them the nastiest names you can think of."

"You don't cuss. It seems wrong to speak the words in my mind right now to you." She slid into the chair, and he put a cup of coffee in front of her. "Why don't you cuss? I've always wondered about that. I mean, you're around guys all day long whose every other word starts with an F."

His gaze shifted to the window over the sink. "That's a story for another day."

"The coffee's perfect," she said after taking a sip, changing the subject as it was obvious he wasn't going to share.

"Half coffee, half vanilla-flavored cream, and three spoons of sugar."

She lifted a brow, surprised he knew how she took her coffee.

"Jake told me how to make it for you."

His smile was sweet. Why couldn't she have fallen for him instead of bad-boy Jake? Jamie was a gorgeous man, blond and blue-eyed, and a friend to everyone. He wouldn't have left without saying good-bye. No, she had to go and want a man who would probably forget about her within an hour of heading back to Pensacola, and would probably have another woman in his bed by nightfall.

Jamie tilted his head and studied her as if debating what to say. Probably wanted to warn her about Jake. "I know what you're thinking, the same thing my brother would say if he were here. Stay away from Jake, he'll only hurt you."

"Actually, you're wrong. I probably shouldn't say this, and if the boss heard me he'd kick my butt halfway to China, but I'm going to say it anyway. Jake's halfway in love with you, but the fool just doesn't know it."

She jerked her gaze to his. *What?* "Would you repeat that, please? I don't think I heard you right."

"You heard me. He's brushing it off to lust, but he's never looked at another woman the way he does you. There's not another woman he's been with—and you know as well as me there's been many—who he would fret over whether or not I had their coffee preference memorized. He doesn't know I saw him, but he stood in front of your bedroom door and glared at it for five minutes this morning before he left."

Well then. The day just turned brighter. "Why are you telling me this? I mean, I expected you to warn me off, but it sounds like you're doing just the opposite. And what should I do about it?"

"I'll answer your questions, but first tell me this. Are you in love with him?"

Before she spoke, she took a moment to examine her feelings toward Jake. There had been something between them from the very beginning, but he'd put up a wall and a "Do Not Enter" sign on the door. Partly, she suspected, because of her age but mostly because Logan had threatened Jake with death if he came near her.

"I take it as a good sign that you're giving it some thought instead of immediately popping out a 'yes,' which I half expected you to do."

"Okay, here's your answer." Her phone buzzed with an incoming text. She pulled it out of her pocket, read it, and smiled. "It's from Jake. He wants to know if you made me breakfast and if I ate it. I think I'll text him back and tell him you tried to feed me an omelet with broccoli and green peppers."

Jamie laughed and grabbed her phone. "Jake's the cook, not me." He typed some words and handed it back. "Send it," he said.

She read his message. *Saint could give you lessons on cooking for me. I think I'm in love with him.* "Oh, Lord." She grinned. "You dare me?"

"It'll drive him crazy. His mom was a chef before she retired, and he prides himself on his cooking skills."

"I didn't know that." Why hadn't she? What else didn't she know about him? "Here goes nothing then." She pushed "Send." What she wouldn't give to see Jake's face when he read it. Would he get a pang of jealousy? He'd know it was a joke but, still, if he felt something for her it should bother him that Jamie was with her instead of him.

She slipped the phone into her pocket. "Okay, back to my answer. I don't love him, but I think I could. I like him a lot though, and I really believe if he met the right woman he could change. That could be just wishful thinking and he could end up hurting me, but it's a risk I'm willing to take."

"The boss won't be happy if you and Jake hook up, but it's your life and you're all grown-up now, able to make your own decisions. I say go for it. Buchanan needs his life turned upside down." He stood and collected their cups. "So, what's the plan for today?"

"I have classes from ten to four, then I need to make arrangements to clean out my apartment. Hopefully, I can salvage a few things."

"If we leave in thirty minutes, we'll have time to stop for breakfast."

She glanced at the clock. "Great, I'm hungry all of a sudden."

When she got out of the shower her phone beeped. Another text from Jake. She read it and burst into laughter. *You won't be happy with Saint. His pecker's only an inch long. Mine on the other hand . . .*

Maybe he was jealous. After considering her reply, she texted him back. *So you claim. I wouldn't know since you left without even saying good-bye, much less showing me your goods.*

———— ❧ ————

Jake finished his breakfast and glanced at the bill. His phone buzzed, and he read Maria's response. She wasn't happy with him. Like that was a surprise. So what if it'd been five in the morning? He should have told her he had been ordered home.

Outside of the diner he stared back down the road he'd just traveled. He was half tempted to turn around and go back. It would mean the loss of his job, but there were other places he could work. Of course, he'd have to move and then he'd never see her.

Disappearing from her life would probably be the best thing he could do for her. It would sure as hell make the boss happy. With a sigh, he turned the car in the direction of home—only a few miles away. He was feeling rather selfish where Maria was concerned, and until he figured out just what he wanted from her, he'd best not make Kincaid any madder.

She had better be kidding about thinking she was in love with Saint. The man would make a perfect husband, but he'd bore her within a month. Maria was all fire and passion. She'd burn through Saint so fast he wouldn't know what hit him.

She had a little more than a week of school left, which meant Saint would be glued to her until it was time for her to come home. What if she did start to fall for him? Jake clinched his teeth. He should be with her, protecting her. What if Fortunada somehow found her?

He pulled into his driveway and turned off the car. Snatching his phone out of his pocket, he called Saint.

"I've asked her to marry me, and she said yes," Saint said in greeting.

The man wasn't as funny as he believed. "I already told her your pecker's only an inch long, so I know you're lying."

"Ah, but it grows to an amazing length for her."

"Shut up, Saint."

"The girl's getting to you. Never thought I'd see the day. So, what's up? You home?"

"Just pulled into the driveway. I wanted to make sure you're not letting her out of your sight and that you're keeping an eye out for Fortunada."

"Rest easy. I won't let anything happen to her. I've gone through your report, and the Tango's mug shot's imprinted on my brain. She's got classes until four today, then we're going to her apartment to see what can be salvaged."

He should be with her when she returned home. "Not much I'm afraid. The bastard did a thorough job of destroying her things. Do me a favor and keep in touch. If something goes down, I'm coming back whether the boss approves or not."

"No problem. By the way, what's with that cat of hers?"

"Whatcha mean?"

"He growls at me. Won't let me near him. It's weird because I like cats and usually they like me."

Jake developed a sudden fondness for the fat fur ball. "He's my bud. You can't have him."

"Got it. Hands off the girl and her cat."

"Damn straight." He clicked off. Just as he entered his condo his phone buzzed, and he glanced at the ID.

"Yo, boss."

"You home?"

"Walking in my door as we speak."

"Good. I'm working from home. Don't want to leave Dani. Be at my house in thirty." As usual, he hung up without saying good-bye.

Some time to get his act together before facing Kincaid would have been welcomed. Jake tossed his tote on the bed, shaved, changed clothes, and was out the door in twenty. He pulled into the Kincaids' driveway two minutes early. Dani opened the door when he knocked.

"Good God," he said. "Are you having triplets?"

"Actually, I think I'm having a cow. A full-grown one." She pressed her swollen belly against his stomach and kissed his cheek. "How are you, Jake?"

Now there was a loaded question. "I've been better, and I've been worse. If you could steal us some time, I'd love to have a private conversation."

"Consider it done."

Dani Kincaid was one of his best friends, a woman he could talk to and trust to keep their conversations private, even from her husband. She'd been married to Evan Prescott, the boss's closest friend, when Jake first met her.

After Prescott had been killed in Afghanistan on a mission, Kincaid had gone to their home in Asheville to protect Dani from a stalker and the two had fallen in love. She'd softened her husband's hard edges, but the edges were still there, and Jake didn't doubt he was about to be on the receiving end.

He followed her through the kitchen out to the deck where Kincaid sat drinking coffee, his computer open in front of him. The day was cloudless, the Gulf barely making a whisper as the waves lapped the shore. Jake had always loved Kincaid's house, and idly wondered if there were any like it for sale in the area. Not that he could afford a place this grand, but Maria . . . Damn, what the hell was wrong with his brain? Slamming the door on thoughts of her, he put on his game face, a wise thing to do before an encounter with the boss.

"Coffee, Jake?" Dani asked.

"Would love some, but sit down. I'll get it." She was so big and ready to pop out their son that just walking back into the kitchen might trigger labor. He knew his way around and after filling his cup, returned to the deck and took a seat opposite Kincaid.

The boss leaned over and soundly kissed his wife. "Now, get lost, sweetheart. Buchanan and I have some serious talking to do."

Dani glanced at Jake and winked. "I don't think so. You're angry with him right now, so I'm sticking around to make sure you don't kill him."

If anyone else refused Kincaid's orders, there would've been hell to pay. All he did in response to his wife's disobedience was chuckle. Jake would love to know her secret. Especially now. He made a million-dollar wager with himself that he could guess the first words out of Kincaid's mouth.

Cold black eyes focused on him. "Anything go on between you and my sister you'd rather me not know about?"

Bingo. It was the moment of truth, so he lied. A bit. "Not a thing and not because I'm not interested."

"She's not for you, Romeo."

Christ, he hated that name. He'd once been proud of it—the proof of his manliness—back when he was stupid enough to think his conquests said something about who he was.

Dani placed her hand on her husband's arm. "Logan, that's not for you to say. Maria's a grown woman. If she wants Jake, that's for her to decide."

"He's going to hurt her."

And there it was. What everyone believed, even him. He'd thought it, worried about it, and had then decided he wanted what he wanted. In his scenario, they both tired of each other at the same time and she wouldn't be hurt. Who was he kidding?

"And if he does, that's still her decision," Dani said.

Kincaid closed his laptop. "There are very few times I tell you to butt out, Dani, but this is one of them. Maria's not for Buchanan. If he touches her, he'd better find a job on the other side of the world. There's nothing either of you can say to change my mind. End of discussion."

"You're a pigheaded man, love. Excuse me for a minute, gentlemen."

Jake pressed his lips together to keep from telling the boss to go to hell. Apparently, he had two choices, his job or Maria. He wanted both. Until he had time to consider his options, he'd best keep the angry words locked tight in his mouth.

A flock of pelicans flew over, single file, and Jake watched them until they disappeared from view. Two dolphins soared out of the water, twisted, and made a splash as they came down on their backs. The nine-o'clock sun had already turned the Gulf's waters to an emerald green as pretty as anything one would find in the Caribbean Islands.

Could he give up everything for Maria? The boss had just made it clear that his job was on the line. He wasn't a forever man, and whatever they had between them wouldn't last. But what if it did and she was the one?

Dani returned, looking pale. Jake was about to ask if she was all right when Kincaid spoke.

"You're leaving Wednesday."

"Going where?" He was being sent away, intentionally, he was sure.

"Egypt. Nineteen-year-old kid decided a year ago the life his rich parents offered wasn't for him and changed his name from Chad Sinclair to Abdul Haq."

"Servant of the Truth," Jake said.

"Yeah, and the truth he learned was the fun of being a terrorist wasn't all it was cracked up to be, and now he wants to come home. Guess he missed beer and girls. His parents didn't hear a word from the time he disappeared until a week ago when he managed to send a coded e-mail, which his father turned over to his good friend, a CIA code breaker.

"Unfortunately for our boy, he's a whiz on the computer and the bad guys don't want to let him go. Daddy's friend worked a deal with his superiors on behalf of the family. If the kid comes home and brings all the intel he's got access to, they'll go easy on him. It's your job to retrieve him."

Because of Dani, Jake swallowed his first response. "Well hell. Who's on this operation with me?"

Kincaid slid a folder across the table. "Everything you need to know is here. You're going in as a reporter. Bayne's your cameraman and Stewart's your soundman."

Jake picked up the file and stood. "I've always wanted to be on TV."

"Logan, can't you send someone else?" Dani asked.

"No, Saint's taken the last two operations. I'm due," Jake said as he thumbed through the dossier. "Think I'll head over to the office and start planning the operation." He pressed Dani's shoulder.

"We'll talk another time." Until this mission was over, he couldn't afford distractions, and Chiquita was definitely a distraction.

She tensed under his palm and pressed her hands over her stomach. "Oh . . . Oh."

The boss turned over his chair in his haste to kneel in front of his wife. "How far apart?"

"Three minutes. Oh . . . crap, that one hurt."

"Dammit, Dani, why didn't you tell me when the contractions started?" Kincaid said.

"Anything I can do?" Jake asked. It was the first time Jake had ever heard fear in the boss's voice. Even in a fierce firefight, the Iceman was always cool and calm.

"Yeah," Dani said. "Ask Mrs. Jankowski to grab my overnight case."

Happy to be useful, he ran through the house calling for Mrs. Jankowski. Dani's five-year-old daughter, Regan, ran out of her bedroom as he raced up the stairs.

"Jake! Did you come to play with me? Mommy wrote me a book about my real daddy and we can read it together. He died in the war when I wasn't born yet. Did you know that?"

The awful night was etched in Jake's memory. He knelt and brushed a strand of damp hair from her face. "Yes, sweetheart, I did know that, and I knew your daddy. He was a very brave man, and I do want to read your book with you but I can't right now. I promise I'll come back soon so you can share your daddy book with me." Standing, he started down the hall. "Where's Mrs. Jankowski?"

Regan jogged along beside him. "She's in my bathroom. We're giving Luke a bath."

He made an about-turn. "You still have that rat?" Not only had Kincaid rescued his wife when she'd been kidnapped, but he'd also brought Luke back with him.

Regan giggled. "I keep telling you he's a doggie. Why can't you remember that?"

The girl was adorable and the very image of her mother except for her eyes, and those were straight from Evan Prescott, her daddy. "Mrs. Jankowski!" he called at the door to Regan's room.

She peeked around the corner of the bathroom. "Goodness, what's all the yelling about?"

"I need Dani's overnight bag."

"Oh my, is it time?" She hurried off, and a soaped-up Doberman took the opportunity to escape.

"Luke, come back," Regan yelled, chasing after him.

"Here you go. You call me as soon as that baby comes," Mrs. Jankowski said, handing Jake the tote.

"I will." Jake grabbed it and ran down the stairs.

Dani and Kincaid were in the car, the engine running, when Jake reached them. He opened the back door and tossed the case in.

"Do me a favor, Jake, and call Maria. Let her know," Dani said.

As it was Friday and she would be out of classes for the weekend, that meant she would come home. His mind needed to be on his new mission and not on Maria. He'd lock himself up with his team while she was in town and avoid her as much as possible. After he brought the kid back from Egypt, he'd decide whether he was prepared to risk it all for her.

CHAPTER TEN

———— ❧ ————

I just realized I need to stop by my apartment and get a book I need for today," Maria said after leaving the IHOP. One benefit about having breakfast with Jamie was he didn't give the stink eye to her chocolate chip pancakes topped with syrup and whipped cream.

When they pulled into her parking slot, Maria's stomach gave a sickening roll at the thought of going inside and seeing her destroyed apartment again. "I don't want to go in there."

"It's that bad?" Jamie asked.

"He destroyed it. I need to get past these last few days of school before I deal with it."

"Tell me where the book is, and I'll get it for you."

She handed him her keys. "On the kitchen table, there're two of them. I'll need both. And the notebook they're sitting on." Hopefully, they'd not been destroyed. She had been too upset to even notice if they were still there when she'd first discovered her apartment had been ransacked.

"Keep the doors locked. I'll be right back." At the front of the car, he stopped and scanned the area in a full circle before jogging up the sidewalk.

Maria slipped her phone out of her pocket, clicking it on. Nothing else from Jake. Fine, she needed to concentrate on her last few days of school anyway. Once she was done with her exams, she could go home and then . . . What? Wait for him to call? Call him? She was twenty-four years old and should know how the dating game worked, but she was pathetically clueless about such things.

The window crashed in on her, a rock landing on her lap and glass hitting her in the face. The startled scream died in her throat at the sight of Fortunada reaching in and grabbing the door handle. For a split second, she froze, unable to believe this was happening.

Then her brain kicked in and she scrambled over the console, intending to jump out the driver's side door. Fortunada caught her by the foot, and for a few seconds a tug of war ensued as she desperately held on to the steering wheel. With the heel of her sandals, she kicked at the fingers digging into her ankle.

"Fucking bitch."

He reached inside and stomach punched her so hard she reflexively clutched her waist and struggled to get air back into her lungs. Before she could catch her breath, he opened the door and dragged her out of the car. At the last moment, she grabbed her phone from where it had fallen on the floor and pushed it into her bra.

When she fell in a heap on the pavement, he dragged her up, almost pulling her arms out of their sockets. Oh, God. Where was Jamie? He'd come out any second, she just had to keep Fortunada from carrying her off first. Hoping Jamie or her neighbors would hear, she screamed and kept screaming. Unfortunately, the majority of the residents were college students and would've been on their way to class by then. No one would sleep in and skip final exams.

Fortunada fisted her hair around his hand and dragged her behind him toward the complex's pool house. With the way he had hold of her, she was helpless to do anything but stumble along behind him. Was he so enraged he didn't hear her yelling for help or did he just not care? The last thought frightened her the most.

Think, Maria! A trail, she should leave a trail. She stepped out of one of her sandals, hoping he wouldn't notice. At the beginning of the sidewalk leading up to the pool house, she kicked off her other shoe. When they reached the door the maintenance guys kept locked, he yanked it open and pushed her inside. Just before he did, however, she managed to drop her watch on the grass next to the sidewalk.

That the door was unlocked meant he'd lain in wait for her to return home. *Oh, God. Oh, God. Oh, God.* Was he going to kill her?

He flipped on the light switch and just stood there, staring at her with the coldest eyes she'd ever seen. As she backed into the corner, she frantically searched for anything she could use as a weapon. There were lots of things: pool vacs, nets on long poles, and large bottles of chlorine. If she could get one of them opened, she could throw it in his face. If she went for one though, he'd be on her before she could get the cap off.

She heard a whimper and knew it had come from her. "What do you want?" The sound of her voice surprised her, her heart pounding so hard she hadn't thought she was capable of forming words. The back of her legs bumped into something and her knees gave out. Glancing down, she saw she was sitting on a pile of bagged grass fertilizer. On the floor next to the bottom bag was a trowel.

"What do I want?" He took a step toward her. "You owe me, bitch. Because of you, the cops are looking for me."

As subtly as possible, she shifted, sliding her foot over the trowel to keep him from seeing it. "I didn't do anything."

Another step brought him closer. "Why were you at my house?"

"I-I . . ." If she told him she might be his daughter would it keep him from hurting her? Before she could decide what to say, he lunged. She twisted so that he came down on her back; she reached down and grabbed the trowel.

With her stomach pressed to the bags of fertilizer and the weight of him on top of her, it was impossible to turn around. With one hand, he cradled her head and smashed her face into the plastic bag. The other hand pushed its way under her and into the top of her capris.

There'd been too many times growing up in her mother's house when she'd had to fight off the advances of men, many of them drunk. No way was the bastard trying to fondle her going to be the one to take what she'd never willingly given. That he might be her father sent a rush of adrenaline racing through her, a resolve to keep the unthinkable from happening.

If only she could get herself turned around, she could aim the trowel at his throat, even better, one of his eyes. Knowing she didn't have his strength and couldn't move as long as he was on top of her, she went limp, pretending to pass out.

When his weight suddenly left her, she thought her plan had worked. She twisted and brought the trowel up, preparing to plunge it into him, father or not. He wasn't there. Instead, he and Jamie were in an all-out fight on the floor of the pool house. Maria pushed herself up and fumbled in her blouse for her phone. Her hands shook so hard, she dropped it and it skittered across the room. As she crawled to it, a toolbox against the wall caught her eye. Scrambling to it, she found a hammer inside, then snatched up her phone. A better weapon in hand, she watched for a chance to bring the hammer down on Fortunada's head. The two men were rolling and moving too fast. Afraid she would hit Jamie, she stood back and watched, feeling helpless as her shaking fingers tried to dial 911.

After giving the dispatcher their location, Maria kept the phone line open, but set her cell on a nearby shelf. The hammer clutched in her hands, she watched the two men fight. Neither man seemed to be aware of anything but doing as much damage as possible to the other.

Sirens finally sounded in the distance, and she hoped they were responding to her call. In a move that happened so fast she gasped in surprised, Jamie hooked his leg around Fortunada's, flipped him, and straddled his back. A gun appeared as if out of nowhere and Jamie pressed it to the man's head.

"You move, you die, you fucking bastard."

If he hadn't used words she'd never heard Saint say before, she wouldn't have known how upset he was. He wasn't even breathing hard and he'd sounded like he was talking about the weather—all cool, calm, and collected.

The sirens were earsplitting now, and she sank onto the bags, her legs suddenly refusing to hold her up. The hammer fell out of her hands, clanking as it hit the floor. The next twenty minutes passed in a daze as she answered Detective Nolan's questions. Finally, the patrol car drove off with Fortunada in the back, and a few minutes later the detective left.

Jamie led her to his car, his hand protectively clasping her elbow. He made her sit in the back while he used a shop vac he'd found in the pool house to clean the glass from her seat. All she could think about—just couldn't get it out of her mind—was that her possible father had tried to rape her. She shuddered, afraid she might lose her breakfast.

"I think you should skip your classes today," Jamie said when he finished.

"I ca-can't. It's a review for . . . for one of my last exams next week." And hopefully, it would help get her mind back where it needed to be.

He studied her for a moment before sighing heavily. "Then I need to go back inside and get your books. You're coming with me."

The last thing she wanted was to see her destroyed apartment again, but she didn't want to be alone either, even knowing the cops had Fortunada. *Paranoid much, Maria?* "I'll stand just inside the door."

A few minutes later and they were back in the car. Hot wind was blowing in the broken window and battling with the air-conditioning Jamie had turned on high.

"I'm sorry."

She reached over and gave his arm an awkward little pat. "I know, and you don't have to keep saying it. There was no way for you to know he would be there." It hadn't occurred to either of them that Fortunada would be inside her apartment, behind the door. That he'd hit Jamie over the head with her bronze statue of Lady Justice just seemed wrong.

"I should have been prepared for the possibility."

She heard the disgust—aimed at himself—in his voice. She'd been around SEALs long enough to know they took failure to heart, and nothing she could say would keep him from beating himself up about it. Maybe he should have considered Fortunada to be a devious rat bastard, and Logan would no doubt blow his top when he heard, but what was done was done.

"How's your head? You really should have it checked." Both she and Detective Nolan had tried to get him to go to the hospital, but he'd refused to leave her side. She was grateful he hadn't been knocked out for long.

"It's fine."

Okay, he wanted to stew about it for a while.

He slapped the heel of his hand against the steering wheel. "If you hadn't left me a trail to follow, I might not have found you in time. I'm not sure I could've lived with that."

So that's what was really bothering him. She shifted in her seat to face him. "Jamie, you did find me in time and I'm okay." Not true, but he was doing a fine job of wallowing in guilt without any help from her.

He looked at her for the first time since they'd gotten in the car. "Are you? Really?"

Wanting to see the guilt in his eyes go away, she smiled. "I am. I won't deny he scared the crap out of me, but nothing happened and I wasn't hurt. He's a creep, one I don't plan to think about after today." And how she wished that were true. It would probably be easier to get him out of her mind if she knew for sure he wasn't her father.

"Good." Jamie flipped on the blinker to turn into the school's entrance.

How hard was it going to be to get him to keep this between the two of them? "I don't think we should tell Logan and Jake about today."

"No can do."

Well, it was worth a try. She'd expected he would feel obligated to tell her brother. "Just Logan then. Jake will likely freak out and do something stupid like come back here. Then Logan will get pissed . . . well, you can see how that would play out."

"I'll leave it up to the boss whether or not he wants to tell Jake."

"Fair enough." It was better than nothing, and she would ask Logan not to tell Jake. Jamie parked the car and walked her to her classroom, taking a position against the wall outside the door. She knew he wouldn't move from that spot until she came out.

CHAPTER ELEVEN

Four o'clock finally arrived and Maria was free until Monday. When she walked out of class, Jamie stood exactly where she'd left him. Poor man, he must be bored out of his mind.

"You need to call Jake." He pushed away from the wall and stepped next to her.

"He knows?" Damn, that was the last thing she wanted.

"No. Just call him."

Handing her books to him, she dug in her purse for her cell. Turning it back on, she punched *3, speed-dialing Jake.

"Hey, Aunt Maria," Jake said.

Because she was used to being called "aunt" by Regan, it didn't register at first.

"Maybe I should say, new Aunt Maria."

"Oh, my God, Dani had her baby?"

"Two hours ago. Evan Elijah Kincaid—nine pounds, two ounces, twenty-one and a half inches."

Named for Regan's father and his twin brother. "That sounds really big. Is it? How's Dani? How's the baby? How's Logan?"

He laughed. "Slow down, Chiquita. Yes, apparently that's bigger than normal, but no record set. Dani's doing great. Baby Evan's doing great, all ten fingers and toes accounted for. Your brother's in the middle of a nervous breakdown but still sane enough to pass out cigars to all the nurses, doctors, and if they'd let him, to all the babies in the nursery. You'd think he managed having his son single-handedly, but I've never seen him happier."

Maria squeezed her eyes shut against the burning in them. Her brother was a father, something he'd once thought he'd never be. This was just what she needed to get her mind off Fortunada, and she wanted to be there. "I'm coming home tonight. Tell Dani and Logan I'll see them in about four hours."

"I figured you would. Well, I'd best go see if I can calm down the new dad. Later."

Later? That was all? "Jake, wait."

"Yeah?"

She opened her mouth, but didn't know what to say. After all that had happened earlier, she felt the need to tell him how special he was to her. Even over the phone, though, she sensed he'd put his walls back up. "Nothing. See you soon."

"Sure," he said and hung up.

"What's his problem?" she muttered, giving the phone a nasty glare. Other students jostled her as they streamed out of the College of Law building, off to start their weekend.

Jamie moved behind her, protecting her with his bulk. "He's not a happy camper right now. You've got his boxers twisted in knots, and now the boss is sending him on a mission."

When she stopped, he put his hands on her shoulders. "Keep moving, or else we're gonna be stampeded. These people take their TGIF seriously."

"That they do," she said as they walked out into the blinding Florida sun. "What's this about Jake? Logan's sending him off? When and where?"

"Sometime next week."

Jamie opened her car door, then came around to his side. "As

111

to the where, I can't say. If the boss wants you to know, he'll tell you."

She slipped on her sunglasses. "At least tell me if it's some-place dangerous." When he didn't answer, she knew. What if Jake got hurt, or worse? Sweat trickled down the back of her neck. She pulled a band out of her pocket and bound her hair up into a pony-tail. "Turn the air up, will you? I'm burning up with this hot wind coming in the window." He turned the knob to high, and she leaned her face close to the air blasting out of the vent.

"I guess you want to put off going to your apartment until next week?"

What she wanted was for Jake to avoid danger. She wanted to turn the clock back a day for Jake to be there instead of Jamie. "Yeah, that can wait. I just need to stop by the house, throw a few clothes into a bag, and put extra food out for Mouse."

"No problem. With my window busted in, we'll need to take your Mustang."

The three-hour drive home on I-10 was boring, and one she'd made countless times. It gave her plenty of time to think about Jake. Had she disgusted him? No, she believed him when he said he wasn't like Jonathan. It was probably her inexperience. Why would he want her when he could crook his finger and have just about any woman who caught his eye?

Jake wouldn't blow off Logan's warnings, but if he really wanted her, that wouldn't stop him. He'd find a way to make it right with her brother. So, that left . . . what? That he saw her as more than a one-night stand? Well, she hoped so. It was a role she would never agree to play. She wasn't her mother and had no inten-tion of having a revolving door into her bedroom.

If he saw her differently from the women he was used to, then it probably scared the hell out of him. What if he thought he couldn't be faithful? Between not wanting to hurt her and Logan's threat, Jake would put on the brakes and try to back away, which seemed to be exactly what he was doing.

"He's afraid of commitment," she murmured.

"Bingo."

Had she spoken aloud? She glanced at Jamie. "But aren't all men?"

"To one degree or another, I think, but I'd put Buchanan at the top of that scale."

Out of curiosity, she asked, "Where are you on the scale?"

He grinned and winked at her. "Why, you interested in me?"

She should be. He was a gorgeous man with a great personality. "And if I were?"

That got her a laugh. "Then I'd say you're a liar. No, you only have eyes for bad boy Jake."

"So what do I do about it?"

"Just keep coming at him. He'll fight you, but if you don't give up on him, he'll come around—realize it's what he wants."

That sounded easier said than done, but her heart wanted Jake—had for years—so she had to at least try. She also needed to convince Logan to back off. Maybe his attention would now be on his new son, and he'd stop trying to interfere in her love life.

Jamie seemed as willing as she not to talk about Fortunada, and for that she was grateful. She didn't want to talk about him, think about him, and especially didn't want to wonder if he was her father. If he was, that would make what he'd tried to do to her in the pool shed gross, even if he didn't know it was his daughter he'd tried to molest.

To take her mind off all men, and because she needed to hit the books, she spent the remainder of the trip studying for her upcoming final exams.

By the time they reached the hospital, it was the dinner hour, and Maria found Logan and Jake in the cafeteria. She and Jamie grabbed trays and slid them down the line. The only things she found that she would eat were macaroni and cheese, and a dried-up hamburger patty. She supposed it was too much to expect a hospital to serve fried chicken, mashed potatoes, and gravy. Deciding to pass on the patty, she ended up with a bowl of mac and cheese, and two chocolate chip cookies.

Jamie pressed his arm against hers. "Your boy hasn't taken his eyes off you since you walked into the room."

Her heart gave a happy little flutter. Maybe she could talk Jake into leaving Jamie to babysit Logan and taking her to Steak 'n Shake. She slid into the seat next to Logan, putting her across from Jake.

She leaned over and gave her brother a kiss on the cheek. "Congratulations, Daddy. I'm surprised you're not upstairs with Dani."

He pushed his empty plate away. "She's sleeping, but I'm going back up now."

Jake snorted. "Bullshit, boss. You're headed back to the nursery so you can press your nose to the window and stare at your son."

Logan shrugged. "So what if I am? It's not every father who can claim his baby is the most handsome one there."

A giggle escaped her. Although her brother tried for nonchalance, he couldn't hide the proud gleam in his eyes. "I can't wait to see him. I'll come up as soon as I finish eating."

"Walk with me a minute," Logan said.

Oh, boy. He wasn't gonna wait until later to discuss Fortunada's surprise attack. "I'll be right back," she told Jake and Jamie, exchanging a glance with Jamie.

In the hallway, her normally undemonstrative brother grabbed her in a tight bear hug.

"Jesus Christ, brat, you're going to give me a heart attack yet. Are you okay?" He leaned back and searched her face.

"Yeah, I am." As she'd done for Jamie, she assured Logan she was perfectly fine. These larger-than-life heroes were prone to do whatever it took to protect those they loved, and she didn't want him deciding he needed to go after Fortunada personally. Another reason not to tell Jake. God knew what he'd get in his head to do.

"Saint said you don't want Buchanan to know, and I agree it's probably for the best right now. I'm sending him on an operation, and he needs to be focused."

"Where to?"

He tapped her nose with his finger. "All you need to worry about is your last few days of school."

With that, he turned to walk away. "Don't be mad at Jamie, okay?" she called after him.

Coming to a halt, he turned. "That's between me and Saint."

Oh no, he wasn't happy with Jamie. Not that she expected him to be, but it really wasn't Jamie's fault. She returned to the cafeteria and as soon as she sat, Jake stood.

"I'm off, too. I've got a lot to do before Wednesday."

He'd ignored her since she'd arrived. Obviously, he wasn't going to make it easy to follow Jamie's advice. "I was going to ask if you'd take me to get something to eat after I saw the baby." She wrinkled her nose at her plate. "I'm starving, and this food pretty much sucks."

He met her gaze for a mere second, then his eyes slid away. "I'm sure Saint will be happy to feed you."

"You bet," Jamie said.

Maria watched, fascinated, as Jake glared at Jamie, some kind of male stare down going on between the two of them. "What was that all about?" she asked after Jake strode away.

"He won't admit it even to himself, but he's not liking me any-where near you."

That was a positive sign, wasn't it? "Come on. Let's go see the most beautiful baby in the world." She'd think about Jake and the next step in her campaign to wear him down later.

———— ⁗ ————

Jake pushed the papers aside and pressed his fingers over the bridge of his nose. This was what happened when you let a woman get under your skin. You couldn't concentrate, and in this business that was deadly.

His stomach growled, and he glanced at his watch. It was only nine, and he'd intended to spend several more hours mapping out a plan to rescue the spoiled, rich kid/terrorist-in-the-making. He could head over to Buck's on the Beach and find Rosie, or Connie, maybe Karen—didn't really matter which one—and try his best to get Maria out of his mind. Yeah, that's what he'd do.

After flipping off the lights and setting the alarm, he stood outside the K2 building and looked up at the sky. Nothing but stars, a perfect night for drinking on the beach. He got behind the wheel and pointed his car toward his favorite pickup bar.

As always on a Friday night, Buck's was packed. Jake made his way out onto the back deck and claimed the one empty seat at the bar.

"Jake, my man," Buck greeted, sliding a bottle of Dos Equis toward him.

"You got uglier since the last time I saw you," Jake said, catching the beer before it slid past.

The old man gave a hearty laugh. "Good thing the girls don't think so."

He estimated Buck to be around seventy, and his beach bar had been a hot spot for as far back as Jake could remember. The story was that thirty or forty years ago, Buck had sat on a chair in the sand, and without any building plans, had told the construction workers to put a wall here, one there, a bar to the left, a stage to the right, and so on.

Jake believed it. The place looked like the Mad Hatter had built it with mismatched pieces of wood that had washed up on the beach. The only reason city officials hadn't closed it down for not meeting code was because the locals would run them all out of office if they tried to mess with Buck's place.

Buck glanced over Jake's shoulder and grinned. "Looks like Carly's headed your way."

Hell. "Her boyfriend around tonight?"

"Should be getting off duty in about an hour. Why don't you just give in and fight the man? I'll set up a ring out on the sand and you two can go at it. Unless you're *ah-skeered* of him." Buck cackled and moved down the bar.

Jake grunted and took a sip of the ice-cold brew. He could take the dude on, but just didn't see the sense in tangling with a cop. No good could come of it.

"Hi, Jake." Carly squeezed in next to him.

"Hey, Trouble."

"Aw, you say the sweetest things. That's why I like you. Come dance with me."

"I get anywhere near you, beautiful, and Mr. Big Bad Policeman's gonna trump up a reason to throw me in jail. Go find someone else to play with."

Full, red lips formed a pout. "I want to play with you. Pleeease."

Not happening. He'd danced with her before he knew she had a jealous cop for a boyfriend. The man had gunned for him ever since. No woman was worth fighting over. *Maria is,* said a voice in his head. Dammit. He was here to get her out of his mind.

"Buck," he called and held up his empty bottle. Carly's hand found its way to his thigh, and he sighed. There must be a hundred plus men here tonight. Why him? His beer came sliding down the length of the bar. Jake picked it up and stood.

"Here, have a seat."

When she was settled, he noted that her miniskirt barely covered her crotch. She was trouble, all right. "Later," he said and walked away.

Was this to be his existence? Hanging out in bars, looking for the next pickup, and fighting off women who were trouble. He hadn't thought much about it before—had rather liked his life, the danger of his job, the fun of deciding who he'd take home. He still loved what he did for a living, but the glitter of his nightlife was quickly fading.

An image of him at fifty or sixty—the hair from one side of his head swept over to the other in a futile attempt to hide his bald spots—and hanging out at Buck's hoping to score played through his mind like a bad movie.

Damn you, Maria. She was messing with his head, not to mention his nightlife.

Eight, maybe nine beers—maybe more—and two hours later, he'd danced with Rosie, Karen, and several women he'd never met before. All had been willing to go home with him, and he'd fully intended to end his night with one of them. He just couldn't find the desire to follow through.

"Hit me," he called to Buck, stumbling as he aimed for a bar stool.

The old man came over empty-handed. "I think you've had enough, son. You ain't driving tonight, are you?"

Jake laughed. "How the hell you thunk . . . think I got here?"

"Still driving that Challenger?"

"Uh-huh."

"They got special keys, don't they? You know, cool ones with all those buttons you can push."

He dug into his pocket, found the fob and stared at it, trying to bring it into focus. "Yep."

"Let me see."

Next thing Jake knew, Buck had his car keys and wouldn't return them. "That was a dirty strick . . . trick. Gimme them back."

"Nope. Never seen you drunk before, Jake. Don't much like it. Now call a friend to come get you."

Hell. He didn't exactly have a friend. Well, the boss was a friend of sorts, but he wasn't about to call him. If he called Saint, another sorta friend, he'd never hear the end of it. He could call any number of K2 employees, but didn't want them talking about having to drive Romeo home. Rosie or one of the other girls would be more than happy to drive him, but they'd expect to come inside with him. Nah, not in the mood.

He fumbled for his cell and finding it, scrolled through the blurry numbers, flipped past Maria's, then back to it. She was his friend, right? Why the hell not call her since she was the reason he was drunk. He pushed her number.

"Jake?"

"How'd ya know it's me?"

"Ah, a little thing known as caller ID."

"You're being scar . . . shar . . . sar–cas–tic. It's not becomer . . . becoming."

"What's wrong with you? You sound drunk."

"You been talking to Buck?" He glared at the old man.

"Who?"

Jake handed the phone to Buck. "She wants to talk to you."

Twenty minutes later, Maria, his friend, stood next to him. He grinned. "Hi, Sha . . . Chiquita, my best friend."

She leaned away. "You smell like cigarettes."

He grinned. "That's 'cause I smoked some."

"You don't smoke."

"Oh."

She glanced at Buck. "What does he owe you?"

"He's good for it, just get him home and put him to bed. You the reason he's messed up?"

The two shared a look Jake couldn't interpret before she turned to him and tilted her head, studying him. "I don't know, am I?"

He nodded. "Yep." Buck had told her to put him to bed. He liked the sound of that.

She put her hand on his leg and squeezed. "Come on, Tiger Toes, let's get you home."

"Kay." He slid off the bar stool. Why did her hand feel so much better than Carly's? Also, he was starting to like "Tiger Toes." He really must be drunk.

Trying not to lean too heavily on her, he let Maria—his best friend in the world—lead him to his car. "Where'd ya get those?" he asked when she hit the button to unlock the Challenger.

"What, the keys?"

"Yep."

She opened the passenger door and pushed him inside. "From Buck."

Tomorrow he was going to kill the old man, but tonight he loved the sneaky bastard for getting Maria here. He just might love her, too. Tomorrow, he'd figure that one out. Looked like tomorrow was gonna be a busy day.

CHAPTER TWELVE

———— ❦ ————

"Missed you," Jake said as she turned out of the parking lot, then he promptly fell asleep.

Maria didn't like seeing him drunk, but couldn't help liking the things he said when not at his best. He probably wouldn't remember any of it when he sobered up. Unable to sleep, she'd been reading one of Dani's books when he'd called. His slurred speech had alarmed her. In all the years she'd known him, she'd never seen him the slightest bit tipsy. What did it mean if he was in this state because of her?

She pulled up in front of his condo. "We're here." He responded with a snore. She turned off the iginition and twisted in her seat. Half tempted to take a picture of him drunk with his mouth hanging open, she shook her head and resisted the urge. If Jamie was right and Jake was half in love with her, then it was time he stopped fighting it. He was flying out on Wednesday, and she wanted things settled between them before he left.

"Why you staring at me?" One eye slitted open.

She shrugged. "Why not?"

"Tried to get you outta my head." Surprising her, he leaned over and gave her a clumsy kiss.

He smelled like booze, cheap perfume, and cigarettes. "God, you stink." Of the three, some other woman's perfume on him was the worst. The only way he could smell like that was if the woman had climbed all over him, and obviously, he'd allowed it. Rat bastard.

"Then we need a shower." He opened the door and stumbled out. He made it halfway up the sidewalk before he realized she wasn't with him and turned around, weaving his way back to the car. "Come," he said, tapping on the window.

Did he think they were going to have sex? No way. He was drunk. She'd seen too many wasted men, many of them mean, fumbling in their efforts to screw Lovey Dovey, sometimes knocking her around. Not that she believed Jake would mistreat her, but he wasn't particularly appealing in his current state. If she was smart, she'd go home and bring the Challenger back to him in the morning.

He opened the door and tugged on her hand. "Come on." A lopsided grin appeared on his face. "Please."

Apparently, she wasn't smart. Besides, she had the keys to his condo and doubted he could manage to find the keyhole. She'd at least unlock the door for him, maybe make a pot of coffee. He could sure use some.

This was the first time she'd been inside his condo, and she looked around with interest, surprised at how nice it was. She'd expected something messy—clothes and magazines strewn about—the furniture worn and cheap.

It was, instead, understated elegance, and as neat as a pin. She hoped he never saw her room. If he was responsible for the décor, then he had a good eye. A brown leather sofa, a matching Euro chair, and a glass coffee table, were the only pieces of furniture. A sand-colored seagrass area rug covered part of the dark wood floor, the biggest TV screen she'd ever seen hung on one wall, and a painting that appeared expensive was on another.

She walked to the picture and studied it. The scene was the back of a young woman with long black hair wearing a knee-length yellow sundress looking out over the Gulf at the rising sun. Barefoot, she stood ankle deep in the water, and the breeze lifted her hair and the hem of her dress, showing a glimpse of one brown thigh.

Maria felt Jake's breath on her neck, which would have been nice if he didn't smell like a brewery. "This is a nice picture."

"She's you."

Wow. He'd bought a painting because it reminded him of her? That pleased her to no end, but she would bet her cat he'd deny it to hell and back when his brain wasn't pickled. She turned around. "Why don't you jump in the shower while I make you some coffee?"

"You don't know where the kitchen is. Come with me and we'll find it together." Again, he gave her a drunk, lopsided grin. "After we shower me." Grabbing her hand, he tried to pull her with him.

She pulled away. "Oh, no. I'm not bathing with you tonight, much less sleeping with you. If I do, you'll be angry with both of us in the morning. When it happens between us, I want you to be fully aware of what you're doing. I don't want regrets, Jake. Now off with you." She waved a hand toward the hallway.

"You're no fun," he grumbled and weaved away.

The kitchen wasn't hard to find as it opened to the great room. She found the necessary supplies and had a strong pot of coffee waiting when he returned. The man who walked into the room wore only a pair of damp red boxer briefs, his hair dripping water, his chest and long, muscular legs glistening with droplets. The air swished out of her lungs. *Holy moly.*

She tried to think of something to say besides, "Holy cow, I want to jump your bones," and settled for, "Did you forget how to use a towel?" Thankfully, her voice sounded only a little raspy.

He scrunched his eyebrows. "Huh?"

"It doesn't look like you dried off."

His chin lowered and he stared at his chest. "Knew I was forgetting something." He lifted his head, a very wicked smile on his face. "You could dry me off."

I'd love to. "Some other time. Here, come drink this coffee."

"Okay, and then you can dry me."

Not weaving as much as he was before his shower, he made his way to the table. He brought the cup to his mouth, took a swallow, and then jumped up. At the sink, he spit it out. "Jesus Christ, Maria. How much coffee did you put in this?"

She'd tripled the normal amount figuring it would help sober him. "Too strong?"

In answer, he turned on the tap, let it run to hot, poured out half the contents of the cup, and refilled it with water.

"Next time you're too drunk to drive, call a cab." Still hurt at smelling the perfume stinking up his clothes, she snatched the keys off the counter and headed for the door. He could have his damn car back tomorrow.

He moved faster than she would've thought possible while under the influence, blocking the doorway. "Don't leave."

A drop of water roamed its way down his chest, past a nipple on its way to his stomach. She clamped down on her bottom lip to keep from licking it. He put a finger under her chin and lifted her face, staring into her eyes.

"I'm sorry."

"For what?" The only thing she really wanted him to apologize for was smelling like he'd had women climbing all over him.

"I don't know. For this, maybe?" He lowered his mouth to hers.

His mouth was hot and tasted like coffee and mint toothpaste. When his tongue tangled with hers, she put her hands on his hips to steady herself. Muscles flexed under her palms. Even though there'd been those few times with Jonathan, intimately touching a man was still new to her. She could get used to it, could learn to crave it even.

He wrapped his arms around her back and pulled her against him. His erection pressed against her belly and an ache began deep in her inner core. If she wasn't careful, he'd have her in his bed in two minutes flat. Not happening. He wasn't stumbling drunk any longer, but he was certainly still buzzed, and the probability of him getting all wonky about it when the buzz wore off was still high.

She pushed away. "No. Go to bed, Jake, and sleep it off. I'll bring your car back in the morning."

"Don't leave. I won't kiss you again." He glanced at the clock on the microwave. "It's going on two, and I don't like the idea of you out by yourself in the middle of the night."

"I live less than ten minutes away. I'll be fine."

"No, there's night monsters out there roaming the streets looking for beautiful women. If you insist on going home then I'll drive you."

She rolled her eyes. "You're in no condition to be driving anywhere."

"Then I guess that means you're staying. We'll just sleep, I promise."

"You swear?"

"Boy Scouts' honor." He put two fingers over his heart.

Maria snorted. "You were never a Boy Scout."

"Shows what you know." He took her hand and led her to his bedroom.

Fool that she was, she let him. After he pulled back the covers, he put his hands on the waist of his briefs, and she held up a hand. "Whoa. What're you doing?"

He gave her a puzzled look. "Taking these off. I sleep in the nude."

"Not tonight you don't. Leave them on or I'm outta here."

"Damn. Guess that means you're sleeping in your clothes?"

She'd thrown on a T-shirt and shorts after his call. "The shirt and my panties are staying on."

His body took a tumble into the bed, and he scooted under the covers, holding them up. "Come on then. If all we're gonna do is sleep, let's get to it."

This really was a bad idea, but she unhooked her bra and slipped it and her shorts off before climbing in next to him. He pulled her against him, wrapped his arm around her waist, spooning her, and nuzzled her neck.

"Jake, stop it."

"Not doing nothing, promise. You just smell so good. You always do."

"Thank you. Now go to sleep."

He chuckled and then went quiet. His arm was heavy on her body, but she liked it, liked how it felt to be snuggled up with him. It was like being in a safe cocoon where nothing could hurt her.

"You leave your car at Buck's?"

She grabbed the hand inching its way past her stomach. "I thought you'd gone to sleep."

"Almost there. Just wondering about Sally."

Like she would leave her Mustang unprotected in a bar parking lot overnight. "Mrs. Jankowski dropped me off."

He lifted on his elbow, leaned over her shoulder, and peered at her. "You told Mrs. Jankowski?"

There was hurt and anger in his voice. It obviously embarrassed him to think her foster mother knew he had to be driven home. "I told her you called, and I was meeting you for a few drinks."

"Oh." He plopped back down and nestled their bodies together to his satisfaction. "She won't expect you home tonight?"

"Mrs. Jankowski isn't my jailer, nor has she ever tried to be. I'm a big girl, and she trusts my judgment."

"That's good. The boss know you're with me?"

"He stayed at the hospital with Dani tonight. Talked the nurses into putting a cot in her room."

"That's good, too. He'd probably kill me if he knew you were here. He makes damn cute babies though."

"God, you're a talkative drunk. Go to sleep."

"Kay."

And just like that, he did. She listened to his even breathing and fell asleep wondering what it'd be like to be with him every night, how they'd be as a couple.

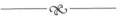

Jake opened his eyes and stared at the strand of black hair wrapped around his hand. He lifted it to the pale light coming in the window—it looked damn familiar. Frowning, he brought it to his nose and sniffed.

Maria.

She lay on her stomach, her face buried in the pillow, but he didn't need to see her to know. He could find her just by her scent in a dark room filled with a hundred women. Keeping her hair pressed to his nose, he tried to remember just how she'd come to be in his bed.

Snatches of the night before flowed through his mind. He'd gotten stinking drunk, something he never, ever did. He'd needed a ride home and Buck had said something about calling a friend. Had he called her?

Apparently, he had, but why was she in his bed? Had they done anything? No way. That, he would remember. So, why was she snuggled up next to him? Not that he minded. He rather liked waking up to find her there.

Easing onto his side, he slid the covers down to her thighs. Damn. If thong underwear wasn't the best invention ever, he didn't know what was. He leaned over her back and trailed his mouth over her skin, starting just below her neck and following the line of her spine down to her beautiful ass.

She moaned and turned over. Sleepy black eyes blinked at him. "Jake?"

"Shhhh. Let me love you." He slipped his hand under her shirt and cupped a breast, flicking his thumb over the nipple.

"Are you still drunk?"

Had he made a fool of himself? "Yeah, I'm drunk on you." He was so hard for her, his cock wanted out of his briefs, needed to be inside her. Now.

Puzzled, he lifted the cover and peeked at himself. Why did he have underwear on?

Maybe this wasn't a good idea. If he'd been a total ass, the last thing she'd want was to make love to him. Until he figured out if he had something to apologize for, he should keep his hands off her. Not to mention his mouth tasted like something had died in it—she'd probably gag if he tried to kiss her.

He glanced at the clock to see it was six. "We should get you home." When he sat up to get out of the bed, she grabbed his arm.

"Not yet."

"Are you sure?" He wasn't. No matter how badly he wanted her—and he did, more than anything—there were too many things to consider. She truly was a friend, and he didn't want to ruin that. What he should do was put her in his car and take her home.

She smiled.

How was he supposed to resist that warm smile and those sleepy brown eyes? He put a finger on her lips when she opened her mouth to speak. "Tell you what. I need to brush my teeth and take a quick shower. You think about it, decide if it's the right thing for you. I can't make you any promises, Maria. Can you live with that?"

She didn't answer.

In the bathroom, he brushed his teeth, his tongue, and then gargled with mouthwash. After a quick shave, he jumped in the shower. The slight buzz left over from the night before faded as needles of warm water struck his skin. It had always pissed off the guys that he never suffered the ill effects of a night of heavy drinking. With Maria in his bed, he was more thankful for that fact than ever.

What had he been thinking to get that drunk? He snorted. Stupid question as the answer awaited him in his bed. What would she decide?

If she was smart, she'd be dressed and ready for him to take her home. A naked female body passed by the shower door before it opened. Maria stepped in behind him. Jake squeezed his eyes shut when she pressed against his back, slid her arms around his waist, and rested her face on his shoulder.

"I'm sure," she whispered.

So much for doing the right thing. He twisted around and crushed his mouth to hers, nudging his cock between her legs. She arched against him and wrapped her arms around his neck. With his hands on her hips to steady her, he thrust between her legs, groaning when she clamped them together, tightening them around his erection. One more minute and he'd get really stupid. *Note to self. From now on, keep a supply of condoms in the shower.*

He pulled away and trailed his palm over the curve of her hip, down through her curls, and slid a finger inside her. Her sheath was hot—and so damn wet—and he found her clit with his thumb, rubbing tiny circles while his finger thrust in and out.

She whimpered and draped a leg around his thigh, opening herself to him. When she wrapped her lips around his nipple and sucked, he about lost it. Her hand encircled his throbbing cock, stroking him from the base of his shaft to the tip and back down.

Her breath hitched in time with his until they both gulped for air. A shudder traveled through her, his name passed her lips, and he let go, climaxing with her. *Jesus.* He leaned his forehead against hers, the sound of their heavy breaths filling the confines of the shower. He wanted her in bed. Now. Reaching back, he turned off the water, picked her up, and carried her to the bedroom.

"We're gonna get your bed wet," she said.

"I don't care." He tossed her onto the mattress and followed her down. Finally, he had her where he'd wanted her for almost four years. Droplets of water dotted her skin and he set about licking her dry. Each place his tongue touched, goose bumps appeared and little shivers passed through her when he found her sensitive places. He memorized each time she reacted—just there on the curve of her breast, the spot on her neck just below her ear, here on her inner thigh—all points of pleasure for her he'd pay special attention to as he loved her.

But first, he had to taste her. Needed to. He pressed his face between her thighs and inhaled the earthy musk scent of her arousal. He adored the little noises she made when she came, and he set about enticing her to make them again. A low growl escaped him when she lifted her hips to meet his tongue. Using his mouth, his tongue, and the scrape of his teeth, he brought her to her second climax of the morning.

She tasted so incredibly sweet that he feared no one but her would do for him. When her body calmed, he reached over and pulled a condom out of the night table drawer. Tearing open the package with his teeth, he started to put it on.

"Let me," she said and sat up, her gaze intent on him. "I've never put one on a man before. Show me how."

"Didn't your ex-boyfriend use them?"

"He always went into the bathroom to put it on. I guess it was a private thing."

Jake decided her ex-boyfriend had been a fool, but then, he already knew that. He handed her the condom and lifted to his knees, which put his hard, pulsing erection near her face. "Leave it rolled, start at the tip, and unroll it as you cover me." Damn if she didn't lower a fascinated gaze on his cock and the thing jerked, trying to reach her mouth.

She flicked a finger over the tip catching the drop of moisture there, then stuck her finger in her mouth, tasted him, and grinned. "You taste like salty seawater."

"You're killing me, Maria. Put the damn thing on me."

It was as if she were performing a sacred ritual, so slow and precise did she unroll the condom over him, the whole time her gaze focused on his shaft as her fingers touched him to cover him with the rubber. Jake gritted his teeth, clinched his fists, and bore it.

"Now what?" she asked when she finished.

"Now this," he said and pulled her onto his lap so that she straddled him. Twisting them around, he leaned back against the headboard. With his hand, he guided his cock into her. "Ride me."

She snickered. "Like a horse? Why not, you're built like one."

He looked into her eyes and smiled. "I seriously doubt that, but hey, I have no problem with you thinking so." She sank down on him and he hissed. "You have no idea how long I've thought of us doing this."

"Me, too, Jake. Me, too."

She then obeyed and rode him hard. Had she thought of them together like this for as long as he had? Her breasts bounced in front of his face as she found a rhythm she liked, and he gave into the temptation to suck a nipple into his mouth. Yeah, maybe he could be faithful to one woman as long as it was Maria. He stopped thinking as a pressure built deep within him, a need to claim her, make her his.

"Jake!" She stilled, then trembled, as she shattered around him. Her inner muscles clinched around him, and she buried her face against his neck, her breaths warm on his skin.

"Maria," he answered and let go, coming so hard he stopped breathing for a second. "Maria," he gasped, his mouth pressed into the valley of her breasts. *Maria.* Her name a song, one too beautiful to ever belong to him. But there she was—his fantasy—straddling him and calling his name.

She nuzzled his neck. "When can we do this again?"

He chuckled and slid his hand down her side, cupping her bottom. As soon as possible he wanted to say, but he needed to think about what he was getting into with her. Then there was the conversation he needed to have with her brother, hopefully without any fists involved. He wouldn't sneak behind Kincaid's back to see the man's sister.

Jake gave her one last long kiss. "Up, Chiquita. We need to get you home."

Her eyes searched his. "Damn you, you're already sorry."

She pushed hard on his chest and swung her legs over the edge of the mattress. He grabbed her hand. "You're wrong. I'm far from sorry, but I have to put all my focus on the operation. You're a distraction I can't afford right now."

"Whatever." She pulled away and headed for the bathroom.

"I hate that word," he muttered.

CHAPTER THIRTEEN

———— ❧ ————

Maria grabbed an orange soda from the fridge. "Where the hell have you been all night?"

She squeaked and spun, banging her hand on the refrigerator door. "Ouch! Crap, Logan, you scared me." Reaching over to the light switch, she flipped it on. Her brother sat at the kitchen table, a cup of coffee in front of him. "I thought you were spending the night at the hospital."

"I did. Came home to shower and change. Answer my question."

"None of your business." She plopped down at the table. "I'm twenty-four years old. I don't need your permission to spend the night away from home."

His lips thinned. "He's no good for you."

"You're probably right, but then again, he might surprise us both." She traced a finger through the condensation the soda bottle had made on the table. "I want him, have for a long time. The only way you're gonna stop me from going after him is to lock me in my room. Even if you dared to, I'd find a way out and head straight for Jake."

"Then understand this. The day he hurts you, and that day will come, I'll fire him. After I kill him, that is."

She reached over and grasped his hand. "No, you won't. If he screws up on the job, then fire him, by all means. But I'm going into this with my eyes open, and you can't get rid of him if it doesn't work out for us, no matter the reason. That just isn't fair to Jake."

One of the best scowlers in the world scowled. "You really piss me off sometimes, you know that? First you won't listen or take my advice, then you tie my hands so I can't beat the shit out of him when the time comes." His eyes softened. "I just don't want to see you hurt, brat. Is that so wrong?"

God, she loved her brother, her protector. She stood and walked behind him, wrapped her arms around his chest and kissed his cheek. "No, and I love you for it. I need to change and get over to K2. Jake will be there all weekend planning his mission, and I intend to help. I want everything to go as safely as possible for him and his team." She also wanted to make sure he didn't end up back at one of his hangouts later. No more cheap perfume on Jake if she had anything to say about it. Logan's grunt said he'd give her the necessary rope to hang herself.

He pushed away from the table. "I'm headed back to the hospital, but I'll stop by later."

After changing into jeans and a sleeveless top, her hair pulled up in a ponytail, Maria backed Sally out of the garage and drove to K2. She wished Logan hadn't assigned this mission to Jake—she didn't have a good feeling about it—but it was what Jake did for a living, and she wasn't about to complain.

As it was Saturday, the front door of K2 was locked. Maria pushed the code on the inner door, and walked into the main room. Jake stood over a table with maps spread out in front of him as his two team members, Rick Bayne and Brad Stewart, looked on.

"Hi," she said.

Rick and Brad gave her big smiles, but Jake's expression remained blank. He wasn't happy to see her. Too bad. "I'm here to help. Give me something to do."

"There's really nothing I can think of," Jake said.

She met his gaze, let him see the determination in her eyes. "Then think harder."

"What about letting her confirm our in-country contact's able to fulfill our list of requirements?" Rick suggested.

"After that, she could do the background on our target," Brad added. "Both those chores together would save one of us three or four hours computer time."

Maria shot Brad a grateful smile. The guys had nicknamed him "Elaine" because he had the hots for Elaine on *Seinfeld*. Rick they'd named "Tennessee." She could sit and listen to him talk in that sexy southern drawl all day.

She took Jake's sigh as a sign of surrender, and grabbed a pen and paper off the table. "Contact and target's name?"

Information in hand, she left them to their planning and walked into the office she used whenever at K2. As soon as she graduated, it would be hers permanently; the plan was for her to take over the legal side of the business. From the day Logan had bought her a computer at the age of ten, she'd fallen in love with the thing and all the wonderful information hidden in such a little box.

Growing up poor and considered trash by her schoolmates, she'd spent her lonely hours looking up famous actors, reading about their privileged lives, envying them. From there, she'd ventured into studying ways to get rich so she could one day buy a pretty dress or spend a day at a spa. She'd learned the stock market inside out, researched companies and their potential for investment.

When she was fifteen, she'd begged Logan to give her a thousand dollars to play with. Bless her brother, he'd handed it over without the first blink, and she'd appreciated that it hadn't been easy at the time for him to come up with that much money. In eight years, she'd grown that one thousand to over fifty thousand, and she now handled all of her and Logan's investments.

There was nothing she couldn't find on a computer, and the thrill of discovery still elated her. Brad had claimed it would take one of them four hours, but it took her a little less than two to complete. She was contemplating what she could do next to help when Jake stuck his head in the door.

"How's it going?"

She slid a file to the end of her desk. "Here's the background on Chad Sinclair, aka Abdul Haq. Everything's in there from the moment he took his first breath to now, what he likes to eat, his first girlfriend, and so on. Your contact in Egypt has managed to obtain all the items on your list but two—three pairs of night vision goggles and the C4. Why do you need C4?"

He grinned. "Never know when you might want to blow something up."

Jeez, boys and their toys. He better not blow himself up. "Well, anyway, he e-mailed that he's meeting a source tonight and should have everything you asked for."

"Good." He approached her desk and picked up the file on their target. "The guys want to go to Seaside for a fish sandwich. Want to come with us?"

"I really should run by the hospital and say hi to Dani. Why don't you come with me and we'll get a quick burger or something after."

He glanced at the doorway, indecision on his face. "Probably better if I don't," he finally said. "You don't need to come back. Go and enjoy your new nephew and the rest of the weekend."

Stupid, stubborn man. "I'm coming back this afternoon, and I'll be here tomorrow. This operation is happening too fast, and you guys need all the help you can get." She stood and picked up her purse. "See you in about two hours."

Deciding to turn the tables on him and see how he liked it, she stopped at the door. "I want to thank you for last night. It was the most amazing night of my life, but I'm putting whatever's happening between us on hold until you're home safe. I suggest you do the same."

It was the most amazing night of her life? Jake stared at the empty doorway. He'd tried all morning to put her out of his mind, but she was there anyway. Her soft sighs, the way she clinched around him when she came, how she'd called out his name when she'd shattered—how was he supposed to put that on hold?

He could give her a thousand amazing nights, wanted to. Angry she could so easily put them on the back burner, he slapped the file against his thigh. Striding into the main room, he thrust the folder at Bayne. "Memorize this. You, too, Stewart."

Sally was backing out of the parking space when he opened the passenger door and jumped inside the Mustang. He glared at Maria and dared her to say one damn word. All he got from her was a sweet smile and silence. Why he was so pissed off, he hadn't a clue other than the fact she was very talented at messing with his mind.

Hadn't she just given him the space to concentrate on his mission? Wasn't that what he wanted? He'd never been so indecisive in his life about anything, and now she had him acting like a yo-yo on the end of a string. This was all new to him, this wanting only one woman, and he didn't have a road map for the trip she was taking him on. Small wonder he'd gotten drunk the night before.

Halfway to Pensacola's Baptist Hospital, Maria reached over and slipped her fingers around his. As the warmth of her hand seeped into his, his blood pressure lowered along with the irrational anger. There wasn't another woman on the planet who could have such an effect on him. That had to say something. He just had to figure out what.

He expected her to say something funny or, more likely, a snarky comment. God knew, he deserved it. She didn't say anything, just held his hand and drove. He leaned his head against the seat and let everything go except for the way her hand felt in his—like that was where it belonged.

When she had walked into K2 earlier, he'd had to bite his tongue to keep from ordering her to leave. As part owner, she had as much right to be there as he, more even. His fear she would disrupt his concentration had been groundless. She'd stayed out of their way and he'd been comforted by her presence in the building. For sure, she'd saved them a lot of time.

"Thanks, by the way," he said.

"For what?" She glanced at him with those warm chocolate eyes.

"For helping us out."

A pleased smile spread across her face. "No problem."

That was another thing about her. He'd known her for years, and she was always ready with a smile, rarely got upset about anything. It wasn't that she never lost her temper. She did, and when it happened it was something to behold, but it never lasted long and next thing he knew, she was laughing again. Maybe because of the horror of her childhood she'd learned not to let things she couldn't change bother her. Someday, he'd ask her.

"Here we are. I can't wait to see baby Evan again. I hope Dani's awake so I can tell her how beautiful my nephew is. She was asleep yesterday when I was here." She chatted on about babies and how she couldn't wait to get Evan home so she could spoil him.

Jake walked by her side, listening to her as they rode the elevator up to the fourth floor, smiling in amusement at the way her hands were constantly in motion as they walked down the hall to Dani's room. If he tied her hands together could she still speak?

She came to an abrupt halt. "Why are you chuckling?"

Because . . . he was happy, content. *Contentment.* He rolled the word around in his mouth. It was something he'd never strived for, but he liked the feeling. He put his arm around her shoulders and got her moving again. If he told her he was laughing at the way her hands waved around in the air when she talked, she would probably slap him with one of them.

"I was chuckling over your enthusiasm for babies. I just never realized you liked them so much."

"Well, who doesn't? I adore Regan and love playing with her. Now I'll have two kids to spoil rotten."

The sparkle in her eyes as she talked about babies mesmerized him. Did she want to have children someday? He'd always pictured her as a lawyer, a career woman running K2 alongside her brother. Never had he imagined her as a mother, but suddenly he could see her with a babe in her arms, a little girl or boy with black hair and coffee-colored eyes.

"You want kids?" he asked.

Her lips formed into a soft smile. "Yeah, someday."

Something very new to him took root and branched out, traveling through his veins like a fast-growing weed to all parts of his body. A possessive need to bind her to him—to be the one to give her babies—hit him with such force that he almost turned and walked away.

Snotty-nosed kids running around at his feet had never been on his agenda. He needed a vacation. Alone and somewhere quiet so he could think all this shit through. Was he ready to give up his lifestyle for a wife and kids? Even a week ago, he'd have given an adamant "no, not happening." Now he was picturing a woman—specifically, this woman—with *his* baby in her arms and liking it.

It was too much, too fast.

Still reeling, he followed her into Dani's room. The boss didn't comment about his being with Maria, but his expression wasn't particularly friendly.

"Hey, you two. Isn't he beautiful?" Dani said of the bundle cradled in her arms.

"You make a beautiful mother, Dani," Jake said. And she did. There was a glow about her, a shining kind of thing he couldn't put his finger on. Would Maria look like that when she held her child in her arms?

Maria perched on the edge of the bed and trailed her knuckles over the baby's cheek. "Oh, he is beautiful, and his skin's so soft."

Jake glanced at the boss. Damn if he didn't glow, too. The new father's eyes shone with pride as he gazed at his son, and Jake found himself envying Kincaid. He needed to get out of this room before he started begging Maria to make a baby with him.

"Your son's a handsome devil, boss. Fortunately, he takes after his mother in looks. Listen, I'll step outside and give you guys some privacy. Dani, it's great seeing you. I'll stop by the house tomorrow after you get home. I have something for little Evan."

Dani lifted her gaze from the baby and smiled. "I'll look forward to it. Thanks for stopping by, Jake."

He fled the room and walked down the hall a ways before stopping and leaning back against the wall. What was wrong with him? All that domestic bliss scared the bejesus out of him . . . at least, it used to. Now, here he was staring at babies as if he had a damn biological clock ticking inside him.

"Get your act together, Buchanan," he muttered. He needed his mind to be alert and not cluttered with thoughts of a sexy, black-eyed girl holding his child in her arms.

"How's the operation planning coming?"

Hell. He'd not even noticed the boss approaching. That just proved his point. If he didn't concentrate on the task at hand, someone was going to get hurt . . . or not come back at all. He pushed off the wall.

"Good for the short amount of time we've had to work on it. Maria's been a big help by saving us a lot of time on the computer."

Kincaid's eyes, always intense, glinted with a hard stare. "I know she spent the night with you."

Jake resisted the urge to look away. "She tell you?" That surprised him. He hadn't thought Maria would've spilled the beans.

"No, I was home when she came back this morning. I all but forbade her to see you again, and she all but told me to butt out of her life. So, even though I don't like it, that's what I'm gonna do. You're going to end up hurting her, Romeo, but she's also made me promise not to fire you when you do."

He would've liked to have been a fly on the wall during that conversation. "I guess you can still kill me, though."

"No, she also managed to get me to promise not to do that either." Kincaid hardened his eyes. "That part really pisses me off."

"You know, I just might surprise you and make her happy."

"Funny, she said the same thing."

"Are you done with your bitching? I was headed to the bathroom." He had no wish to discuss Maria with her brother.

"For now. I have to be in Washington Thursday. My flight leaves a few minutes before yours, so I'll pick you up." He turned away and headed back to his wife's room.

"Hey, boss." Jake waited for him to turn around. "Don't ever call me Romeo again. I'm done with it."

Kincaid gave a slight nod of his head. "Fair enough. What should we call you?"

"I'm sure you'll think of something."

As he walked away, the man gave a chuckle that sounded a little too evil for Jake's comfort. He could hardly wait to hear what Kincaid came up with.

So Maria believed he could make her happy. Could he? As he'd never attempted to try and keep one woman happy, he didn't know, but something in him wanted to prove her right.

The reason for the upheaval in his life walked out of Dani's room. "Hey, Tiger Toes," she called, a bright smile on her face. "Let's get lunch. I'm starving."

Her brother came out behind her and by the smirk on his face it was obvious he'd heard her. A hundred bucks said he had a new nickname.

Jake traced a finger down Maria's arm. "Hey, yourself. Go on to the car, and I'll be down in a minute. I need a word with the boss."

"How much?" he asked after Maria left.

"How much what, *Tiger Toes*?"

"Dammit, boss. You're having so much trouble keeping a straight face your lips are quivering. I'll never hear the end of it if you call me that in front of the team. How much will it cost to buy you off?"

"There's not enough money in the world, Tiger Toes, but I'll make a deal with you. As long as you keep Maria happy, I'll shorten it to Tiger. One tear falls down her pretty face and all bets are off."

"You're a mean bastard, you know that?"

"Just keep a smile on her face, Tiger Toes, and you got nothing to fear from me."

"Stop calling me that."

"Tiger Toes. Tiger Toes. Tiger Toes." Kincaid finally gave in to his laughter.

Jake gave him the finger and strode away. Once his back was turned, he grinned. He couldn't explain it, but he didn't mind Maria calling him that. As for the boss, it was great seeing him laugh, something he never did before Dani. However, the first one of his men to call him Tiger Toes would get a fist in his face.

After lunch at the Hot Dog House—where Jake ate a hot dog for the first time in years—he and Maria returned to K2 and went to work. Saint came in around two, Kincaid at three, and between all of them a plan took shape. They'd have the next day to refine it and then two days after that to go over and over it.

As they wrapped things up for the day, the boss said, "I have an announcement to make."

Jake didn't like the look of amusement in Kincaid's eyes when the man glanced at him. What was he about to say?

Kincaid put his hand on Jake's shoulder. "As of today, you'll no longer refer to Buchanan as 'Romeo.' That name's been retired." He gave Jake a hard look. "At least, until I say otherwise. His new handle's 'Tiger . . .'"

Jake tensed and narrowed his eyes. *Don't you fucking dare.*

Kincaid answered Jake's silent message with a grin. "So, Tiger, looks like your plan's coming together. I'll stop by tomorrow afternoon and review your progress. Anyone got questions?"

Bayne and Stewart shook their heads. Jake hadn't worked a mission with either one before and that worried him a little, but they had come up with some good suggestions so that eased his mind.

Maria popped her head out of her office doorway. "Logan, Jake, I need to see you a minute."

"We have a problem," she said when they followed her into her office. She closed the door. "I thought it might be a good idea to hack into your target's computer . . . you know, just see if all was kosher. Turns out someone else hacked him, and I followed that trail back to a computer in Afghanistan. My educated guess is it's the Taliban, and they've been watching Sinclair for over a month, which means they know he's sent messages to the States. Whether they've been able to decipher his code, I have no way of knowing."

Jake exchanged an uneasy look with Kincaid.

She handed her brother a printout. "Just thought you would want to know. You have a code specialist contact at the CIA, right? I'd send this to him and ask how easy, or hopefully how hard, your guy's message would be to decrypt."

Jake was beyond impressed. "You're amazing, Chiquita." Not caring that the boss stood next to him, Jake stepped in front of her and soundly kissed her.

"Good God, Maria, are you sure I can't kill him?"

Maria glanced over at her brother. "Get lost, Logan."

"With pleasure. Call me later, Tiger Toes. We need to talk about this."

"Why'd he call you that?" she asked after Kincaid left.

"Who cares?" He pulled her back into his arms. "Have I told you how amazing you are? Yeah, I think I did, but it bears repeating." Jake lowered his mouth to hers and just before he resumed kissing her, said, "You've turned my world upside down, girl. I think I just may like it."

Her mouth was warm against his and he vowed then and there no man's lips but his would ever touch hers. He reluctantly pulled away. "Got any plans for tonight?"

"I do."

The level of his disappointment surprised him. His first reaction was to demand to know what her plans were and with whom, but his pride took over and he didn't ask.

"Don't you want to know what I'm doing tonight?"

He caught the little twitch of her lips. Ah, she was teasing him. "Couldn't care less. I have plans of my own," he said and kissed her again. "Have a nice evening." He turned to go and she grabbed his arm.

"Hey, weren't you about to ask me out?"

"Possibly, but you said you're busy, so I guess I'll see you tomorrow." Two could play this game, and he rather liked the fire flashing in her eyes. "I think I'll just swing over to Buck's, check things out. The place is always jumping on Saturday night."

She huffed a breath. "Fine. Go play with your girlfriends until you stink of cheap perfume. Just don't call me to come get you this time."

He didn't doubt he'd smelled like the inside of a whorehouse by the time she'd arrived at the bar. Had she been jealous? This was the point at which he backed off—or always had in the past. The first possessive sign on the part of a woman had him out the door before it could slam on his ass.

With this one, though, he wasn't eyeing the door, anxious to be gone. Imagine that. He slipped his hand around hers. "You could cancel your plans, come with me . . . keep me out of trouble."

She gave a little snorting sound. "You could use a keeper, for sure. Just give me a minute to call my lover and let him know I can't make it tonight." Pulling her hand away, she walked to her desk, picked up the phone, and dialed.

Her lover? Hadn't she just been teasing him with her pretend plans? Who the hell was she calling? His cell rang. When he saw her name on his caller ID, he glanced at her and raised a brow. "Hello."

"Hi, lover boy. Listen, I'm really sorry, but something's come up, and I'm gonna have to beg off tonight."

"But I have tonight all planned—it involves champagne and corn dogs, warm oil massages, maybe a little body painting before we're done."

"Champagne and corn dogs? Wow, how am I supposed to resist that? Hold on a sec." She put the phone on hold, then shrugged. "I don't think I can get out of my date with lover boy. Why don't you call Jamie, have him babysit you?"

He formed his lips into a pout. "But Saint doesn't drink or carouse."

She grinned. "Exactly."

"No, I think I'll just go home and sulk." He walked out of the office, his phone to his ear. He'd never played games like this before and even though it was kind of silly, it was novel . . . and fun. She was a constant surprise, and he was going to like having her for a girlfriend.

"I'm back, lover boy. What time are you picking me up?"

After a quick glance at his watch, he said, "Eight." That would give him a little over an hour to get everything ready.

"Can't wait," she said and disconnected.

Where the hell did one buy body paint?

CHAPTER FOURTEEN

———— ✤ ————

When in Pensacola, Maria lived with Logan and Dani. It had been generous of them to invite her to continue living in their home after they married, but once she was back for good, one of the first things she planned to do was find her own place. One where a nosy brother wouldn't be lying in wait whenever she walked in.

In her room, Maria tried on three outfits before deciding on the yellow sundress. It was soft and easy to get out of, but most of all, the girl in his painting—the one he'd drunkenly admitted reminded him of her—wore one like it. Running out of time, she'd let her hair air-dry after showering, leaving it to flow naturally down her back.

She had managed a few hours of study between her time at K2 and visiting Dani at the hospital. Fortunately, she only had two exams left, and they were her easiest classes.

Regan bounced in; her Doberman, Luke, by her side. "Maria, you wanna watch my mermaid movie with me and Luke?"

How many times had they watched that movie together? A hundred, at least. Maria sat and pulled her niece onto her lap. "Can't tonight, sweetheart."

"Why?"

"Cause I have a date. I'll watch it with you tomorrow, I promise."

"What's a date?" Luke pressed himself against Maria's legs and laid his chin on Regan's lap. Maria idly scratched the Doberman behind his ears. "A date is . . ." How did one explain a date to a five year old? "You know how your mom and dad say Saturday nights are just for them and they go out for dinner or a movie? That's a date."

Regan's lips puckered and her eyes filled with tears. Luke, always sensitive to Regan's moods, whined. "Mommy went away to get me a little brother, but I don't want one. I want Mommy and Daddy to come home."

"They'll be home tomorrow, sugar pie. Come here and give me a kiss."

"Jake!" Regan jumped off Maria's lap and went running to him, Luke fast on her heels.

Almost as at home in Logan and Dani's house as Maria, it wasn't a surprise that Jake now stood in the doorway of her bedroom. So why was her heart doing summersaults?

With Regan wrapped around his chest and Luke's nose stuck against the back of his knee, he came into her bedroom. "Hi," he said.

At the heated look in his eyes, Maria's brains turned to mush. "Hi." It was the only word she was capable of saying. God, he was so hot she wanted to lick her lips in appreciation. He wore black dress pants and a blue button-down Oxford shirt, and looked like he'd stepped off the cover of some magazine.

Mrs. Jankowski followed him into the room. "Regan, my girl, there you are." She took the child from Jake. "It's time for popcorn and your movie."

"Hi," Maria said, walking up to Jake.

His lips twitched. "Hi again."

Yeah, she'd said that already. "Sorry." In the eleventh grade, she'd had a crush on a cute guy in her class. He'd stopped and talked to her once and she had gone all tongue-tied. Like now. She'd known Jake for years, and this awkward feeling didn't make sense.

The corners of his eyes crinkled in amusement. "Maybe if you stopped clasping your hands together you could talk better."

She didn't get it.

"Never mind," he said and chuckled. "Ready for our date?"

Until she managed to calm down a little, maybe it would be best not to speak. She nodded.

He took her hand and led her out of the house to his car. When he slid into the driver's seat, he leaned over the console and kissed her. He smelled like sandalwood and spicy aftershave. She brought her hand to his cheek, feeling the smoothness of his skin. Something warm and fuzzy slithered through her knowing he'd dressed up for her, shaved even. God, he smelled good.

"Another minute, Chiquita, and I'm going to have you under me right in your brother's driveway." He inhaled a deep breath and started the car. After he backed out of the driveway, he took her hand and placed it on his thigh.

She liked that he seemed to want her hand on him. Making circles with her fingers, she caressed his leg, feeling his muscles ripple under her touch. He didn't speak, and the silence between them felt intimate, as if words weren't necessary to know their desire for each other simmered in the air. Leaning her head back against the seat, she closed her eyes and narrowed her focus to nothing but the feel of the soft fabric of his slacks covering a muscle-hard leg.

Her fingers roamed to the inside of his thigh and he made a low humming sound, its timbre vibrating in hot waves throughout her body. She barely noticed when he pulled into a parking spot in front of his condo.

"Maria."

"Hmmm?"

He took her hand and pressed it over his erection. "See what you do to me?"

She turned her head toward him and smiled. "That's nice."

"Nice?" His laugh held the sound of amusement. "Right, nice. Let's see if I can get something better than 'nice' out of you." He exited the car and came around to her side. Opening her door, he held out his hand.

As she walked beside him, her hand in his, she thought she'd never been happier in her life. He glanced at her and winked. Well, that was just sexy.

She leaned her head against his shoulder as he slid his key into the lock. "After yesterday, you can't know how happy I am to be here with you." The door swung open and she stepped inside.

"What happened yesterday?" he asked, following her in.

Crap, crap, crap. Why hadn't she kept her mouth shut? Seeing the painting he'd said reminded him of her, she walked over and stood in front of it. She considered telling him the last few days of school had worn her out, but even as she thought it, she couldn't bring herself to lie to him.

"Maria?" His hands came down on her shoulders, and he turned her around.

There was no getting out of it, but he wasn't going to like it. "Fortunada's finally in jail."

"So the cops found him and you didn't tell me?"

Oh, yeah, he wasn't happy and it was only going to get worse. "Not exactly."

He backed away and shoved his hands in his pockets. "What exactly then?"

"Well . . . he . . . Fortunada, kind of attacked me yesterday morning."

"He *kind of* attacked you? Where the hell was Saint?"

Icicles should be dripping from his mouth, his voice was so cold. "It wasn't his fault." She rushed on to explain what had happened, unnerved by his hard stare.

"And you didn't tell me this yesterday because?" he asked when she finished.

"I didn't want to worry you, you know, with the mission and all, you didn't need the distraction."

"You need to get one thing straight. It's not your job to protect me."

Jake had never been so angry in his life, and the hurt shimmering in her eyes at his declaration only made him madder. The bastard had gotten his hands on her, and she wasn't going to tell him out of some misguided idea he needed to be coddled?

Soft music played on his speakers, and the lights were dimmed to a golden glow. He'd set the stage for a seduction before leaving to pick her up. Things had changed though. He flicked off the stereo and turned on the lights to full brightness.

"You're overreacting, you know. I did what I thought was best for you." She sat on the sofa and clasped her hands between her knees.

He opened his mouth, then snapped it shut before he said something he couldn't take back. How she could say that with a straight face was beyond him. A battle raged inside him, half of him wanting to yell at her for trying to hide the fact Fortunada had had his hands on her, the other half wanting to wrap his arms around her and keep her there where she'd always be safe.

Turning on his heels, he went into the kitchen and filled a glass with water. If he took his time drinking it, maybe he would calm down. He wasn't used to losing control of his emotions, could keep his composure on a battlefield with bullets whistling past his ears and bombs raining down around him. How then did one slip of a girl turn him into something he just wasn't?

Maybe he wasn't meant for a long-term relationship, didn't have the right DNA for it or whatever the hell it was that made a man want to stay with one woman.

Footsteps sounded behind him, but he didn't let on he'd heard her. She slipped her arms around his waist and pressed her face against his back. Resisting the urge to turn so he could hold her, he set the glass down and braced his hands on the sink. There was no way to make her understand she had all but said he wasn't man enough to handle knowing she'd been attacked.

"You're right and I'm sorry," she said. "I should have told you. I just didn't want to worry you when you're about to leave on a dangerous operation."

"Yes, you should have." He felt her arms tense, a barely discernible squeeze on the sides of his waist. What did she want from him, that one little "I'm sorry" returned his man balls back to their place?

"You know what, Jake?"

When she didn't answer her own question, he pried her hands away from his stomach and turned. "No, can't say I do." Even as he said the words, he knew he was being an ass, but she'd pushed his buttons. He didn't know how to unpush them.

If the flare in those black eyes had been real fire, he, she, and the kitchen would've just gone up in flames. In zero to sixty, his cock went rock hard. Obviously, his brains had decided to relocate south.

She took a step back from him. "I was going to say get over it, but now I think I'll just say to hell with you. Good-bye."

"Get over it?" Before she made it past the kitchen table, he moved in front of her. "To hell with me? You planning to walk home, Chiquita?" The flinch she gave at hearing his pet name for her only spiraled his blood pressure.

"If you can't understand I only did what I did because I'm worried about you, then screw you." She pushed at his chest.

"You really should stop talking, Maria." Any hope of reason deserted him, and he backed her—step by step—against the nearest wall and seized the hands poking at him. To make good on his threat, he captured her mouth with his and kissed her as if his life depended on it.

He'd gone insane. He didn't care.

Only when he'd yanked his zipper down did he think of needing a condom. A sliver of reason returned and he rested his forehead against hers. "There're two possible answers to my question, and I may or may not agree. Do you want to go home?"

"I don't know."

"Not the right answer." He scooped her up and headed down the hall.

"I don't want to go home, but I'm also mad at you."

"Then we have something in common," he said as he dropped her to her feet next to his bed. "I'm mad at you, too." In two seconds flat, he had her dress off. Since he liked the way the lacey, yellow bra and matching panties looked against her tanned skin, he decided to leave them on. For now.

"Lie down."

CHAPTER FIFTEEN

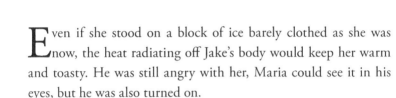

Even if she stood on a block of ice barely clothed as she was now, the heat radiating off Jake's body would keep her warm and toasty. He was still angry with her, Maria could see it in his eyes, but he was also turned on.

"I said lie down."

"You're awfully bossy," she said, not moving. The words were no sooner out when she was lifted and tossed on the bed. Although she'd never admit it, this domineering side of him excited her. When she started to scramble to the other side, he came down on top of her, none too easy.

"Going somewhere?" He ground his erection against her. "Think again."

He took her mouth then, and his tongue—hot and wet—scraped across her teeth. He tasted like mint-flavored candy. No, she wasn't going anywhere, and she twisted the collar of his shirt in her fingers, locking herself to him. Lifting up, he stared at her for a few seconds before angling his head and devouring her mouth again.

The buttons on his shirt rubbed over the bare skin of her stomach, reminding her he was still clothed. Wanting him skin to hot skin, she tried to undo the first one. When her fingers fumbled with the button, she pulled the two sides of his shirt apart.

He raised his head and watched the button fly across the room, then ping against the closet door before dropping to the carpet. "Damn, Chiquita, this is my best shirt."

She popped the next one. "I'll sew them back on later."

For the first time since she'd let slip that Fortunada had attacked her, amusement lit his eyes. "Yeah, right."

"Okay, then I'll buy you another one." Why were they talking about shirts and sewing? "Either take it off yourself or the rest are going too."

He nudged her legs apart with his and knelt between her thighs, popping off the remainder of his buttons with one pull. After yanking off the shirt, he tossed it to the floor. His gaze roamed over her, his hazel eyes now darkened to a mossy green.

Captured by the hunger she saw in them, she lifted a hand to touch him. Before she could, he seized it and the other one, lifting her hands above her head and holding them there. Something fierce glittered in his eyes, sending liquid heat straight to her groin. She tried to squeeze her core muscles together to keep from soaking her panties, to keep him from knowing what he did to her with just a look.

His eyelids slid closed and his nostrils flared as he inhaled deeply. A wicked smile curved one side of his mouth. He was smelling her! Warmth crept up her neck and into her cheeks.

"Does it embarrass you that I can smell your arousal?" he asked, following the words with a chuckle. Not waiting for an answer, he pushed under the elastic of her panties and swirled his finger inside of her. "What about if I taste you? Will that turn your cheeks red too?" He stared at his finger, glistening with her juices, as if contemplating something. "What about if we taste you together?"

Unable to form words, she watched as he rubbed his finger over his mouth. A low ache began and grew with each throb of her pounding heart. "I-I—"

"Don't talk," he said just before lowering his mouth to hers.

Her taste combined with his in an exotic mix of musk, mint, and saltiness. One of them moaned as their tongues dueled in a furious battle for supremacy. That she wanted him to win, to take command of her and her body, was a surprise and not something she'd ever thought to want from a man.

The questions scattered to oblivion when he rocked against her, his erection rubbing over her clit. Even with the material of his slacks and her panties between them, she could feel how hard and big he was. She tried to pull her hands free so she could touch him, but he tightened his grip.

"Here're the rules, Chiquita. You keep your hands above your head. Grab hold of the pillow if you have to. No touching until I say you can and no talking."

"Who made you—"

He tsked. "Already, you're breaking them. Before you say another word, you might want to know your punishment."

At the rise of his brow when she opened her mouth to respond, she snapped it shut. This arrogant, dominant side of him shouldn't be such a turn-on.

"Good, you're catching on."

He lowered his mouth to a breast and sucked on the nipple through the lace of her bra before biting down with his teeth. Pleasure pain spiraled through her bloodstream. If this was her punishment, she had no complaints.

"Like that, do you?" he murmured, then blew on the damp material, soothing the ache.

"Yes." God yes. The sly glint in his eyes clued her in to her mistake.

"You should know I can be a cunning devil when it suits me. That's two punishments on the score sheet so far. Care to take a guess what you can expect?"

Priding herself that she learned from her mistakes, she pressed her lips together, nor did she chance even a nod of her head.

A grin lifted the corners of his mouth. "Smart girl. I'll take it for granted you want to know." He put his mouth next to her ear. "I'm going to make you want to come so bad it hurts, Maria, but I'm not going to let you until I decide you can. Two times now, I'm going to torture you. And again if you break another rule. Before I'm done with you, you'll be begging me."

His breath blew warm on her skin, and the whispered words sent shivers down to her toes.

"I hope you remember the rules because I'm not going to repeat them."

She cited them in her head to make sure she remembered them and even as she ticked them off, she knew she might willingly talk or touch him if it turned out she liked his definition of torture and wanted more.

When he took the nipple of her other breast in his mouth, she dug her fingers into the pillow. She wanted to beg him to remove her bra so she could feel the scrape of his teeth directly on her. *Not yet, Maria. Don't give him the satisfaction. Make him wait for it.*

Two could play this game. As sure as she knew her name, she knew he wanted her to break another one of his rules. Little did he know she'd learned how to be invisible at an early age, a talent that included keeping her mouth shut.

When he leisurely licked his way down her stomach, she thought of a case study to keep from crying out his name. Thank God he hadn't made it a rule she had to be still. That would have been impossible.

He took the elastic of her panties between his teeth and tugged them down her hips. When he'd bared her, he gave a grunt that sounded like one of satisfaction. Maria twisted the end of the pillow around her fist at the first feel of his tongue on her. Making good on his threat, he played with her, toyed with her until she wanted to scream at him to let her come.

Each time she came close to the edge, he moved away, trailing kisses down her legs or giving her stomach little nips. To keep from pleading with him, she bit down hard on her bottom lip. Was it possible to die from intense sexual frustration?

"You think you can't take any more, but I'm going to prove otherwise," he said, sounding gravelly and a little unsteady.

No, she knew she couldn't take any more and could only hope the tremor she heard in his voice meant he too was nearing his limits. Minutes that felt like hours passed, and she finally, absolutely, couldn't bear it. She would give him the satisfaction of begging.

Except somehow he knew. His tongue and teeth performed a magic act, and white, shimmering stars exploded behind her eyelids. The pleasure was so powerful it ripped a scream from her throat, and her heart pounded a roaring noise in her ears. "Oh God oh God oh God."

Suddenly, he was holding her in his arms. "I've got you, Chiquita."

Had she fainted? She had no sense of him moving until he was holding her close and murmuring comforting words. "Jake." His name slipped past her lips before she could stop it, and she prayed he didn't hear the notes of love embedded in it.

"I'm here."

She burrowed her face against his neck, and when her tongue flicked out to taste a salty drop of sweat, he gave a little shudder and groaned. The climax he'd brought her to had rocked her world, and could it be he'd been affected too?

"Can I talk now?"

"Yeah, baby, say anything you want." He pulled her tighter into him.

"Thank you. Take off your pants, please."

His chest shook as a chuckle grew into an all-out laugh. "Not exactly what I was expecting to hear," he said, then covered her mouth with his.

When he'd finished kissing her until she didn't know what day it was, he rolled onto his back and lifted his hips to slide his slacks down his legs.

"You're not wearing underwear." Her gaze automatically fell on his erection and the drop of moisture glistening on the tip.

He turned onto his side to face her and grinned. "Was pretty sure I wouldn't need any tonight. Like what you see?"

"I certainly do." She caught his gaze and held it. As far as she was concerned, the game had ended in a tie, and she wanted to make sure he understood that.

"I won't beg, Jake. Begging's for someone who's desperate. I'm not there yet." Maria knew she was playing with fire—daring him, taunting him. Her blood simmered, hot and heavy in her veins, as his smoldering gaze raked hungrily over her. It was a look that promised she would indeed be begging before the night was over. Maybe she would let him win. Or maybe not.

It was at that moment Jake realized he'd truly met his match. "Careful, Chiquita. I'm not a man you want to issue that kind of challenge to." Although he'd set out to punish her, he wasn't sure the tables hadn't been turned on him. Anger had first fueled his intention to prove . . . he was no longer sure what he meant to prove. There was something he wanted to make sure she understood, but it would come back to him. Later.

The only thing that mattered was meeting her challenge—he needed to hear her beg. He grabbed a condom from the drawer and rolled it on, watching her watch him. "Take off your bra."

A finely arched brow rose. "Say please."

"No. Take it off." He'd noticed earlier she seemed to like being dominated, and the way her brown eyes dilated and turned almost black confirmed his hunch.

She unsnapped the front clasp, then held it closed with her hand. "And if I don't?"

How far could he take this game? He guessed she was daring herself as much as him. Without doubt, her history—growing up with the kind of mother she had—affected her natural tendencies. Even with all she'd seen and heard, he didn't think she understood how deeply sensual and passionate she was. All she really knew was the message her brain kept sending her: she didn't want to be like her mother.

Deciding it best to slowly teach her there was a world of difference between a whore who put out for any man with a buck in his pocket and a woman freely expressing her needs, he restrained his urge to up the level of play and punishment.

He wrapped his hand around his cock. "If you don't, then I'll just take care of myself." Heat flared in her eyes when he slid his hand to the bottom of his shaft and back up again. "I'll admit it's not as pleasurable as being inside you, but it's close enough."

It was a near thing, but he managed to hold back his laugh when she yanked off the bra, then spread out her arms and her legs, reminding him of a snow angel.

"That's my girl," he said, moving to kneel between her thighs. He stroked his fingers along the skin of her inner legs. She sighed and her eyes slid closed. Dew glistened on her curls from their earlier play, and he almost came just from taking in the beauty of seeing her opened to him.

"Maria."

"Mmm?"

"Open your eyes and watch."

She lifted onto her elbows and lowered her chin, focusing her gaze on his cock. The damn thing jerked up, preening for her. Jesus, this wasn't going to last long. His balls were so hard and tight, the skin encasing them felt like it had been stretched around a basketball.

This might kill him, but now that she'd put it in his mind, he *had* to hear her beg. When she did, then he'd know she needed him as much as he needed her. Taking himself in hand, he rubbed the tip up through her folds to her clit. Pausing there, he circled the little nub until it puckered and her hips lifted off the bed. Sliding back down, he held still at the entrance of her sheath.

"Jake, please."

Not good enough. He slid into her an inch and stopped. When she rocked forward in an attempt to take him in, he leaned away and teased her again. This was meant to torture her, but he was the one who'd soon be begging.

Without warning, she reared up and clamped her teeth down on his shoulder. "Damn you. Now, Jake," she all but growled against his skin before spearing herself down on him. "Please, now."

That was good enough. It was what he'd needed from her. Jake pulled her legs behind him, and she immediately caught on, clasping her ankles against his ass. He cupped her bottom in his palms to support her, then lost himself in the feel of being inside her. She was tight, hot, and wet. Her movements were awkward at first, but when she caught his rhythm, he had a brief thought that it had never been like this with any other woman. Then thinking ceased. If the earth was blown to bits at this moment, he was too far gone to care.

Pressure built as he thrust into her, so intense he couldn't hold it back. "Come, Maria," he demanded. The muscles in her sheath clinched around him as he sought out her lips and kissed her with the hunger of a starving man as he exploded inside her.

"Je . . . sus." He twisted and fell back onto the bed with her sprawled across him. "Jesus, Maria," he said between gulps of breath.

Minutes later, when he breathed normally again, he lifted his head and looked down at her. She'd fallen asleep, and he lowered back down and stared at the ceiling.

Although his ego liked that he'd apparently knocked her out cold, couldn't she have at least first said it was good, maybe even amazing?

CHAPTER SIXTEEN

———— ❦ ————

I think I aced it," Maria said to her friend as they walked toward the exit. "How about you?"

Gina shrugged. "I think I did good, but you know how I freeze up on exams. I really hate essays. I sure miss your bodyguard though. He was some kind of eye candy."

"Admit it. You have the hots for him." Since Fortunada was now in jail, Jamie was back doing whatever he normally did before bodyguard duty. He'd driven Maria back to Tallahassee on Sunday so he could get his car, and Gina had been disappointed when he hadn't shown up with Maria on Monday.

"What woman in her right mind wouldn't?" she said rolling her eyes. "Your guy's not so bad either, but those blue eyes of Jamie's?" She waved her hand in front of her face as if she needed cooling off.

No denying Jamie was hot, but she preferred hazel eyes that went as dark green as moss after a rain when they were turned on. Three days had passed since she'd seen Jake, and she missed him so much it sometimes hurt to breathe.

Gina shifted her books to her other arm. "I'm starving. Wanna grab a pizza?"

"Sure. Let me check my messages first." Jake would be boarding his flight in five hours and she was hoping he'd call before he left. It had been hard to concentrate on her final exam knowing he was about to put himself in danger. Saying good-bye to him Sunday morning without telling him she thought she was falling in love with him had been hard, but his attention needed to be on his mission. Nor was she sure he'd want her to be in love with him.

He'd given no sign that being with her wasn't just another fling for him. If his history with women was any indication, he'd soon tire of her and move on. It was too depressing to think about that with her last exam coming up, along with worrying about him having to go to Egypt.

That wasn't even taking into account Fortunada, and not knowing whether or not he was her father. She just couldn't deal with it yet. When her exams were done and Jake was home safe, she'd face that and try to figure out her feelings. Besides, there were two other father possibilities, so maybe she was worrying for nothing.

Turning on her phone, she saw she had one message and her heart beat in anticipation. It wasn't from Jake, though, and she listened to Angie's message. Her stomach grumbled at the thought of missing out on a double cheese, pepperoni pizza.

"Sorry, but I'm going to have to pass on lunch. That was a message from Angie, the girl I told you about. She's upset and needs to see me. Something to do with her mother."

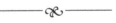

Jake gave one last critical study of the suitcase open on his bed. He didn't like that he couldn't strap a gun or knife on him before boarding the plane, but if their contact spoke true, everything they needed would be waiting when they arrived.

He had three hours before Kincaid picked him up, and he decided to call Maria. She should be out of her last class about now. "You a lawyer, yet?" he asked when she answered.

"Almost. One more day and then next step, the bar."

"I'm proud of you, Chiquita." And he was. He wanted to be there when she walked out of school for the last time. It was a milestone he wished he could share with her. "You headed home to study?"

"I'm on my way to see Angie for a few minutes and then, yeah, it's hit the books for the last time."

"Something wrong?"

"No, I think her mom's having a meltdown, and Angie hopes I can help calm her down. Jake . . ."

Just the way she said his name and then stopped alerted him that something between them was about to change. "Yeah?"

"I lo . . . Never mind, just stay safe, and I'll see you soon."

He fell heavily onto the bed. Had she almost said she loved him? "Take care, Maria." He clicked off and stared at the phone as he tried to decide if he was sorry she hadn't taken that next step—if that's what she had been about to say.

His finger tapped on the face of the cell, itching to call her back and demand she finish the rest of the sentence. "Damn." He tossed the phone on the bed. This wasn't the time to tangle his mind up with anything but the mission.

All he had to do was get through the next five days and he'd be home where he could give his full attention to Maria and their future. After a lengthy shower—probably the last one until he was back in the States—he grabbed a bite to eat.

The boss honked his car horn at precisely 1700 hours and Jake picked up his duffel bag from next to the front door, locking up behind him. After he was belted in, Kincaid handed him an envelope. Jake took it and checked both sides, but there was no writing on it. "What is it?"

"How the hell would I know? It's sealed and Maria made me promise not to open it. I seem to be making a lot of promises to my sister lately because of you, Tiger Toes. I don't like it."

"Get used to it." Jake slid a finger under the flap and opened it. He peeked inside and grinned. She'd sent him a picture of her taken on the beach with her back to the camera like the girl in his painting. Only difference, Maria wore a bikini that showed off her very fine ass.

It hadn't occurred to him to ask for a photo, and he was pleased she'd thought to give him one. When he returned home, he'd get one with her facing the camera—one he could put in his wallet to show off to anyone wanting to know what his girlfriend looked like. Damn, he had a girlfriend. He slipped the picture back in the envelope and tucked it into his shirt pocket.

"What was it?"

"None of your business, boss."

"See, that's what I'm talking about. All of a sudden you both have secrets. I don't like it."

"You already said that."

"Bears repeating," Kincaid muttered.

After parking and entering the airport, they parted ways. As Jake waited to board, he studied his men who had joined him at the gate. Stewart seemed calm, but Bayne was on edge. As second in command at K2, Jake had read the background reports on both men when they were hired.

Kincaid only hired ex-SEALs, so the two men were experienced in military operations, but Bayne had once been captured and held for five days by insurgents before being rescued. Even under torture, Bayne hadn't given anything away, and that was impressive.

Jake worried, however, that they were putting him back in action too soon. "I'm thinking this little operation's gonna be a cakewalk compared to what we're used to. Our biggest problem will be babysitting the kid until we can turn him over to his dad."

He waited for both to nod their agreement. "But that doesn't mean we treat it like playtime. We stay alert, we follow the plan, and we watch each other's backs. When we get home all safe and sound, beer's on me."

"Works for me," Stewart said.

Bayne shrugged one shoulder. "Sorry, but I'm a scotch man, myself."

"You got it." Jake glanced at his watch. They should've started boarding ten minutes ago. About the time they were due to depart, an announcement came over the speakers that the flight would be delayed for one hour.

That was annoying. He was ready to get this mission over with. Considering it would be the next day before they reached their destination, Jake decided to break the K2 rule of no alcohol on an operation. Besides, he didn't count it as starting until they were on the plane—wheels up.

"Let's wait in the bar." He almost warned his team one drink only but held his tongue, wanting to see if either was stupid enough to get drunk. Thirty minutes later, he and Stewart still nursed their one beer, but Bayne had ordered a second Scotch. Jake's unease increased.

As he listened to Stewart boast about his latest conquest, it struck him that he was glad he'd left that lifestyle behind. He'd wondered if he might miss partying, but he didn't. All he wanted was Maria.

Somehow, she'd performed a magic act and made his issue with commitment disappear. He had no desire to have anyone in his bed but her, and the part of him that had believed he couldn't be faithful no longer worried. That he was starting to think he wanted only her for the rest of his life was some kind of miracle.

She'd said she planned to stop by Angie's, but by now she was probably back home studying for exams. Was she having trouble sleeping without him like he'd had since she'd returned to school? He considered calling her, but he'd probably blurt out that he thought he might be falling in love with her. When he told her, he wanted it to be in person.

"They should've called for boarding by now," he said, checking his watch. "Looks like another delay."

His phone buzzed and he answered, listening with a sinking heart to Detective Nolan. "The bastard has Maria," he said, standing up so fast he knocked his chair over. How the hell did they let Fortunada post bail?

"Who has her?" Bayne asked.

How was he supposed to get on a plane and travel sixteen hours away from her knowing she was in trouble? He couldn't. Kincaid's flight had left already so there was no way to get in touch with him. Even if he could, he'd still be headed for Tallahassee, and if it cost him his job, he didn't give a rat's ass.

"What's going on?" Stewart asked.

Jake jerked his head up. "What?"

The airport's speakers crackled to life and announced boarding would commence for their flight in ten minutes. Options raced through his mind.

"Who's got Maria?" Bayne asked again.

"The bad guy. I don't have time to explain. Here's the plan. You two go on ahead, and I'll catch up with you at the safe house . . . Friday night, latest." Was he making a mistake sending them off without him? They were experienced soldiers, but this was their first K2 mission. Yet, if someone didn't show up to meet their contact, the dude might get spooked. He pulled two twenties out of his pocket and handed them to Bayne.

"Pay the tab. We'll wait for you at the gate." Time was wasting and he needed to get to Maria. What was the fastest way?

"Listen," he said when he had Stewart alone. "Bayne's a little jumpy. Do what you can to settle him down. I'll be there no later than Friday night, probably sooner. Assure Har-Shaf that everything's proceeding as planned. Don't even think of leaving the safe house and venturing into Egypt on your own. Spend the time going over the plan. It'll give you both something to do."

"And if you're not?"

"Then you'll come back home, but I'll get there." As soon as he rescued Maria and could see for himself she was safe. "I'll keep in touch and let you know when to expect me. By the way, Har-Shaf means terrible face, but it would be a mistake to ask him about his nose. He's rather touchy on the subject. One reason he likes us is we don't make fun of him like his countrymen."

"What happened to it?" Stewart asked.

"Rats ate it off when he was a baby."

"Jesus."

"Stewart's got the lead until I arrive," Jake said when Bayne caught up with them.

"Go kick ass," Stewart said.

"That's the plan." As he strode down the concourse, Jake dialed his friend, Bob Michaels, who not only owned a Lear based at a nearby private airport but was in possession of a few things he'd need. If his flight had left on time, he wouldn't have known Maria was now a hostage until he'd changed planes in Miami. Thanking whatever fates were at work, he caught a cab to take him the short distance to Executive Airport and the jet that would take him to her.

The only advantage he had was the tracking device he'd taped under the lining of her purse, and he hoped to hell she hadn't changed purses. When he'd made a detour to K2 Sunday morning before taking her home, she'd questioned the necessity of his precaution now that Fortunada was in jail. He couldn't explain his unease and attributed it to knowing he'd be out of the country and out of reach.

"The bastard's blaming you for all his problems. He's come after you once, and he'll do it again given half a chance. If nothing else, knowing we can track you should something happen makes me feel better, all right?"

She'd looked at him then, brown eyes damp with unshed tears, and said, "Can I put one on you so I'll feel better too?"

Because he couldn't make sense of what was going on with his heart, he'd simply answered her with a kiss.

CHAPTER SEVENTEEN

————— ❧ —————

Maria glanced at the fuel gauge. "If you're planning on us going very far, we'll need gas. The gauge is on empty." Did he even know where he wanted to go?

"You got money?"

"Just a few dollars." If she steered the car off the road, could she manage hitting a tree and killing Fortunada without killing herself?

When she'd knocked on the door, it had opened and she'd walked in, never expecting to see Carol and Angie bound and gagged. The door had slammed behind her before she could turn and run. Now, she was driving Carol's Taurus to God-knows-where with a man—who might or might not be her father—who was in possession of a gun, one pointed at her. At least he'd left Carol and Angie behind, and by now they'd surely found a way to get untied and call the cops.

"We need a different car and some money," he said, looking at her as if she could snap her fingers and make that happen.

The last thing she wanted was a different car. The cops would be looking for this one, something that had obviously occurred to him. Knowing her car would be easy to spot, she'd suggested they take her Mustang, but he'd given her a suspicious glare and ordered her into the Taurus. Lesson learned. Next time she wanted him to do something, suggest the exact opposite.

"How much money's in your account?"

As if she'd tell him there was enough for him to easily disappear into Mexico and live comfortably for a long time. The lie came easily. "About five hundred dollars."

She glanced at him. He really wasn't bad looking with his Latino features, but as hard as she tried to find any semblance to her, she couldn't. No way this man was her daddy, she decided, and prayed it was true.

"Find an ATM," he said, lifting the gun.

"Unless you want to be sitting on the side of the road out of gas, you need to let me find a station first." Where this courage to speak up to him with the black hole of a gun barrel pointed at her came from, she didn't know, but she wasn't going down without a fight. What she couldn't decide was whether or not to tell him he might be her father. Would that help or make things worse?

"There." He pointed to a Shell station ahead on the right. "You get out and fill the tank and don't try anything funny. Don't think I won't shoot you."

There went taking off when he got out. On to plan B. She slipped her purse onto her shoulder before leaving the car. Plan B was to run inside the station, but he was waiting at the back of the car when she came around the trunk.

Plan C then. She dug out her credit card and swiped it. "I have to pee," she said after removing the nozzle from the car's tank and putting it back on the pump.

"No, you don't." He lifted his chin. "Get in."

Although the gun was in his pocket, so was his hand. No doubt he had his finger on the trigger. She crossed her legs. "Yes, I do. Please, I don't want to pee in my pants."

He glanced from her to the station and back. "You try anything and not only will I shoot you, but also anyone else nearby."

He grabbed the bathroom door before she could pull it closed behind her. "I'll be right here. Hurry up."

She did have to pee, or at least she had to before a crazy man with a gun stood on the other side of the cracked door. Unable to bring herself to pull her panties down with him standing there, she hurriedly rummaged through her purse for her phone. Unable to talk with him listening, she wondered whose number she should call. Jake was on his flight by now, and her brother was on his way to DC. That left one person. She dialed Jamie's number.

"You have thirty seconds before I come in."

In a panic, she pushed the phone into her bra, hoping Jamie answered and not a recording. Then she prayed he was smart enough to catch on and listen. She flushed the toilet, then turned on the tap. When she went to grab her purse from the door hook, she remembered the tracking device Jake had put in it.

"Thank you, Jake," she whispered. Afraid Fortunada might take her purse away at some point, she fumbled with the lining until she felt the device, pulled it off the tape, and stuck it too in her bra. As long as Fortunada didn't make her strip, she at least had two ways for them to find her.

The door flew open, and startled, she shrieked, dropping her purse. "It's a sad day when a girl can't even pee in private," she muttered, bending down to pick up her purse. "Not that a Shell station is my favorite place to pee," she added, praying Jamie was listening.

"Whatcha got in there," he said, snatching the strap out of her hand.

"That's mine, Mr. Fortunada." *Did you hear who I'm with, Jamie?* God, she wished she knew if he was listening.

Ignoring her, Fortunada rummaged through it, finally settling on taking the forty or so dollars in her wallet. He pushed her out of the bathroom and with his fingers digging into her elbow, he steered her to the cooler. After grabbing a tall can of beer, he herded her to the counter. As he paid for the beer with her money, Maria tried to catch the attention of the clerk. When he finally glanced at her, she mouthed the word "help." He grinned and in heavily accented English said, "Have nice day."

If only. "Great place you got here," she said. "Never knew there was a Shell station on Lumford Street."

The clerk's head bobbed. "Have nice day."

"Shut up," Fortunada growled as he pushed her out the door.

Back on the road with a full tank of gas, she drove in a wide circle, keeping the Shell station in the center, hoping Fortunada wouldn't notice. So far, he'd been enjoying his beer too much to give her directions. Did the creep even have a plan?

"Find a money machine," he finally said.

The only one she knew the exact location of was near her apartment. "There's one on College, not too far from here." That would get them back into her neighborhood.

"Go there." He crushed the empty can, then tossed it onto the back seat. "Why'd you come to my house?"

Crap. She chewed on her bottom lip, debating whether to tell him the truth. "There's still time to let me go before the cops find you. I'll get you money and you can take the car, go wherever you want."

"No. You're my insurance." He fiddled with the gun resting on his thigh, sliding it back and forth. "You're the reason the cops are after me, so you got this coming."

"I really wish you wouldn't point that gun at me." If she could only figure him out, she might be able to decide what to do. Sometimes it seemed as if he was confused as to how he'd gotten in this mess. Other times, he'd look at her with so much hate that she feared he'd pick up the gun and shoot her just because it would please him to do so. Every once in a while he would eye her as if he were trying to undress her.

A shiver traveled up her spine at the thought of him putting his hands on her. Somehow, she had to get away before he either shot her or touched her. Although she continued to check in the rear-view mirror for any sign of a police car, she saw none.

"Turn here," he said all of a sudden.

"Governor's Square Mall. I love the stores here," she said, still hoping Jamie was listening.

"Shut up." With the nose of the gun, he pointed. "Go there to the back."

Twenty minutes later, they were back on the road in a stolen car. "I'm really impressed you know how to hotwire a car but if we were going to steal one, couldn't you have picked something nicer than a green Ford?"

"Do you ever shut up?" He changed the radio from a talk show to a country station, then turned the volume up.

That was going to make it harder for Jamie to hear her if he was listening.

⸎

"He just stole a car, a green Ford. Don't know what model or year. She let us know he's got a gun."

The bastard was a dead man. Jake walked up the sidewalk to Carol and Angie's house, the phone to his ear. "She's still got the tracking device on her, right?"

"We're assuming it's on her and not riding around in someone else's car," Saint said. "She hasn't said anything about Fortunada tossing her purse away. We're following its movements on the big screen, and the direction jibes with everything she's saying. Right now, they're on College, a few miles from State Street. You gonna tell the cops we're tracking them?"

"And risk a shoot-out? Hell no. I'll tell them about the change of cars, and to search the back of the mall for Carol's Taurus. Maria's car's here; I'll take it to go after them. I'll call you back as soon as I'm gone from here."

A uniformed cop answered his knock. "I need to see Detective Nolan."

"He's busy."

"Yeah, so am I," Jake said, pushing past the man.

"Hey!"

Jake jerked his arm away when the cop grabbed it.

"It's okay, Grabowski, let 'em in."

Nolan held out his hand and Jake shook it. "I was hoping the next time I saw you it would be while we watched Fortunada get sentenced to prison. Whose bright idea was it to let him out on bail?"

"Sorry to say, it was out of my hands. Why are you here, Buchanan? Tell me you don't got it in mind to play superhero."

Okay, he wouldn't tell him. Jake glanced at Carol and Angie, huddled together on the sofa. Tears streamed down both their faces.

"I-I'm so sorry," Angie said, following it up with a hiccup. "He made . . . he made me call her."

Jake knelt in front of her, covering her hands with his. "I know. You did what you had to do to keep you and your mom safe, and no one blames you. Does he have only the one gun?"

She nodded. "I think so."

"How do you know he's got a gun?" Nolan asked.

The door burst open and Eddie barreled in, running headlong into Grabowski. The two of them fell to the floor, a tangle of legs and arms.

"Jesus," Jake muttered. He pulled Eddie up by the collar. "What the hell's wrong with you?"

"Why are all those cop cars out there? Where's Angie? What's going on, dude?"

"Angie's fine. Go sit with her on the couch and try to be quiet."

Nolan looked at Jake and rolled his eyes. "Shoulda just sent out invitations. Now, you were going to tell me how you know our perp has a gun."

No, he wasn't. "Let's talk in the kitchen."

Rummaging in the refrigerator, Jake found a bottle of water. "Want one?"

"I'd rather have a double shot of scotch, straight up, but that'll have to do." Nolan took the bottle and opened it. "Talk, Buchanan."

Jake unscrewed the cap to another bottle of water and downed half the contents, then set the water on the counter and crossed his arms. "I'm more of a beer man myself. Let me ask you something. What happens when a cop spots Carol's car? He's gonna call for backup, then they'll surround the car, guns drawn, right? Or, if he's a hothead, he's not going to wait for backup and will try to pull them over instead, then there'll be a high-speed chase with the likelihood of a crash. You disagree?"

The detective set his bottle on the counter next to Jake's, then crossed his arms, mirroring Jake's stance. "Where you going with this?"

If he'd been in the mood, he would have laughed at the old police ploy of aping a subject in an attempt at intimidation. But time was wasting and he had no tolerance for games at the moment. "I notice you didn't disagree. Why? Because you can't. I won't risk Maria being in the middle of a shoot-out."

"So you think you can save her all by your lonesome, Lone Ranger?"

"I know I can." He prayed it was true. "I'll call and tell you where you can come collect your man."

"Where you going?"

At the kitchen doorway, he stopped and turned. "To rescue a damsel in distress." His damsel. "By the way, you can find Carol's car behind the Governor's Square Mall. Your *perp* stole a green Ford."

He walked out to the sound of some mighty fine cussing. Although he'd thought he would have to break into the Mustang and hotwire it, he found it unlocked and her keys in the cup holder. "Maria, Maria," he tsked.

Since he knew she usually pocketed her keys, he could imagine her upset by Angie's message and her hurry to get inside. He'd told Nolan he would call and tell him where to come get Fortunada. What he neglected to add after Fortunada's name was "dead body."

Although her Mustang was souped up, it didn't have a GPS. From the pouch around his waist, he took the one Michaels had brought, along with two guns—a Glock and a SIG Sauer—a knife balanced perfectly for throwing right between someone's eyes, a flashlight, a whistle, and a grenade.

"A whistle and a grenade?" he'd said when examining the contents of the pouch.

"Why not? Who knows, you might want to blow something up. And that's a dog whistle. I'm never without one."

Michaels had grinned at his own words, and all Jake could think when seeing the demented twist of his lips was that he was damn glad the man was his friend. "Scares me straight to know our government has a psycho like you on their payroll," he'd said as he packed the toys back into the pouch.

With the GPS turned on and sitting on the dash, he backed out of the driveway. His foot heavy on the gas, he headed for College

Street, her last known location. When he had her safe in his arms, he'd give her holy hell for taking ten years off his life.

"Where's she now?" he said when Saint answered his call.

"They just left the ATM. He told her to get on I-10 and go west. She'll be turning onto the entrance in seven."

The bastard was running. "How much longer you think her phone battery will last?"

"Two hours at most. Even if it dies out before you get to her, we're still able to track her. Don't lose your cool, Jake."

"Easy for you to say when you're not in love with her." The declaration so surprised him, he almost hit the car next to him. "I mean, that's easy for you to say when you're not here."

"I know what you meant," Saint replied, sounding as if he really did. Then his voice turned serious. "I finally tracked down the boss. He's catching a plane back tonight, but he said the only way he'd fire you for not being on a plane headed for Egypt was if you didn't show up tomorrow with his sister standing next to you."

"Just keep me informed on where they are or anything she says." He disconnected and concentrated on weaving in and out of rush-hour traffic. If the bastard harmed one hair on her head, he really would be sent to hell in a body bag.

CHAPTER EIGHTEEN

———— ❦ ————

Jake ran the red light at the entrance onto I-10 West. An oncoming car's brakes squealed and the driver flipped him a finger as he sped past. "Yeah, yeah, back atcha," he said as he floored it up the entrance ramp.

He dialed Saint. "I'm on I-10. How far ahead of me are they?"

"They got on the Interstate twenty minutes ago. She just asked where they're going and he didn't answer. She's starting to sound scared. We don't think she knows for sure if we're listening, and I'm guessing she's beginning to think she's on her own."

How could she not know he'd come for her no matter what? "Call me if anything changes." He dropped the phone onto the passenger seat and swerved into the right lane, passing a van traveling at least five miles under the speed limit. "Slower traffic keep right," he yelled as he moved ahead of the idiot. What was wrong with these people?

Hoping she'd keep to the seventy-mile-per-hour limit or under, he calculated how long it'd take to catch up with them if he drove ninety miles per hour. In a little over an hour—as long as no cops got in his way—he'd have her in his sights.

That she'd thought to turn on her phone was impressive. Although the tracking device would lead him to her, it helped that someone was listening and evaluating her stress level. So far, it appeared she was keeping her cool, but how long would that last?

Less than twenty minutes later, his phone buzzed and he grabbed it, punched "Speaker" and set it on the console so he could keep both hands on the wheel. "Whatcha got?"

"We're listening in on all the police radios . . . city, county, and state. The owner of the Ford reported his car stolen so the cops have the model and tag number. It's a 2009 Fusion, moss-green metallic, and they've got an APB out on it."

Jake memorized the tag number Saint gave him. Another forty minutes at most and he should catch up to them. He glanced at the speedometer and eased off the gas, bringing his speed back down to ninety. As much as he'd like to push the Mustang to its limits, someone would probably call 911 on him if he blew by them doing over one-twenty. Last thing he needed was a cop on his ass.

"Uh-oh."

He heard someone speaking in the background. "What? Talk to me, Saint."

"A state trooper just radioed in and verified the tag number. He's behind them."

"Does he know the bastard's got a gun?"

"Hold on a sec."

To hell with watching his speed. Hoping people would assume he was an undercover cop, he turned on his lights and his hazards, then pressed the pedal to the floor. The Mustang shot ahead as if it'd been catapulted out of a slingshot. Thank God Maria loved fast cars.

"Okay, the trooper turned on his siren about two seconds before his supervisor told him to wait for backup. Fortunada's ordering Maria to run, but she's refusing. I'm putting Maria on speaker so you can listen for yourself." Jake steeled himself to hear her voice, wishing there was some way to let her know he was listening.

"He's probably stopping us because I was going a little too fast. If we run, he'll have every cop in the area after us, maybe even helicopters. You need to stay calm, Mr. Fortunada, or he'll get suspicious. And keep that gun out of sight."

Good girl, just keep staying cool. Hearing her voice, Jake wanted to crawl through the phone and snatch her out of danger. A car changed lanes in front of him and he laid on the horn, passing it on the shoulder. Once a year, Kincaid signed all of them up for a week of intensive race car driving school, and Jake suddenly felt a deep appreciation for the man's foresight.

"Take that exit, then pull over."

Damn, Fortunada sounded panicky. "How far away am I from them?" he asked, knowing Saint would be tracking his phone.

"As fast as you're moving on my map, I'd say twenty minutes."

Too much could happen in twenty minutes. "What exit are they taking?"

"The Caryville exit, 104. Unfortunately, it's isolated. No stations or food joints."

Jake had a bad feeling the situation was headed south fast. This was no traffic violation stop, and the trooper would be as on edge as Fortunada. As he listened to the heated conversation between Maria and Fortunada, it was obvious they were both losing it.

"What the hell's going on?" he asked when their voices faded in and out.

"Either her battery's dying or there's spotty service where they are. Ken thinks it's a service problem."

If their tech geek said it was the service, then that's what it was. Straining to hear over the static, he could only make out a word here and there. With what he could pick up, it sounded like the trooper was ordering them out of the car and Fortunada was refusing.

Suddenly, gunfire filled the air. "Who's shooting, Saint?"

"Don't know. Hang tight a minute. Ken's got his eyes squeezed shut and his earphones on, trying to listen."

Another shot exploded through the speakers, followed by a scream from Maria, then silence. "Talk to me. What's going on?" The trucker he flew past blew his air horn and, startled, Jake jerked the wheel and almost ran off the road. "Dammit, man. You scared the shit out of me."

"What?"

"Just having a friendly conversation with a trucker. Is Maria okay?" If she wasn't, he'd go on a rampage, and God help anyone who got in his way.

"All we know is they're on the move again . . . at least, her purse is."

He should've planted a tracking device under her skin. When he had her back and safe again, that was the first thing he was going to do.

"You might want to slow it down. There're two state troopers coming up behind you, going fast."

Jake let off the gas and pulled into the right lane. Two minutes later, he heard sirens. A check in the rearview mirror showed the trooper's cars in the fast lane, red and blue lights flashing.

After they passed, he pulled out behind them and sped up. What he'd like to do was give them a piece of his mind. If their pal had left well enough alone, he'd be almost caught up with Maria by now and would have delivered Fortunada to them, a shiny red bow plastered to his forehead.

He followed them off the Caryville exit, slowing and gawking like a regular driver would at the sight of a trooper lying on the side of the road. "Hope you're okay," he said as he drove by.

"Saint, you there?" he asked, halting at the stop sign. Nothing. Now that he'd verified for himself there was no cell service here, all he had to decide was whether to go left or right.

———— ❧ ————

"You shot him! Why'd you do that? Couldn't you have just tied him up or something?"

Maria swiped her fingers over the tears streaming down her cheeks. Her vision was so blurry she could barely see where she was going. What she couldn't stop seeing though was the officer jerking backward, then crumbling into a heap when Fortunada had shot him.

It was her fault. She hadn't been speeding like she'd told him and had rejoiced at the thought she was about to be rescued. It had never occurred to her it would come to this.

From the moment she'd opened her mother's stud book, she'd grabbed at the idea of finding her father, dreaming that he would take one look at her and love her. Instead, all she'd done was get a cop killed. Why hadn't she burned the stupid book?

She wanted Jake but by now, he'd be on his way to Egypt with no way of knowing how much she needed him. She didn't even know if Jamie was listening in on the phone she'd stuffed into her bra.

Oh, God. She'd gotten a cop killed.

"Stop."

Maria slammed on the brakes. Fortunada had already killed one person and the gun leveled at her head spoke volumes. She peered around them through her tears and froze at the sight of a gray-haired woman sitting on her porch. Then her gaze settled on the old car parked at the side of the small house and she knew what he wanted.

"No." No way she was going to be responsible for hurting someone's grandma, especially just to steal a car left over from the Stone Age.

Fortunada put his thumb on the revolver's hammer and cocked it. "I just want her car. You've been a pain in my ass from the first so it makes no difference to me if I kill you now."

"Promise you won't hurt her." God forgive her, she was a coward.

He pressed the gun to her head. "You got three seconds to drive this car behind that house."

The part of her that wanted to live screamed at her to obey him, but the decent side of her decided this was where a line had to be drawn. "No." She waited to die but nothing happened, so she ventured on. "You can't go around killing people. It's just not okay. I have no problem with stealing her car, but you have to swear you won't hurt her. She's just a little old lady."

"If you were my wife, I'd be beating the shit out of you about now. Just get us the car."

If she was his daughter, would he also beat her? The debate on whether or not to tell him it was a possibility raged on, and still, she couldn't decide. She turned onto the dirt driveway and slowly approached the house. *Please, lady, please get up and lock yourself in the house.*

The woman stood and shaded her eyes with her hand, watching them. "Hello," she called and cheerfully waved when Maria stopped the car. "If you're selling, I ain't buying. Best if you know that up front."

"Park around the back, out of sight," Fortunada said.

Maria furiously blinked her eyes at the woman, hoping she'd catch on that things weren't right. "I'm just going to drive the car around the house. I'll be right back." The subtle message apparently hadn't worked as the lady was standing in the same spot when they walked back to the front of the house, Fortunada behind Maria with his gun poking into her spine.

"Don't try anything or she gets hurt," he growled into her ear.

As incentives to behave went, that one was right up there. "Hello, ma'am. We need to borrow your car."

The woman put her hands on her hips. "What's your name, girl?"

"Maria." She put her foot on the bottom step. "Maria Kincaid. This is Mr. Fortunada and he's in something of a hurry." The sooner she got them away, the less likely he'd do something stupid.

"Well, Miss Maria Kincaid, I'm Mrs. Watkins, and you can't borrow my car. Looked to me like yours worked just fine."

A cat appeared and wound itself around her legs. Maria picked it up and held it above her face, debating the wisdom of tossing it at Fortunada.

"His name's Mr. Kitty."

"Nice to meet you, Mr. Kitty." He began purring and she brought it to her chest, wishing she were home and it was Mouse she was holding. Her poor cat was going to think she'd abandoned him. Tears burned her eyes that she might never see him again. Or Jake. Or Logan, Dani, and the kids.

Get a grip, Maria. She couldn't afford to fall apart now. Fortunada prodded her forward. Mrs. Watkins took a step back, finally seeming to realize something wasn't right. *I'm so sorry. I really wish you'd locked yourself inside and called the cops.*

"Here," Maria said, handing the woman her cat. "If you'd just give us the keys to your car, we'll get on our way and leave you be."

"I've already told you no, young lady." She turned toward her front door.

"Give me the fucking keys, lady," Fortunada said, stepping around Maria.

"You need to watch your language, Mr. Fortunada. The Lord don't take kindly to those kinds of words." Her eyes widened when he lifted the gun and pointed it at her. "Oh, my." She clutched her cat to her ample breasts.

Maria put herself between the woman and the gun. No way she could stand by and let him shoot anyone else. "Please, Mrs.

Watkins. If you'll just do what he says, he won't hurt you." God, she prayed that was true.

As if backing away from a rabid dog, the woman slowly shuffled toward the house. "You two wait right here, and I'll go get them."

"So you can call the cops?" Fortunada caught the screen door and pushed Maria inside.

"I need to use the bathroom," Maria said, hoping for a chance to see if her phone was still working. As before, he stood in the hallway and made her leave the door cracked. Only difference this time was he made Mrs. Watkins stand with him. She really did have to pee and tried to be as quiet about it as possible.

The sink wasn't visible through the gap. She turned on the water, then pulled her phone out. Damn. Damn. Damn. No service. Not only that, but her battery didn't have much charge left.

Fortunada rapped on the door. "You taking a bath, or what?"

Leave it on or turn it off? Since the lack of service would have disconnected her from Jamie, she turned it off and slid it back into her bra. Afraid the tracking device might fall out at some point, she tucked it into the pocket of her capris.

"I'm just washing my hands," she said. After shutting off the water, she grabbed her purse from the counter and walked out.

"Now, I gotta take a leak. You two stay right where I can see you." Fortunada put his hands on his zipper as he headed for the toilet.

"Oh, sweet Lord, is he going to make us watch him?" Mrs. Watkins said.

Maria turned and wrapped her arms around the woman and the cat still clutched against her bosom. "We'll just close our eyes while we say the Lord's Prayer so we won't hear him." It was the only prayer she knew, one she used to recite to block out the noises coming through the thin walls of her mother's bedroom. It certainly couldn't hurt to try and get the Lord's attention right now.

A minute later, Fortunada followed them through the living room and into the kitchen.

Mrs. Watkins sat the cat on a small table, then opened the pantry and removed a black patent leather purse. "Robbers would never think to look in there for my pocketbook," she said with obvious pride at her ingenuity. Then her eyes narrowed at Fortunada. "Don't be thinking to come back and steal it."

Ignoring her, he opened the fridge. "You got any beer in here?"

Mrs. Watkins appeared sorely affronted. "No, sir. Mr. Watkins didn't cotton to spirits and neither does the good Lord."

He grunted and snatched a bottle of soda. Eyeing the old-fashioned wall phone, he walked over and pulled the wires from the socket. "Give her your keys, and whatever money you got in there you can give me."

"Thank you, Mrs. Watkins, for the use of your car," Maria said, holding out her hand. *And as soon as we're gone, you walk to your nearest neighbor and call the cops.*

The woman dangled a key ring above Maria's hand. "Mr. Watkins bought this car when it was brand spanky new, and it was his pride and joy. It ain't going nowheres without me."

Oh, no, no, no. "No ma'am, that's really not a good idea."

"Actually, it is," Fortunada said. "Cops won't be looking for a little ole lady. But we'll wait until it gets dark. Better that way."

Maria spun. "No, I refuse to go anywhere if you take her. Leave her be."

"Fine, I'll just shoot her instead. Your choice."

Would he really? Why not? He'd put a bullet in a cop so what difference would it make if he shot a sweet old lady? Cold black eyes stared at her, daring her. She lowered her head in defeat, unable to risk finding out if he was bluffing.

When this was over, she was signing up for every kind of martial arts class in existence and would never leave the house again without a knife strapped to her thigh and a gun in her purse. If she got out of this alive, that was.

At the sound of a low-flying helicopter overhead, everyone froze. "Quiet," Fortunada said.

Maria prayed they would spot the Ford, but it was unlikely. He'd made her park it under a large oak tree, and unless they landed they'd never see it.

"Don't see as how they can hear us all the way up there, Mr. Fortunada." Mrs. Watkins picked up her cat and headed for the door.

"Where you think you're going, lady?"

The old woman gave him a look that said he was stupid. "You got a gun Mr. Fortunada. I ain't having no shoot out in my house, no sir. I'm gonna go out there and wave at them, otherwise they're gonna send someone to check. I seen that one time on the television. There was this murderess on that show—"

"Christ, woman, I don't give a shit about no TV show. You go out there and wave, but don't you think about trying something." He brandished the gun at her. "I'll be watching you."

"Your cussing offends me, sir." She huffed, then walked out onto the back steps with Mr. Kitty and gave a merry wave. The helicopter hovered a few more seconds before moving away.

All rightly then, I've fallen down a rabbit hole. Maria only wondered how soon she'd get to meet Alice.

CHAPTER NINETEEN

———— ❧ ————

Jake checked his phone again. Still nothing. He needed to turn around and go back to where he'd had service so he could call Saint and find out where Maria was. Maybe right had been the wrong direction to take, but he'd once heard that when people were lost, they tended to make right-hand turns.

There'd been no sign of her, the Ford Fusion, or Fortunada for the last twenty miles, and he was ready to tear something apart with his bare hands. As soon as the oncoming car passed, he'd make a U-turn and head back to the Interstate.

Ahead, a low-flying helicopter approached. When it was within thirty yards, it hovered, forcing him to stop. Jake kept his hands visible on the wheel. He didn't have time for this. The bird approached off to the side, and the pilot looked him over before giving a curt nod and flying away.

Jake watched in the rearview mirror as the chopper disappeared. If nothing else, he'd learned they'd yet to find Fortunada. Deciding to check his phone one last time before he turned around, he clicked it on. Sweet Jesus, yes. Two bars should be enough to get through to Saint. "Don't know if I'll fade out so tell me quick where Maria is," he said when Saint answered.

"One sec. Okay, got you. She's six point seven miles to the

northeast of you. You need to stand by for instructions. Kincaid's here and . . ."

Static garbled Saint's next words, then the call cut off. "And he's organizing a rescue," Jake finished for him. Maria was minutes away and the hell with standing by.

When he had her back, it was entirely possible he'd turn caveman: throw her over his shoulder and carry her off somewhere private. He needed to touch her, feel her under him. Or over him, he didn't really care. Needed to lose himself in her and know she was where she belonged. With him.

"You're a goner, Buchanan," he muttered. Hearing it said aloud rammed the truth home. Acceptance settled in, sweeping the last of his doubts out the door. From the night he'd first made love to her, he'd considered her his. Mine, his brain had declared the second he'd sank into her wet heat. What he hadn't done was give her the gift of him . . . all of him.

Although he'd decided he wanted a relationship with her, he hadn't completely shed Romeo. He'd assumed the lust would eventually wear off for both of them and they'd move on. And although his heart had done a funny little flip when he'd thought she was going to say she loved him, it had also scared the bejesus out of him.

Amazing, I'm in love and the world hasn't stopped spinning. It was something he'd keep to himself until he returned from Egypt. Not once in his life had he told a woman he loved her, not even to talk her into his bed. When he told Maria, he wanted to do it right, and he'd need to do some planning.

First though, he had to rescue his lady. The few houses along the road were all small, old, and spread apart by a few acres. They all looked pretty much alike; a few more run-down than others. At the six-point-seven-mile mark, he studied the house with a 1950s model Buick parked under a carport. No sign of the Ford. In case anyone was watching out the window, he didn't slow. He needed to find a place to hide the Mustang and then do some reconnoitering.

A quick check of his cell showed he was back to no service, but he wouldn't call Saint even if he could. Last thing he wanted was to be ordered to stand down. The sun was setting and it would be dark soon, making it easier to prowl around.

A half mile down the road, he saw what appeared to be an abandoned house. He pulled the Mustang into the carport and rolled down the window. As much as he wanted to charge over to the targeted location and snatch Maria away from the bastard, he knew that was how mistakes were made. She had better be in that house though.

With his eyes closed, he listened to the sounds around him, especially for any barking dogs. Off in the distance he heard one, but it was to the right, and Jake's interest lay to the left. Crickets began to chirp as dusk gave way to night, and an owl hooted nearby. Turning off the overhead light, he eased the door open, stepped out of the car, then quietly closed the door.

The windows at the back of the house were boarded up with cheap plywood, verifying the place was vacant. Jake sat on the back stoop and removed the pouch from around his waist. Out of habit, he checked the guns, then slipped both of them into the waistband of his jeans. He slid the knife out of its sheath and held it up to the waning light. It was a wicked-looking thing, and he tested its weight before putting it back in its holder. Standing, he stuck it into a back pocket.

For a few seconds, he stared at the grenade. With a shake of his head, he put it back in the pouch and secured it back around his waist. The small flashlight went into the pocket opposite the knife.

Dark surrounded him as he disappeared into the scrub oak

behind the abandoned house. On high alert, he eased the balls of his feet down first, testing the ground under them for limbs or leaves that would make a crackling sound. Five minutes later, he stood as still as the tree next to him in the backyard of the house where he thought Maria was. He scanned the area, his gaze coming to rest on the Ford Fusion parked under the massive limbs of an oak tree and impossible to see from the air.

He'd found her.

When his heart settled back into its normal beat, he slipped through the dark to the Ford and punched a hole in all four tires with the knife. Making his way into the yard as far as he dared, he stopped next to a bush of some kind and waited.

A male figure walked past the window, outlined by the dim light behind him. Even though Jake couldn't make out his face, every bone in his body knew it was Fortunada.

"I'm coming for you, you bastard," he murmured. He unzipped the pouch, pulled out the whistle, and blew it. All he could hear was a sound like a rush of wind, but if there was a dog inside, the high-pitched noise would incite it to bark.

A cat jumped onto the window sill and stared out. Jake waited and his patience paid off. A woman too heavy to be Maria came into view and picked up the cat. Unless she'd known Fortunada beforehand and this had been his destination all along, there was now another hostage to rescue. Question was, did she live alone or was there another man in the house?

He made his way to the Buick and jammed the knife into the right front tire, the one anyone coming out of the side door couldn't help but see. The car was a real beauty, and he slid a hand over the glossy paint of a fin as he quietly apologized for hurting her. Now that any means of escape was disabled, he hugged the outer wall and slid along it to the back window where he'd seen the cat.

The old house didn't have air-conditioning, and he was counting on some open windows. Pleased his hunch paid off, he stayed to the side of the screen and listened.

"Fix me some dinner, then we're taking off before the cops start knocking on doors."

Fortunada's voice was close, and Jake flattened against the wall. The cat he'd seen earlier jumped back onto the sill, pressed its face against the screen and meowed. *Go away, cat.*

"Hope you're not in a hurry. Wednesday's fried chicken night," an older-sounding woman said. "Come on, Mr. Kitty. I'll fry you up some livers."

Mr. Kitty was gone in a flash and Jake let out the breath he'd been holding. The woman's tone had been friendly and not at all fearful. Could she be Fortunada's mother or sister, a friend maybe?

"Why don't you just take the car and go? You don't need me anymore, and I won't let you hurt Mrs. Watkins."

Maria's voice! He chanced leaning his head enough to see inside. She had her back to him, and a rage lit fire to his blood at the way Fortunada was eyeing her breasts. The bastard wasn't long for this earth.

"Whatcha gonna trade me for leaving her here?"

A lead ball fell down Maria's throat to her stomach, one she fought to keep from throwing right back up. She recognized that look in Fortunada's eyes, had seen it too many times on the faces of the men her mother brought home when she hadn't hid fast enough and they caught sight of her.

Taking a step back, she shook her head. "Don't even think it. Just take Mrs. Watkins's car and go." A predatory smile curved his lips, and she realized she'd made a mistake by showing fear. It excited him, and if she was to survive this, she had to hide her escalating terror.

"I'd rather do this," he said, grabbing a breast with the speed of a striking viper and squeezing it hard.

Tears burned her eyes from the pain. Maria brought her knee up, but he anticipated it and twisted to her side. The cold barrel of his revolver pressed against her temple, and she went still.

"The old lady said dinner's gonna take a while. I think we'll spend the time testing her bed. Start walking."

"Please, we can't. You're my father," she blurted, desperate to stop him. Some stupid, naive part of her mind had thought he'd lower the gun in surprise. All she got was a laugh.

"Nice try." He pushed her toward the hallway.

"No, it's . . . it's true. That's why I came to your house that day."

When the gun flew past her, landing on the floor at the end of the hall, she thought she'd shocked him so much that he'd had some kind of knee-jerk reaction. Then his weight slid down her back and she staggered forward, falling on her knees.

The revolver was just out of reach, but if she could get to it before him . . . A grunt and the sound of a fist hitting flesh stopped her frantic crawl toward the weapon. She craned her neck and looked behind her.

Jake! Oh, God, yes. Jake was here. How that was possible, she didn't know and didn't care. Somehow, he'd found her and that was all that mattered. Turning her attention back to the gun, she grabbed it and pushed her back against the wall. Sitting on the floor with the revolver, she watched the two men fight.

Jake would win—she had no doubt—she was prepared to shoot Fortunada if necessary. Fortunada wasn't going down easy though. He fought back with the cunning of a desperate man. The hallway didn't give them much room to brawl, but neither seemed to care as they bounced from one wall to the other.

195

The strangest sight of all, though, was Mrs. Watkins standing several feet behind them, Mr. Kitty draped over one arm and a frying plan held high in the other. The woman's eyes were positively gleaming, and Maria got the impression that this was the most excitement Mrs. Watkins had had in a long time.

"I'm going to kill you for touching her," Jake growled and brought his fist down. Blood spurted out of Fortunada's nose. "And I'm going to do it real slow."

It was then she understood Jake was playing with him, wanting to drag out hurting Fortunada.

"Naw if I ills you irst," Fortunada lisped through a split lip and broken front tooth.

Would Jake really go so far as to kill him? Although she prayed he wasn't, the man might be her father. The wrestling match began again and Maria leaned her head back, closing her eyes.

Why had she started on this quest? She didn't need a father in her life. It was that stupid stud book that had started her longing to have a parent who loved her. Before then, the chance of narrowing down the possibilities was so slim that she hadn't even thought to try. And she'd been fine with that.

She had her brother, Dani and the kids, Mrs. Jankowski. They all loved her, so why hadn't that been enough? Because there'd once been a little girl so lacking in something that even her mother couldn't stand the sight of her. No matter how good she'd tried to be, no matter that she'd brushed Lovey Dovey's hair every night, careful not to pull on it too hard, no matter that she'd catered to her mother's every whim, it had never been enough.

There'd been no kind words for her, no hugs or smiles. When she'd found three names that fit—right year, right nationality—the old longing she'd thought was banished forever returned and she'd wondered: what if?

Tears leaked out of the corners of her eyes, and she buried her head against her knees. Blocking out the sounds of grunts and bodies banging against the wall, she let go of the dream once and for all. She didn't want a father, didn't need one.

If Fortunada was him, she didn't care and didn't want to know. She would appreciate the family she had and if that included Jake, she would rejoice and love him forever. If not, she would still have a full and productive life. She'd survived without her mother's love and she could survive without Jake's. Well, that would hurt. A lot. But it wouldn't kill her, not like it appeared finding a father might.

Suddenly, a helicopter sounded as if it was going to land right in the middle of the living room. Had the cops finally found them? She lifted her head and peered at the ceiling. The two men still going at it didn't seem to notice. Why hadn't Jake put Fortunada's lights out already? He could do it if he wanted, but it appeared he was enjoying beating the crap out of the man too much. Fortunada was still trying to fight back, but just barely. A few more minutes and Jake would be trying to knock the brains out of an unconscious man. It was time to put a stop to this.

She pushed up against the wall, the revolver in her hand hanging down at her side. "Jake, enough." He didn't seem to hear her. Maybe she should tell Mrs. Watkins to bang him over the head with the frying pan.

Before she could figure out how to get through to him, four men dressed in all black slithered up behind Mrs. Watkins. Maria looked into the eyes of her brother, visible through the eyeholes of his black face mask. His gaze raked over her, and she knew he was determining for himself that she wasn't hurt. No, she wasn't, she messaged him back.

Logan nodded, then turned his attention to Jake and Fortunada. Both seemed to be unaware of the scary men watching them with envy in their eyes, every one of them obviously wishing they were in Jake's place.

What was it with men and their loving to punch the daylights out of someone? Maria's only concern now was the heart attack Mrs. Watkins was going to have if she looked behind her.

"Mrs. Watkins, my brother's here with his men. He won't hurt you, I promise."

Mrs. Watkins glanced to the left, then to the right, before turning her body around to see behind her. "I didn't hear you boys knock." She lowered the frying pan. "Are you here to save us?"

"Yes ma'am," Logan said and pulled off his face mask. He gave the woman a killer smile, then stepped past her and rapped the back of Jake's head with his knuckles. "Enough, Tiger. I know you want to send him to hell. So do I, but that would require too many explanations of who we are."

Maria watched as Jake came back to himself and glanced around. Then his gaze settled on her, and the look in his eyes, God, the look in his eyes took the ability to stand right out of her. She sank to the floor in front of him.

"You came for me," she said.

"Did you think I wouldn't?"

He seemed so disappointed and she didn't know how to tell him she'd believed he was on his way to Egypt, putting his job first. She didn't know how to tell him she loved him.

CHAPTER TWENTY

————— ❧ —————

Jake half listened to the older woman tell Kincaid how Mr. Buchanan had done some kind of "chop, chop" on Fortunada's neck and sent the gun flying. He half heard her tell the boss how she'd put three of her sleeping pills in the iced tea she'd planned to give the bastard. All he cared about was the woman kneeling in front of him, surprised that he'd come for her.

That really pissed him off. How could she not know he'd come for her? The caveman scenario had been a fantasy, or so he'd thought until, gone some kind of stupid, he picked her up and tossed her over his shoulder.

"Where the hell you going?" Kincaid called after him. "You're supposed to be on your way to Egypt."

"I will be. Tomorrow," he tossed back. And he would be after he and Maria got a few things straight between them. If it took all night, all the better.

"Damn men in love," he heard Kincaid mutter. *Damn straight*, Jake thought as he kept going.

"Put me down," Maria said when he was halfway to her car.

That she'd kept quiet that long was actually amazing. "No." Fuck no. "You really need to shut up," he said and trudged on. If she didn't heed his advice, he might very well lay her down in the middle of the road and screw her until her eyes crossed and she admitted she loved him.

Wisely, she didn't say another word. Seeing that bastard put his hand on her breast had sent him into a murderous rage. By the time he reached her car, he'd managed to walk off some of the fury threatening to put him over the edge and was able to refrain from claiming her in the cramped backseat of her car parked at the abandoned house. Barely.

In silence, he drove on the I-10 to the next exit where the road sign had three pictures of motels on it. The first one he came to was a Ramada, and if it wasn't his first choice of where he'd like to take her, he didn't care about that either.

"Don't move," he said as he stepped out. After securing a room, he followed the clerk's directions to the back and pulled up in front of room 116.

During the fifteen minutes it took for them to get to the motel, she'd not taken her eyes off him. He knew that, even though he'd not once looked at her. He was afraid to. If he did, he would yell at her for scaring twenty fucking years off his life.

She'd been through an ordeal he'd wish on no one, and it wouldn't be very nice to give her hell about it. But, Jesus, he wanted to. He wanted her to know he would've willingly killed a man tonight for simply touching her. Never mind the bastard had intended much more than that. Thinking about it, he was sorry he hadn't killed Fortunada.

"Jake?"

Finally looking at her, he took in the uncertainty in her eyes. "Tomorrow, I have to get on a plane and fly seven thousand miles away from you. I won't be here to keep you safe, and that just about makes me crazy. But tonight, I'm here and you're mine."

Not giving her time to answer, he got out and went to the door, sliding the key card into the slot. He turned and stared through the windshield until she got the message that this room was where she'd spend the next eleven or so hours.

When she reached him, she lifted on her toes and pressed her lips against his, and Jesus and all his angels, he almost took her against the open door of a Ramada Inn with traffic whizzing by on the road two hundred feet away.

Between the walk to the car and the drive to the motel, enough time had elapsed for some semblance of reason to return. There had been no way for her to know his flight had been delayed, that he'd still been in Pensacola when Nolan's call came. How could she know he'd defy orders no matter the consequences and not stop until he found her?

He'd given her no indication by word or deed that she meant more to him than a bit of fun for a few weeks. The anger at her for not knowing he'd come for her had been entirely misplaced, and he owed her an apology for going caveman on her. And he would apologize, as soon as he had her naked and under him.

What was going through that mind of hers as she stood silent and still, her arms at her sides and her gaze fixed on him? "You're being scary quiet, Chiquita."

"I'm unsure if I'm supposed to talk. Last time you were mad at me, you ordered me not to. Are you going to invoke that rule again?"

"Sweetheart, you can talk my ears off if you want." If she wanted to blabber all night about Hollywood gossip and fashions, he didn't care. All that mattered was he'd found her and she was safe. He trailed his knuckles down her cheek. "For the record, I'm not mad at you, but if my ordering you about turns you on, I'll be happy to oblige."

In response, she threw herself at him and wrapped her legs around his waist. "I was so scared, Jake, and then there you were. I don't know how you did it, but the minute I saw you, I knew I was safe."

With his arms wound tightly around her back, he pressed his face to her neck and inhaled her scent, let the touch of her body against his soothe the lingering emotions of the last few hours. Never—not even in the most intense of battles—had he been so afraid.

"It's over now, baby. Your brother will deliver that bastard to the cops," he said as he lowered her to the bed, coming down on top of her, a grenade pressed between their stomachs.

"Shit." He unclipped the pouch and carefully set it on the nightstand. The guns tucked into his waistband were next, followed by the knife and flashlight.

Her eyes grew wider as the pile grew. "Jeez, you're a walking weapons store."

"By failing to prepare, you are preparing to fail. Benjamin Franklin." How he even remembered the famous quote was a damn miracle when the woman he loved wiggled her body so that the V between her legs aligned perfectly with his cock.

"Does that mean you're prepared for me?"

"You keep moving around like that and I'll fuck you all the way back to the past so you can hear ole Ben say the words in person."

Passion glittered in her eyes alongside a dare. "You could try."

So he would. He kissed her then, hard and needy, and she gave back as good as she got. Her mouth was wet, hot, and spicy sweet, and he couldn't get enough. Would never get enough.

There were other parts of her he needed to taste, and he kissed a path to her neck, then to her earlobe where he traced his tongue around the swirl of her ear. She moaned and slipped her hands under his shirt, scraping her fingernails up his spine.

He'd thought his dick couldn't get any harder. He was wrong. "Clothes. Off."

In a flurry of arms and legs, they shed shirts, jeans, his briefs, and her bra. When he caught sight of her panties, he brushed her hand aside, sat back on his knees, and stared at them.

A furry cat covered the front with the caption, "Pet me." He lifted his gaze to hers. "You better not wear these for anyone but me, Chiquita."

"I thought of you when I saw them. You like?"

"Oh, yeah." And he liked that she thought of him when buying sexy panties, liked the way her eyes went all soft and warm. When she started to push them down her hips, he stopped her. "Kitty needs a pet."

Starting at the head of the cat, just above the line of her feminine curls, he stroked his fingers over the picture. The cat's tummy was situated right at Maria's clit, and he stopped there and circled his thumb over the little peaking nub. Only a few seconds passed before she fisted the sheets in her hands and brought her knees up, feet flat on the mattress.

"You like?" he said, echoing her last words. Her crotch was soaked, telling him she most definitely liked.

She exhaled a rush of breath. "Stupid question."

"You saying I'm stupid, Chiquita?" He slipped a finger under the material and traced her damp outer folds, down one side and up the other. While he played with her, sliding his finger in and out of her sheath, he took his cock in his other hand and stroked from the base to the head and back.

"Did I say something? I don't remember."

The male ego embedded in him from birth sent a satisfied grin to his mouth. "You said I was the hottest man you've ever laid eyes on. Then you said you'd never let another man touch you like this."

He braced one hand on the bed near her waist and rubbed the head of his cock through her slick, wet heat.

"I said all that?"

"You did."

"Then it must be true." Her eyes dilated, going from dark brown to black as she watched him.

So much passion in her and she still had no clue. She was his and he'd kill any man who dared to say otherwise. All he had to do was make sure he didn't screw everything up and lose her. The thought of her with someone else? No way he'd allow that to happen.

"Do you want to come?"

Those eyes shimmering with heat lifted to his. "Yes, please."

"So polite," he said with a chuckle. The hell if she didn't make him want to smile, to grin, chuckle, and laugh, but most of all he wanted to fuck all that pretty politeness right out of her. He wanted her barely able to talk . . . maybe just enough to beg.

"Time for kitty to go," he said as he stripped off the panties.

Maria lifted her hips so Jake could pull her underwear down her legs. Although he'd softened somewhat in the last few minutes, there was something hard and angry in him. Until he'd chuckled just then, his face had been a mask of granite, a little scary and a lot sexy. His cheeks were shadowed with a beard trying to grow back, and it added to his dangerous appearance.

He was so freaking hot in so many ways. His body was a furnace, heat radiating off him in waves, but what a fine body it was. The fury in him, the flames she could almost see licking his skin, the male possessiveness in his eyes, all of it was a massive turn-on. She wanted him feral, she wanted to tame him, she wanted to keep him whichever way he decided to be.

"What?" she said when he just kept staring at her.

"He touched you and I wanted to kill him for you."

An image formed in her mind, and she laughed. She didn't mean to, but it was out before she could stop it.

"That's funny?"

"Yes, I mean, no. It really isn't. It's just when you said that, I pictured my cat proudly dropping a dead mouse at my feet. It's his way of showing he loves me."

His eyes shuttered. Damn, she shouldn't have said that last part. If Jake came to love her, she wanted him to say it without her prodding him or feeling like she'd forced him into admitting to something he didn't really feel.

Not responding, he put his hands on her thighs and spread her legs apart. When his mouth came down on her and he began to explore her with his tongue, she groaned and spread her fingers through his hair. The disappointment that he'd not given any hint as to his feelings for her was momentarily forgotten as he sucked her to an orgasm that had her gasping for air and chanting his name.

When the last of her shudders faded, he crawled up her body, licking her the entire way with pauses at her belly button and her breasts. She was fairly certain she'd died, and if this was heaven, she had no problem with staying.

"Maria."

He'd said her name many times but never like that, as if it were the most precious sound in the world to him. Before she could think how to answer—or even decide if an answer was required—he kissed her and this too was different, almost as if he were trying to show her something he couldn't say. It wasn't the words she wanted to hear, but she would take it.

Not that she'd said them to him either, but she wanted to wait until he returned because . . . because why? If there'd been a reason, it escaped her now. He was leaving on a dangerous mission and if something happened to him, he'd never know.

She cupped his jaws, wonderfully bristly, and let him see the truth in her eyes. "I love you."

Not a word passed his lips, but he held her gaze with a fierce intenseness as he lowered his mouth to hers and kissed her with a possessiveness that said he was claiming her. She fought off the hurt that he'd not said it back.

If your own mother couldn't love you, Maria, why would you think he would? Don't go there, not now. She squeezed her eyes shut and banished the dark thoughts. Or tried to, but they hovered on the edge of her mind, mocking her.

If nothing else, Jake hadn't grabbed his jeans and run out of the room. That was a good sign, right? Still kissing her, his hands began to move over her, sliding over her skin, leaving lines of goose bumps in their wake.

Needing to touch him, too, she trailed her fingers down his sides, over the ridges of his ribs, to his trim waist, then to his narrow hips. His taut butt flexed under her palms and she grasped it, tried to pull him into her.

"Condom."

"You have one?" She didn't want a condom. She wanted to marry him, sleep with him every night, and have his babies, ones who would never doubt their mother loved them.

He grunted as he leaned over the side of the bed and pulled his wallet out of his jeans. Did he always have one on him, just in case? She wanted to beat on his chest in a mad rage at the mere thought of him with another woman.

When he tore off the end of the foil, he glanced at her, then frowned. "What's wrong?"

"Nothing." God, why did her every thought have to show on her face?

His eyes flicked to the condom and then back to her. "You're wondering what every woman wonders at the sight of a condom in her man's wallet. Am I wrong?"

Her man. She liked the sound of that, especially since he'd given himself the label. Her silence apparently verified his guess because after he rolled the condom on, he took both her hands in his.

"Listen to me, Maria. For as long as we're together, I'll never cheat on you. That's my promise to you. I can't see into the future, but I hope it's for a long, long time."

It wasn't a marriage proposal, or even an "I might be falling in love with you," but she believed him. And maybe, just maybe, it was the beginnings of love on his part.

"Fuck me, Jake."

A slow-forming, wicked smile curved his lips. "I love it when my woman talks dirty."

CHAPTER TWENTY-ONE

My woman. Her man.

Some kind of milestone had just passed between them and although Jake knew she wanted to hear words of love, he just couldn't say them. That he felt them, he'd accepted. But he'd created this scenario in his mind of a special night where he romanced her and led up to telling her. This was a first for him and he didn't want to mess it up. There would be dinner at the most expensive restaurant in Pensacola—where that was, he didn't know but he'd find out—and there would be flowers, maybe a walk on the beach in the moonlight. An engagement ring? That one, he hadn't decided yet.

The other thing stopping him from promising her anything was his upcoming mission. He just had a bad feeling about it, one he couldn't shake. If something happened to him, if he was killed or, worse, maimed, he wouldn't have her obligated to him. She was too beautiful, too special to be reduced to a life of playing nursemaid.

So he would wait.

He lowered himself over her, taking his weight on his elbows. "Hang on for the ride of your life, Chiquita," he whispered next to her ear. Her legs immediately wrapped around his hips, and her arms circled his neck in a death grip.

With his body, Jake tried to show her that he loved her.

Weren't women supposed to like talking after sex? Jake smiled as he memorized how sweet Maria looked asleep, tucked up under his arm. Her hand rested over his heart as if even in sleep she needed to know it still beat. Well, it did. For her.

He dozed off, his mind already on the coming days and wanting them over so he could come back and tell her how much he loved her. At three, he slid down the bed and woke her with his tongue. He didn't have another condom so he couldn't bury himself in her slick heat like he wanted. But he pleasured her until she screamed his name. It was the sound he would take with him.

When they got married and had kids, he'd need to build a soundproof bedroom. If they got married.

When her turn came—or was it his?—she slid down his body and teased him with her tongue before sucking him into her mouth. He came with a force that had him reeling, and the words he'd been holding back almost escaped.

Just in time, he stopped them.

Exhausted and sated, he slept a few more hours while holding her in his arms. At six, he eased out of bed and groped around in the dark until he found his jeans. Slipping them on, he quietly walked outside and pulled his cell out of his front pocket, punching in Logan's number.

"I'll have her at the safe house in two hours. I assume Saint's there, waiting." Even though Fortunada was once again in jail, he knew Kincaid wouldn't allow her to be without a guard again until she was back home in Pensacola. Jake was damn glad she'd be in good hands. It was the only reason he'd be able to walk onto a plane that would take him almost seven thousand miles away from her.

A long pause followed before Kincaid answered. "Yes. When you get back, we need to talk."

The boss wanted to know his intentions, but that was between him and Maria. "No, I don't think we do." He clicked off and went back inside to wake her.

———— ❧ ————

Jake studied the weapons spread out on the rickety table, every instinct screaming at him to dump all this shit in the trash and return home with his team. Har-Shaf had managed to get everything on their list, all right. Problem was, it was all just that—shit. There wasn't a piece on the table in decent shape, not a thing had been taken care of the way weapons should be. He picked up one of the AK-47s and slid a finger over the rusted trigger. The thing was just as likely to explode and kill one of them as it was a bad guy.

"Let's see what we can salvage here," he said. "Where is Har-Shaf, anyway?"

The condition of the weapons was worrisome. Har-Shaf had never let them down before. Of course, with the way things were in Egypt these days, it might have been too dangerous for Har-Shaf to put his hands on the best toys.

"Haven't seen him since he dropped us here and said he'd go get some food. That was yesterday morning," Stewart said as he and Bayne pulled up stools and went to work.

Har-Shaf had spooked, and the blame for that belonged to him. If he'd stepped off that plane when he was supposed to, Har-Shaf would now be sitting in this room with them. Hiding his unease, he settled down next to Bayne, picked up a handgun, and began to clean it. Bayne's nerves were showing and that concerned him.

Jake glanced at the empty kitchen shelves. "So there's nothing to eat in the house?"

"Nope, not even running water. We didn't want to get into our MREs, so I slipped out last night after dark and managed to find a little store," Stewart said. "Got us some food for dinner and breakfast this morning, but didn't want to load up with too much and draw attention."

Jake didn't insult Stewart by asking if he'd made sure he wasn't followed back to the house. The house wasn't safe, though, not with Har-Shaf unaccounted for.

"I'm thinking it'd be a good idea to move," Jake said.

Stewart nodded. Bayne stayed silent, keeping his eyes on the gun he was cleaning. Bad vibes. Oh, yeah, Jake was having them. He stood and squeezed Tennessee's shoulder. "I'm gonna call the boss, get us a new safe house. You got any special request? You know, maybe a house where there's a harem of belly dancers waiting for us?"

The chuckle Tennessee gave was forced, and Jake exchanged a glance with Stewart over Bayne's head. It was too late in coming, but they both realized their teammate had no business being on this mission. Jake grabbed the bag with the satellite phone and went into one of the bedrooms, closing the door behind him.

When the boss answered, Jake got right to the point. "Har-Shaf's MIA. You hear anything from him?"

"We sent him a message telling him when to pick you up at the airport. No response. You're telling me he wasn't there?"

"He didn't meet me. Had to find my own way to the house. Our man's not been seen since he dropped Ste . . . Elaine and Tennessee off at the safe house and said he was going for food. We need a new hidey-hole." He'd almost broken the cardinal rule by saying Stewart's name over a phone, even an encrypted one.

There was a long pause and then, "I'm on it."

There was much unsaid in that pause and Jake knew it. The boss wouldn't have missed his near slip. Did Kincaid blame the disappearance of Har-Shaf on him for not getting on that plane when he was supposed to?

"We might have one other problem," Jake said.

"What's that?"

"Tennessee's on the verge of shutting down."

"Not what I want to hear. We put him through the psych tests and he aced them."

Jake walked to the window, lifted a dusty curtain, and peered out. "Yeah, well, I guess it's one thing sitting in a room answering questions and something entirely different when faced with the real thing. We need to revisit our policy on a situation like Tennessee's, but that's a discussion for another time."

"You want to scratch the mission? It's your call."

It was tempting. But they were in Egypt, and their plan was a good one. "No, at least not yet. I'll keep an eye on our boy. The toys we have to play with aren't what we'd hoped for, but we'll make do. Call when you got a place for us to go."

Disconnecting, Jake set the phone on a nearby table and studied the traffic going by on the street and looking for anyone standing around who seemed out of place. It was almost impossible to know if someone didn't belong. Unemployment was high in Egypt these days, and too many men spent their time loitering on the streets, alone and in groups. He dropped the curtain, picked up the phone, and rejoined his team.

By the time they finished inspecting and cleaning the firearms, Jake figured a little more than half were usable, better than he'd expected. Most of the weapons were Russian, but the three helmets were American military and he tried not to wonder who they'd once belonged to. While they worked, he and Stewart attempted to raise Bayne's spirits with jokes, then the talk turned to bragging about the women they'd dated.

"Best tits in the world, hands down, Brenda Johnson," Stewart said, waggling his fingers as if reaching for said breasts.

Bayne nodded in agreement. "Hell, yeah. Best ass, Cheryl Rollins."

Uncomfortable with the conversation, Jake pointed one of the guns at the far wall and sighted down the barrel, tuning them out. There'd been a time when he'd enjoyed this kind of talk with his teammates, but now it seemed kind of stupid . . . even disrespectful to the women in question.

More so, it seemed wrong to think of any woman but Maria, and he certainly wasn't going to share intimate details of her with his men.

When he'd settled onto his seat on the plane, he'd taken out the picture Maria had given him, memorized it, and then tucked it away in his wallet—storing her away in the back of his mind. While waiting to board, he'd almost called her one last time but forced himself not to. It was critical that he keep his attention on the operation and not allow thoughts of her to distract him. Listening to Bayne describe his date with a woman named Erica, it hit Jake hard how much he missed Maria.

Disquiet crept into his mind. This operation seemed to be falling apart by the minute, and his brain wasn't one hundred percent focused on the mission. There had never been a woman before now he'd been anxious to return home to. That should please him. Instead it seemed ominous—something that would be denied him because he wanted it too much.

Maria chewed on her thumbnail and fidgeted in her chair. She'd once thought the hardest thing she would ever do was pass her law exams, but she'd been wrong. As she sat in the situation room at K2 with her brother and K2 staff, waiting to hear Jake's voice come through the speakers topped the list. She slid a quick glance at the man sitting next to Logan. Although he hadn't been introduced, he had CIA written all over him. He briefly met her gaze, but didn't give even the hint of a smile. Logan would've briefed the guy on who she was, but he'd given no sign of wanting her to acknowledge him, so she tried to ignore him.

Jake had been gone for three days, and today was The Day. Any minute, the feed from the team would stream over the speakers as they prepared to sneak into the house and rescue Chad Sinclair. A part of her wanted to leave, or at least cover her ears. If she went back to her office, Logan would come tell her when it was over. He would tell her that Jake was safe.

Who was she kidding? There was no way she could leave. The situation room was the closest to Jake she could get. She would will him to stay safe. Logan had ordered her not to say a word, that if she even muttered something under her breath he would physically pick her up and deposit her outside the conference room door, locking it behind him.

Saint winked at her, a silent reassurance that all would be well. She smiled back and felt her lips trembling. Jake would be okay. He would. This kind of operation was a piece of cake for him.

Yet, so many things had already gone wrong. The weapons the team got belonged at the city dump, they'd lost their in-country contact, and had been forced to move to a different safe house. Maybe it was true that bad luck came in threes and now the operation would get back on track. Maria said a little prayer it was so.

"You in place, Elaine?"

It was starting. Maria's heart went into overdrive at the sound of Jake's voice coming through the speakers.

"Eyes on the back door," Stewart said. "All's quiet back here. No Tangos in sight. Headed your way now."

"Good. Tennessee, ready to rock and roll?"

God, she loved how Jake's voice sounded so sure and confident.

The silence stretched as everyone in the room waited for Rick Bayne to answer Jake. They were supposed to have a video feed but for some reason, it wasn't coming through. She had mixed feelings about that, half wanting to see Jake, half fearing what she might see if things went wrong.

Finally. "Ah . . . yes, sir. I'm right behind you, Buchanan . . . Tiger."

They weren't supposed to use real names—a slipup Bayne should never have made—and Logan's lips thinned. Was he concerned about Bayne? Rick was supposed to have Jake's back. Maria tried to catch her brother's eye, but he wouldn't look at her, which worried her all the more. Logan knew something she didn't, something he didn't like.

Her pulse pounding a kazillion beats a minute, she moved to the edge of her chair. It was three in the morning in Egypt, and hopefully all the bad guys guarding Sinclair were asleep. As planned, Jake and his team were going for the kid two days earlier than he expected.

"Show time," Jake said.

Maria closed her eyes and imagined him creeping up to the front window. They would go in through the lower floor's window instead of trying to get through a locked door. Once inside, Jake, with Rick and Brad covering his back, would find Chad Sinclair and get him out of the house without anyone ever knowing they were there. That was the plan anyway, and she crossed the fingers on both hands.

The radio went silent, the only sound in the room the tick, tick, tick of the clock on the wall. She glanced at it and watched the second hand bump its way past the numbers—a minute, two, and on to three. Unable to take her eyes from it, by the time it hit five minutes, her stomach churned and she feared she might throw up.

"We're in."

Jake's whispered voice startled her so badly she squeaked, getting a glare from Logan. Maybe she wasn't cut out for all this cloak-and-dagger stuff and should wait outside. Although, in the past, she'd sat in and watched or listened to live operations, and it had never unnerved her like this.

God, she was so worried about Jake and wanted this to be over and done with. Quiet descended again, but then she realized this time there was the sound of heavy breathing. Logan tilted his head as if listening closely and frowned, which didn't help Maria's nerves.

Because they had a diagram of the house, she was able to close her eyes and imagine Jake and the guys searching the ground floor, night-vision goggles turning the scene a watery green. All was still quiet, so that meant there were no bad guys waiting to ambush them. Now, they would be creeping up the stairs, cautiously placing their feet to avoid making creaking noises.

Still, the only sound was one of the men's heavy breathing. She guessed it was Rick Bayne. The thought that one of them might be on the edge sent her worry up another notch.

The speakers crackled to life. "Tennessee, stay here and watch our backs."

Jake's whisper was so soft she had to strain to hear him. Maria thought they were at the top of the stairs and wondered if he was positioning Rick there to keep him from bungling the room search. Suddenly, the video sputtered on, and everyone in the conference room focused on the screen. It was too dark to see much, but Maria was still comforted that they were getting the feed. As long as that camera on Jake's helmet stayed upright, he was safe.

A door was opened—she assumed by Jake—and because of the moonlight coming in a window, they could see that there were three beds occupied by sleeping men. Jake eased the door closed.

The screen went blank. Damn, they lost the feed. Maria went back to watching the clock, the ominous ticking hand sounding like something out of a Stephen King novel. Three long minutes passed before she heard Jake's whispered voice again.

"We're here to take you home. Don't talk, okay?"

She imagined Jake's hand over Chad Sinclair's mouth followed by the kid's nod. The man Maria took to be CIA let out a puff of air. Good to know she hadn't been the only one about to come out of her skin. Although her brother appeared to be sleeping, she wasn't fooled and knew just where to look to know how tense he was. A quick glance at his index finger tapping hard against his knee said it all.

The rustling of covers and the faint sound of bare feet hitting the floor sounded in the room. Realizing she was holding her breath, she exhaled. They had the kid and it should take them only a few minutes to get out of the house. As soon as Logan's finger stilled, she'd rest easy.

"Mother fucking bastards!"

Oh, God, that sounded like Rick Bayne. The expletive was followed by the sounds of chaos as a voice yelled in a foreign language. Gunfire erupted, and Jake's voice could be heard calmly issuing orders to his team. Her eyes glued to the clock, for three minutes—what felt like hours—a battle raged. Bodies could be heard hitting the floor and slowly the gunfire tapered off.

They were going to be okay. They were going to be okay. Please let them be okay.

And then she heard Jake's voice. "Tennessee's down! Get the kid out of here, Elaine."

Silence, heavy and ominous, descended. Maria dragged in a ragged breath. *Say something, Jake. Please say something so I know you're okay.* A gun shot exploded in the silence and, startled, Maria reared up from her chair.

"Easy," Logan said and grabbed her hand, pulling her back down. He didn't let go of her, and she held on to him for dear life.

Another shot sounded, followed by an *oomph*, from Jake. "I'm hit," he said.

Oh, God. Maria swallowed bile and closed her eyes, praying harder than she ever had in her life.

CHAPTER TWENTY-TWO

———— ❦ ————

They'd gotten the kid home safe along with a handful of thumb drives the CIA man had just about drooled over. Somehow, they'd managed to get Rick Bayne's body out of Egypt and home without causing an international incident. Maria figured the new Egyptian government probably wouldn't have appreciated a clandestine operation by Americans carried out under their noses.

Today was Rick's funeral and the first time she would see Jake since he'd returned three days ago. If he bothered to show up.

Logan hadn't told her when the team was landing, and had taken Jamie with him to the airport to meet the midnight flight. They'd apparently gone back to K2 for a debriefing. All her brother would tell her was that Jake had been shot in his leg—a clean shot in and back out—and even so, he had carried Rick's body out of the house. After giving his report, Jake had requested and been granted a leave of absence.

He'd not once tried to contact her.

"Give him time, Maria," Logan had advised when Jake ignored her calls and text messages.

"I don't understand what his problem is. Good God, he's a hero."

"Sometimes being a hero comes with a price. He lost a man on his watch and, believe me, he blames himself. The last thing he considers himself is a hero."

She supposed Logan understood better than most, as Dani's first husband had been killed on a mission to rescue a captured Air Force pilot. It had taken her brother years to come to terms with Evan's death. Still, Jake didn't have to be alone. She could help him if he'd only let her.

What if he never got over it?

The day before, she'd given up on waiting for her phone to ring and had gone to his condo. When he didn't answer her knock, she'd turned to leave when a young woman came out of the condo next door and glanced over.

"He's not there. Said he'd be away for a while."

"Did he say where he was going?" The girl was very pretty, and Maria couldn't help wondering if Jake had ever slept with her.

"Just said something about a vacation."

He went on a freaking vacation? "Did he say when he'd be back?"

Earlobe-length, sleek blonde hair swirled around the girl's head when she shook it. "Nope. I'm Sugar Darling, by the way. Just moved in a few weeks ago. Jake's the only neighbor I've met so far. He's a real cutie."

Maria raised a brow.

Sugar rolled her eyes. "Yeah, I know what you're thinking, and yes, that's my real name. I love my daddy, but I'll never forgive him for laying that one on me. He thought since our last name was Darling, Sugar would be just the cutest thing evah to name me."

Her grin was so full of mischief, Maria couldn't help but like the girl. Even if she did think Jake was a cutie. "Okay, thanks." She started to walk away, then turned. "Nice to meet you, Sugar, and your daddy's right. That is the cutest name *evah*. You from South Carolina by any chance? Charleston, maybe?"

Sugar blinked big blue eyes. "Wow, you're amazing. What gave me away?"

"Just a lucky guess. At least you weren't loaded down with two names." Maria'd had a roommate in college from Charleston, and Sugar sounded just like Emma Grace. "Count your blessings he didn't name you Sugar Sweet."

A throaty laugh sounded from the girl. "Oh, Lordie, don'tcha dare suggest that to my daddy."

Maria took two steps before adding, "And by the way, my name's Maria, and Jake belongs to me so don't get any ideas where he's concerned."

"Dang, all the cute ones seem to belong to someone else."

Maria turned and with her back to Sugar, she grinned. "At least, this one does," she murmured. All she had to do was find him.

If he wasn't at the funeral, she'd make Logan tell her where he was. She didn't doubt her brother knew, and she'd make his life miserable until he gave up Jake's location. Deep in her bones, she knew Jake needed her and one way or another, she'd run him to the ground. The poor man had no clue how determined she was.

———— ❧ ————

Maria got to the chapel early and positioned herself in a far back corner. The glossy black coffin at the front drew her eyes. It was an open viewing and she dreaded the moment when she'd have to walk to the front and see Rick. He'd been the newest guy at K2, so she didn't know him as well as the others, but she'd liked him.

Her heart hurt for the life lost and for Jake—the man who blamed himself for getting Rick killed. She blinked against the burning in her eyes and opened the small pamphlet that gave a brief biography of Rick, along with his picture.

There was so much about Rick missing from the pamplet, stuff that only a few people knew: that he'd given his life on foreign soil to rescue a misguided boy; that he'd put food out in the mornings for two feral cats living in the alley behind K2; and that he'd spent his off-hours volunteering at a boys' club. Rick once asked her to go in and talk about college to a group of his brightest kids.

According to his biography, he had no brothers or sisters, and only his father still lived. She glanced to the front to see an older man—his head bowed—on the first pew next to Logan and Dani. She hoped he knew his son was a true hero in more ways than just the job he'd died for.

Her breath caught in her throat when Jake entered, so handsome and somber in a black suit. Her eyes riveted on him, she watched as he walked resolutely down the aisle, a slight limp the only indication he'd been shot in the leg. He stopped next to Rick's father and leaned close, saying something in his ear. The man nodded and then hugged Jake.

When the man embraced him, Jake squeezed his eyes shut and when he opened them, he looked straight at her. Frozen in place by his intense focus on her, she wanted to cry upon seeing the despair in his eyes. She smiled and fought against the trembling of her mouth. He broke the contact between them and slipped into the pew behind her brother and Mr. Bayne.

The air swished out of her lungs. She wanted to go to him, had planned to, but now she wasn't sure if she should. There'd been no warmth for her in his eyes, no welcoming invitation. Logan had said to give him time, but what if he couldn't get past Rick's death and never came back? Not wanting to do the wrong thing, indecision gripped her.

"You should go to him."

Maria leaned her head against Jamie's shoulder. "You just get here? Have you talked to him?"

"Yes, just got here. And no, I haven't talked to him since the debriefing. He won't take my calls."

"Yeah, mine either. He's only talking to Logan, and my stupid brother won't tell me anything. He just keeps saying to give Jake time. Do you really think I should go sit with him?"

"I do. He wants you with him even if he's trying to convince himself he doesn't deserve you."

She peered up at Saint. "You think that's what he's doing?"

"I know it. Go on."

Jamie put his hand on her back and gave her a little push. Maria tossed him a grateful smile over her shoulder and, with her heart banging against her chest, walked to the front of the chapel and slid into the pew next to Jake just as the minister approached the pulpit.

The man who held her heart and happiness in his hands stared straight ahead, his body stiff and unyielding. He might as well have hung a "Keep Off" sign around his neck. The salt from the tears welling up burned her eyes. She blinked hard and glanced at the casket. If she cried, at least everyone would think it was because of Rick, and it would be partly for that reason.

Her tears were also for the man sitting beside her. It was hard to understand, though. If she was hurting as badly as Jake was, the first person she'd turn to would be him. She'd want his comfort, his words of assurance that somehow things would get better and that he'd stand beside her in her time of need.

Yet, Logan had reacted the same way as Jake did—closing up and pushing her away—after Evan had been killed. So was it a man thing? Was their pride so great that if they weren't perfect in every little thing, they blamed themselves for whatever went wrong? Of course, Rick getting killed wasn't a little thing, and there had to be more to the story than she was privy to.

If Jake would only talk to her, tell her what happened, maybe she could find the right words to ease his pain. Even if she couldn't, just getting it off his chest should help him some. They'd been friends before they became lovers and wasn't one of the benefits of having a friend to be able to lean on them during difficult times? There was no doubt in her mind that if she was going through an emotional crisis, Jake would be there for her. Why wouldn't he let her be there for him?

If Jamie was right and Jake didn't think he deserved her after whatever had happened in Egypt, then that was just stupid. She made up her mind that if Jake wouldn't let her in, she'd make Logan so miserable he'd tell her what happened just to get rid of her.

"Please stand for the Lord's Prayer," the preacher said.

"Our Father, who art in heaven."

As Maria listened to those around her join in with the minister's soothing voice, she slipped her hand into Jake's. Expecting him to shake her off, she was surprised—and relieved—when he gripped her hand hard enough to hurt. She didn't care because it meant he did need her, if only he'd admit it to himself.

All through the remainder of the service, he held on tightly to her hand. When the soloist began to sing "Go Rest High on That Mountain" by Vince Gill, a shudder traveled through Jake, one she felt against her shoulder and in their held hands. Maria tightened her grip, bowed her head, and uselessly fought her tears.

"Wait for me," she whispered when the last amen sounded and Jake stood to join Logan, Jamie, Brad Stewart, and two other K2 employees to bear the casket out.

He didn't.

Nor did he show up for the burial at the cemetery. Nor did he appear at Logan's where everyone gathered afterward.

"Where the hell is he, Logan? And if you say I just need to give him time, I swear, you'll never be able to make another baby with Dani."

Three days had passed since the funeral, and Logan had steadfastly refused to tell her anything. Although she'd never thought herself a violent person, she was ready to beat the crap out of him to make him talk.

"Ah, I'd appreciate it if you'd reconsider that particular threat," Dani said, amusement in her voice.

Maria stopped her pacing, giving her sister-in-law a sheepish shrug. "It was the best one I could think of. Make him tell me. I know you can wheedle it out of him if anyone can."

Dani blinked her eyes seductively at her husband. "Tell her, sweetie."

"He's pitched a tent at St. George Island State Park. There, are you happy?"

Deliriously. She glared at her brother. "You mean all I had to do was blink my eyes at you to get you to spill?"

Logan snorted. "No, it only works when Dani does it." He leaned his head back on the sofa and sighed. "Jake doesn't want you to find him, but I think it's time you did. Sit down and listen."

Maria pushed his feet off the ottoman and plopped her butt on it. "I've been wanting to listen to you . . . or Jake, anybody that would talk to me since everything went all wrong. What happened in Egypt?"

Her brother exchanged a look with Dani, who nodded. That was what Maria wanted more than anything in the world, even more than passing the bar, which, until Jake, had always been number one on her list. The kind of silent exchange she watched pass between Logan and his wife—the kind that didn't need words because they understood each other in a way no one else could. She wanted that with the man she loved and was prepared to fight for it with everything that defined her.

As she listened to Logan, her belief that she could overcome anything Jake was facing fell. Because of the decision he'd made to come to her rescue, Jake believed—maybe rightly so—that he was responsible for Rick's death.

Because he hadn't stepped off the plane with the rest of the team, their contact had spooked and it had all gone south from there. Worse, according to Logan, it had been Jake's decision not to call off the mission when he realized Rick wasn't ready to be back in the field. If it hadn't been for her, Jake would've been on the plane with his team. *Stupid, stupid Maria.* Why did she have to go searching for a father who'd never tried to find her?

The guilt of what Jake was going through because of her, the memory of Fortunada's hands groping her, and the too-peaceful face of Rick lying in his coffin while his father stood over him and wept, leveled a hard punch to her abdomen. Her stomach heaved and she ran out of the room, barely making it to the bathroom before losing her lunch into the porcelain bowl.

"It'll all be all right, sweetie. There now, let me help you."

Maria lifted from her bend over the toilet and leaned into Dani's warmth. "It's my fault. Oh, God, Dani, it's my fault Rick was killed. How can Jake ever forgive me or himself?"

Dani brushed Maria's hair from her face. "No, you can't think that way. Let me have Mrs. Jankowski bring us up some tea, and we'll have ourselves a little talk about men and why they get these notions in their heads. Okay?"

Maria nodded. "Okay. I'll wait for you on your deck." Logan and Dani had a deck outside their bedroom with a beautiful view of the Gulf, and Maria stretched out on a chaise. Shaded by the deck's roof, she closed her eyes and listened to the sound of the waves hitting the shore as a soft, warm breeze blew over her. She hadn't slept well the past few nights, and as she felt herself dozing off, she realized she should have come out here to sleep.

Yawning, she opened her eyes to find Dani in the opposite chaise, nursing baby Evan. On the table between them was an empty mug and a glass of red wine. She sat up and stretched.

"I thought we were both having tea."

Dani chuckled. "That was three hours ago, sweetie. It's wine o'clock, and although I can't have any while nursing my little man here, no reason you can't."

"Wow, three hours? I didn't mean to do that." Dani called both her and Logan "sweetie," but when she used the endearment with her husband, there was a different sound to it. More intimate, softer. It was wrong to envy their love for each other, but she did.

"I'm guessing you needed it. Haven't been sleeping too good, have you?"

"No, I'm so worried about Jake, and wish I hadn't gone looking for a father, and . . . and stuff." She'd almost said, "And if I hadn't been so pathetically needy wanting a parent who loved me, Jake would have been on the plane with his team when he was supposed to be." Everything might have gone down the way it was supposed to then. Nothing could change the fact that the blame for the screwed-up mission pointed right at her.

She picked up the glass and took a sip of the rich red wine. Dani grew up in a loving home with parents who adored her, and one where money was never a problem. Even though she knew Logan and Maria's life story, she could never understand the heartache of having a mother like Lovey Dovey, nor what it would have meant to Maria to find a father who wanted her.

"You're blaming yourself, Jake's blaming himself, and you're both wrong," Dani said. "That's going to get you both nowhere." She shifted Evan, who'd fallen asleep, into the crook of her arm and buttoned her blouse.

Maria pinched the bridge of her nose, trying to stop the tears pooling in her eyes. "If that's true, then Jake and I need each other, we need to be together so we can help each other through this. If he loved me, maybe he'd see it differently, but he doesn't and he doesn't want me anywhere near him. How can he not resent me for his not getting on that plane? Jamie said Jake thinks he doesn't deserve me, but I don't really get that. I'm just me, Maria, nothing special."

"Oh, he loves you, sweetie, believe me. You can see it in his eyes every time he looks at you."

"If that's true," and she wasn't sure she believed it, "then what's his problem?"

Dani lifted her gaze to the ceiling and shook her head. "Between you, and Logan, and now Jake, I really should've majored in psychology." She reached across the small table and stroked her fingers down Maria's cheek. "You're an amazing girl. You're beautiful, inside and out, you're soon to be a lawyer, and you're a partner in a business usually only inhabited by men. You can change a nickel into gold just by playing around in the stock market, and there's nothing a computer can hide from you. And you claim you're nothing special? Get real, Maria, and stop feeling sorry for yourself. It isn't becoming."

Maria bit back an angry retort finishing the last of her wine. As Dani's words sunk in, she realized her sister-in-law was right. She was holding her very own private pity party, and it was getting her nowhere. Nor had she ever listed all her accomplishments like Dani had just did. Not bad for a girl with her background.

Gently rocking her baby, Dani continued. "As to Jake's problem, I'd say Jamie called it right. After losing a man on his watch, Jake doesn't think he deserves to be happy, and you're his happy. Men have this pride thing going, Maria. When they screw up, they don't handle it well. Not that he screwed up, but he believes he did."

"So what do I do about it?"

"You do what Dani did with me. You get into his mind so deep, he can't get you out of it."

Maria craned her neck and peered up at her brother. "You been back there eavesdropping all this time?"

"Nah, not that much into girl talk, but my advice is to get in his face and don't take no for an answer. He'll come around." He leaned down and kissed her cheek. "Love you, brat, but I'm missing my wife and son, so I'm stealing them away."

After they left, Maria considered all that was said and decided to give Jake one more day before she descended on him. It was a hard decision to make, because she felt so strongly that he needed her and she wanted nothing more than to jump in her car and head for St. George Island.

She tried not to let it bother her that Jake had talked to Logan but not her. Her logical mind knew the men had a bond no one outside the team could understand. Sometimes one of them could just grunt and the rest would nod their heads as if a full conversation had just taken place. But it tore at her heart that Jake preferred solitude to being with her when he was hurting.

Logan had reacted the same way when Evan had been killed. Even though he hadn't made the mistakes Jake had, he still took on the burden of allowing it to happen. She had witnessed firsthand her brother's withdrawal when he returned from Afghanistan. So, if Logan had done everything right and had still had a hard time of it, what did it mean for Jake when he'd made decisions that he believed resulted in getting a team member killed?

She feared it was something he'd never get over, but she was going to take Logan's advice and refuse to take no for an answer.

Her brother better know what he was talking about.

CHAPTER TWENTY-THREE

"You in place, Elaine?"

"Eyes on the back door," Stewart whispered into his headset. "All's quiet back here. No Tangos in sight. Headed your way now."

"Good. Tennessee, ready to rock and roll?"

The silence stretched and Jake shifted, staring through his night goggles into the shadowed doorway behind him. The watery green image of Bayne's body was the only thing visible, not whatever expression might be on his face. He needed to see Tennessee's eyes, see if they held fear and panic in them. If so, he'd immediately call off the mission, and he and Elaine could come back later after making a new plan. Just as he took a step back, his headset crackled to life and he paused.

"Ah . . . yes, sir. I'm right behind you, Buchanan . . . Tiger."

Dammit, Tennessee knew better than to use their names on a mission. A moment of indecision stilled him. By the time he and Elaine made it back, it would be close to dawn and there would be people on the streets. Less risk to go in now. He'd just keep a close eye on Tennessee.

"He gonna be okay?" Elaine whispered, sidling up to Jake with his hand over the mouthpiece of his headset.

Jake shoved his mouthpiece aside. "That's the question of the day." He glanced back to see Tennessee push away from the doorway and head their way. "You thinking we should shut this down? Me and you come back later?"

A cocky grin appeared on Elaine's face. "Hell, no. We're here and it's a good plan. Let's get this thing over with so we can go home. He'll be fine."

Ignoring his misgivings, Jake nodded as he pulled his mouthpiece back into place. "Show time."

They'd brought glass cutters, but the window was unlocked, allowing them to slip inside. Holding up a fisted hand, Jake paused to get his bearings. The room on the main floor held no furniture except for a two-foot-tall table covered with remnants of what Jake assumed was that night's dinner. Dozens of pillows were scattered around, along with numerous rolled-up prayer rugs. In a far corner was a rustic kitchen with an open fire pit for cooking.

The stairs leading to the bedrooms were at the back wall. "Careful you don't trip on anything," he whispered as he led his team across the room.

A snort from Elaine sounded in his ear. "This ain't my first rodeo, Tiger."

Jake lifted his hand above his shoulder and gave Stewart the finger. Admittedly, that was a stupid thing to say to men experienced in clandestine operations, but he was on edge, too much so. He'd been on missions far more complicated than this one without a second thought, but this was the first time he had doubts about one of his teammates. He would have been happier if it had been Tennessee making the snarky comment.

Call it off, a voice whispered in his mind. Shutting down all distracting thoughts, he headed up on silent feet. At the top, he motioned for Tennessee to position himself on the last stair, the safest place for him. "Tennessee, stay here and watch our backs."

Bayne nodded and pressed himself into a crouch against the wall.

Toe to heel, Jake moved to the first door with Elaine right behind him. Easing it open, he quickly scanned the room to see three beds occupied by bearded men. He stepped back, gently pulling the door closed, then lifted three fingers, letting Stewart know how many Tangos were inside.

They moved down the hall to the second room, and he breathed a soft sigh of relief that their quarry was the sole occupant. Stupid idiots should've posted guards downstairs and at least one with Sinclair. This was going to be a piece of cake after all.

Elaine took up a position in the doorway as Jake moved to the bed and placed his hand over the kid's mouth. Chad startled when Jake shook him, his eyes darting frantically around before settling on Jake.

Jake put his mouth next to Sinclair's ear. "We're here to take you home. Don't talk, okay?" He nodded, and Jake signaled Elaine to keep an eye on the kid while he dressed. Moving to the computer he'd spied upon entering, Jake scooped up all the memory sticks in sight and shoved them into the empty pouch at his waist. Taking a thumb drive from his pocket, he pushed it into a slot in the system's unit and uploaded a virus, wiping out all the files.

Time to get the hell out of this place. The kid was dressed and standing still in the middle of the room, and Jake glanced at Elaine, who nodded, giving the all clear. Pointing to his feet while putting a finger across his lips to tell Sinclair to walk quietly, Jake moved behind the boy to follow him out. Elaine gave another nod and stepped into the hallway.

"Mother fucking bastards!"

Why the hell was Tennessee screaming? Elaine backed up and Jake pushed Sinclair against his teammate, then slid around the doorway just as gunfire erupted.

"Tennessee's down! Get the kid out of here, Elaine."

My fault. My fault. My fault. Jake struggled to find his gun but he was tied up. When had that happened? Jerking against his restraints with all his strength, he came free and fought his way up, but his feet were entangled in something and he fell on his face.

Gasping for air as he lay with his cheek pressed against the nylon floor of his tent, awareness filtered into his brain. Every damn night since he'd returned, the nightmare had come, causing him to relive the operation in minute-by-minute detail. Some nights, the dream stopped at the sound of gunfire, and other times, it continued on to the end, forcing him to stare into Tennessee's dying eyes as he held his teammate in his arms.

It didn't matter. Asleep or awake, he could see the accusation in Bayne's eyes as the life faded from them. "You should've called it off, Tiger," they said.

He rolled onto his back and kicked his feet clear of the sheet. Within an hour of returning to his condo after the funeral, the walls had closed in on him and he'd known he couldn't stay. Unsure where to go, only that wherever he ended up there could be no suffocating walls, he'd thrown a tent and a few supplies into his car and somehow found himself at the state park.

Through the open flap of his tent, a single ray of the rising sun fell on the unopened bottles of scotch. He'd resisted drinking even though on his aimless drive before ending up at the park, he'd stopped and bought three bottles, choosing scotch because he hated the stuff and figured he'd be less likely to drink them than cases of beer.

The throbbing in his leg where the bullet went through made itself known and, to hell with it, he reached for one of the bottles.

Finding it impossible to drink while flat on his back, he sat up and poured the burning liquor down his throat straight from the bottle.

"Go away," he said to Tennessee's eyes, and drank some more. The edges of his vision blurred and he held up the scotch to see almost half of it was gone. If he could get blind drunk—was there such a thing?—then he wouldn't be able to see anything, especially dying eyes. He drank some more.

The last time he'd gotten drunk, Maria had come for him. Would she come this time? Nah. "She wouldn't want a man who gets people killed," Tennessee whispered in his ear. That certainly called for another drink. This stuff wasn't so bad once you got used to it, he thought as he pushed his pillow behind him, stilling at the hard press of cold metal under his palm.

He lifted his gun and turned the barrel toward himself, staring down into the black hole. All his mistakes in judgment and what he'd lost because of them stared back at him. The loss of a teammate headed the list, Maria a close second. Then there was his self-respect and his job, the respect of the boss and the rest of the team. With no job, he'd lose his condo—and on and on it went.

Why bother living?

His finger lightly stroked the trigger as Tennessee's eyes danced in his blurred vision, delighted with this turn of events. "Jesus," he swore and threw the gun across the tent. It bounced against the soft wall and landed halfway back to him.

"Lucky the damn thing didn't go off." That he'd even carelessly thrown a loaded weapon scared him. He pulled on a pair of board shorts, then grabbed the Glock. Hurriedly dismantling it before he got stupid again, he walked down to the beach and into the Gulf. Swimming out as far as he dared, he dropped the pieces to the ocean floor in scattered bits. As drunk as he was, he figured it was only because of his SEAL training that he didn't drown.

That night, Jake strode along the edge of the water, the moon bright enough to allow him to avoid stepping on the jellyfish stranded and dried up from the day's hot sun. The sand under his feet was hard packed, and he could walk miles and miles over it—something he'd done every night in an effort to stay ahead of the nightmares chasing him.

The air was balmy and a nice breeze cooled his face. It was a perfect night for a lovers' stroll. Yet, he was alone.

By choice.

The temptation to call Maria, to ask her to come to him, had teased him since he'd pitched his tent under the stand of scrub oaks. He'd resisted, not wanting to see the pity in her eyes, possibly even disgust. At the funeral, he'd not dared to look at her, so he didn't know what was in them. If he could tell her one last thing, it would be how much it meant to him when she'd slid her hand into his at Rick's service. He wasn't sure he'd have gotten through it without her beside him. That was Maria, though, just being there as a friend, no more to it than that.

Ahead of him, a sea turtle lumbered out of the Gulf and made her way across the sand to a place she deemed perfect to lay her eggs. He stopped to witness the marvel of a mother starting new life. By tomorrow night, the Turtle Patrol would have the area taped off with signs warning against molesting the nest.

For a few magical minutes, he watched her dig a hole and then back her tail up to it. He tried to count each egg and thought she'd laid at least a hundred. Somewhere he'd read only one in a thousand made it to adulthood. If he had any luck in him, he'd wish that all these did.

But he was the wrong man to be wishing for anything—or to be asking God to answer any prayers of his. He had no right to ask for any favors, especially for the love of a woman he didn't deserve.

The mama turtle scooped sand over her nest hole with her back flippers, then plodded her way back into the water, leaving her babies alone to survive—or not. After she was long out of sight, Jake walked to the disturbed sand and dug a crater around the area with the toes of one foot to make it easy for the Turtle Patrol to find the nest.

Sometimes, life just kept tripping on, whatever one wished, but maybe he'd saved a hundred or so little turtle lives tonight. It was far from making up for the mistakes he'd made, though. Too bad a circle in the sand wouldn't bring his teammate back.

He turned and headed back to camp where he planned to test his theory that scotch could keep the nightmares at bay. But first, he had to make a phone call and accept the job offer from Grayson Services International, based in San Diego. It was about as far away as he could get from Maria without leaving the country.

Jake wasn't drunk enough to believe he was dreaming when the soft, warm body nestled alongside his. He didn't have to open his eyes to know who it was. Even blindfolded, he'd know the scent of her, the touch of her.

"Maria," he whispered.

"Hush," she said, and pressed her naked body against his.

Although he knew he should, he couldn't bring himself to say the words that would send her away. If he opened his eyes, her being there would be all too real and he'd say something to hurt her, to make her leave. He needed her too much, and even though he thought it the most selfish thing he'd ever done, he pulled her close and pretended to himself that she was only a dream.

Delicate fingers traced over his chest, across his ribs, made their way down to his ass. And then—oh, Jesus—and then a shudder passed through him when she cupped his balls, kneading them as if she wanted to imprint the feel of her fingers on them. After playing with them for a few minutes, she danced her talented fingers up his shaft, wrapped them around his erection, and rubbed the tip over her clit.

Holy God. Jake clinched his balls, his cock, and his stomach to keep from coming right then and there. He'd once been a man who took his pleasure when and where he found it, as often as he could find it.

Until Maria.

"You're holding back," she whispered, then covered his mouth with hers. "Don't." Her last word vibrated over their joined lips.

He came.

He came in her hand, couldn't have stopped it even if he'd put every ounce of his SEAL training to the effort. Surprising him, she scooted down and covered his cock with her mouth, sucking him dry.

Jesus. Oh, Jesus.

Amazingly, even drained, he was still as hard as a rock. "Maria." There were so many things he wanted to say, but only her name seemed to matter.

She slithered back up his body. "I know. I know, Jake."

"I want you so bad, need to be in you . . . I don't have any condoms."

"Then it's a good thing I do." She reached over, dragged her purse next to the air mattress, and pulled out a foil package.

Somewhere in his drunk brain he thought he should stop, make her go, but the man that needed to be inside Maria—needed her this one last time—allowed her to set the rules. Her slick, hot heat drove all thoughts of anything but her from his mind. As he slid in her and out and back in, he wondered if he might be dreaming after all. This couldn't be real, this slice of heaven not meant for him.

Those fingers he'd already admired for the things they could do to him slid down the crack of his ass and again grabbed hold of his balls. Where the hell had she learned how to do that?

Jake wrapped his arms around her back and pulled her into him, wishing the time wouldn't come when he'd have to let her go. He thrust deep into her, touched her core, and tried to draw her heat into him.

Home. Maria was home and he'd returned to her safe haven. As long as he held her close, he wouldn't see Tennessee's face as he spoke his last dying words. Pushing the thought from his mind, Jake gripped her hips, spread his fingers over her soft skin, and helped her match his rhythm. In and out—slow and easy—in and out. He never wanted it to end.

All too soon, she clinched her inner muscles around his cock. "JakeJakeJake."

The way she called out his name, strung together with no breaths in between, the way it sounded like a plea for something only he could give her, almost severed his control. Gritting his teeth, he waited until the shudders traveling through her body faded. Then he flipped her over, rose to his knees and grabbed her legs, hooking her ankles behind his back.

Because he feared words he had no right to say would flow from his mouth, he clamped his lips together and pressed his fingertips into her thighs. A need to possess every inch of her rose, bringing with it an aggression he'd never felt before with any woman. There was a beast inside him he never knew existed before her, one that craved to mark her as his, one that wanted to kill any other man who touched her.

Afraid this violence welling up inside him would cause him to hurt her, he called on all his years of discipline and training, tempering his movements, softening his touch.

She gave his ass a thump with the heel of a foot. "Stop it. I feel you holding back and I don't want you to. I want you to give me everything you're feeling."

"I'll hurt you," he ground out.

"Never. Give it to me, Jake. I need it."

He couldn't deny her, couldn't deny this new need powering up inside, ready to explode. He let go of the control he'd tried to maintain. Still on his knees, he ruthlessly thrust into her, his fingers digging into her skin hard enough to leave bruises.

"God, yes," she cried out and rose up, pressing her breasts against his chest. Her arms wrapped around his neck and she scraped her teeth across his shoulder, then clamped them down on his skin.

"Jesus, Chiquita," he gasped. The pain was exquisite. Jake cupped her bottom, supporting her and burying his face in her neck, pressed his lips to her pulse point, and inhaled her scent deep into his lungs as he sucked on her skin, satisfying his need to mark her.

"Now. Please, now." She wiggled against him, taking him deeper inside her.

"Maria," he whispered reverently, knowing it would be the last time he would say her name while joined so intimately together. He came hard and fast, his hips rocking, grinding against her pelvis as though he just might be able to disappear into her depths.

"Jake," she answered, whispering too, and tightening her hold on him.

After one last thrust, he eased them down onto the air mattress. Spent, drained to the equivalent of a wet noodle, he combed his fingers through her hair and took a few seconds to regret allowing this to happen and what he was about to say. Although it would hurt her now, she deserved better than him and someday she'd thank him for it.

It would mean never returning to K2 and the job he loved. When she met the right man and fell in love, there was no way he could bear watching her with someone else, couldn't stand seeing her have babies who weren't his. The job on the West Coast was waiting for him, and he'd leave as soon as possible.

She'd fallen asleep, the way she always did after they made love. For a few more minutes he held her in his arms, trying not to think about it being the last time he'd ever do so. He closed his eyes and inhaled her scent, imprinting it in his memory, then kissed the top of her head, his lips lingering on her silky hair.

Refusing to consider his actions, he slipped his hand under his pillow and palmed his knife. At the bottom of her neck, where she wouldn't notice it missing, he cut off a strand of her hair. Curling it around his finger, he held it up to the dim light of dawn. Staring at it, an idea occurred to him. Something he could do for her. He wasn't sure how much he needed, so he plucked a half dozen— probably more than necessary but he wanted to be certain.

So as to not wake her, he slowly stretched his hand to his duffel bag and grabbed his sunglasses case. After tucking his prize inside it, he slipped the knife back under his pillow and allowed himself a few more precious minutes of watching her sleep in his arms. It would be for the last time.

The moment had come to let her go.

Biting back words of love—the things he really wanted to tell her, had planned to say once he'd returned home—he gave her bottom a little slap and forced the hateful words out of his mouth.

"Thanks for the fuck, Maria. Time for you to go home now."

CHAPTER TWENTY-FOUR

What?

Maria struggled up from the sated sleep she'd fallen into after the most amazing hour of her life. What had he said?

"Hey," she said, lifting herself up on her elbow and peering down at him. "I didn't mean to fall asleep."

The gray dawn of morning gave enough light to see his face. Her heart sputtered at the cold in his eyes and the firm press of his lips. Lips that only a few minutes ago had explored every inch of her. How could he love her the way he just had and now look at her as if she were as repellent as a blood-sucking leech?

"I brought coffee and donuts. I thought we could watch the sun come up over the Gulf together. I don't think I've ever seen a sunrise. I'm not a morning person, but you probably already knew that. Or maybe you didn't."

She was rambling—knew it and couldn't stop. She didn't exactly know what he'd just said, but her instincts screamed loud and clear that she didn't want to hear it again. So, she kept talking.

"You probably like mornings. I brought coffee and some donuts." Now she was repeating herself. "I didn't know what you liked, so I got an assortment. I figured you've probably gone all macho . . . you know, living off the land, eating fish and who knows what. The coffee's in a thermos, so it's still hot."

She trailed off and waited for him to say something. Anything. He said nothing, not a word. Nothing but a closed-off, cold stare. What had she done wrong? After he'd loved her so fiercely—so possessively—as if he'd desperately needed her, she'd thought everything between them would be okay.

The insecurity she thought she'd put aside returned. Had she been too shameless, too much like her mother? Acted like a whore? She had so little experience with men, and didn't understand them. What she knew of them, she'd learned by spying on Lovey Dovey. It wasn't until she'd seen the loving relationship Logan and Dani had that she'd started to yearn for that kind of love for herself.

Somewhere, she'd once read men wanted their wives to behave like their mothers, to be all prim and proper little women while their mistresses fulfilled their fantasies in bed. She'd dismissed it as rubbish, but now she wasn't sure. Sex with him had been a little wild from the first, but tonight had been different and some kind of line had been crossed. She'd let go of the last of her inhibitions with him, and maybe he didn't want a whore for a girlfriend.

"I'm sorry," she said, although she wasn't sure what she was apologizing for. That she was apologizing for unknown reasons stirred resentment.

"Go home, Maria."

"Pardon?"

"You heard me. Time for you to go." His gaze shifted to the door of the tent, as if he couldn't bear to even look at her.

"Why? At least, tell me what I did wrong." Now she was begging. Her resentment level rose. She felt like she'd been used, only to be tossed away. Maybe she should take a lesson from Lovey Dovey and charge him for her time.

"Nothing. You did nothing wrong. It's just not going to work between us."

Words tumbled one on top of the other to the tip of her tongue. Begging words, pleading words, hateful words. Maria swallowed every one of them and pushed off the mattress. She'd be damned if she would beg.

"Whatever," she snapped as she snatched up her clothes. "Enjoy the coffee and Danish. They're the last thing you'll ever get from me."

He finally looked at her but with eyes that had grown even colder, if that was possible. "I do appreciate the fuck. Saves me a trip out later to . . ." he trailed off, his gaze sliding away again.

"Bastard." Naked, Maria ran to her car. Thank God no other campers were up to see the nude, crazy woman with tears streaming down her cheeks. After quickly pulling on her clothes, she started Sally and turned the Mustang for home.

By the time she reached Logan's house, her heart hurt so badly she was blubbering like an idiot. How she made it home without crashing into a tree, she didn't know. She sat in the driveway for fifteen minutes until she got her emotions under control. With only lingering hiccups, she slipped into the house. Before heading for her room, she detoured to the kitchen to get the pint of chocolate brownie ice cream she knew was in the freezer. She would eat her heartache away.

"You've been crying."

Maria yelped and turned to glare at her brother. "Dammit, Logan. I hate it when you do that."

Logan smirked. "Lurking's what I do best." His gaze fell on her neck and his demeanor turned hard. "Did he hurt you? I'll kill him if he did."

He probably would, too. She grabbed the ice cream and a spoon before sitting across from him. "Why are you looking at me like that?"

"He marked you. I warned him if he hurt you I'd make him sorry."

She resisted the urge to slap her hand over her neck. "Jake didn't do anything I didn't want him to, so put away your gun." She rolled her eyes. "I swear, why do men have to go all macho on me?"

"Maria."

"Be quiet and let me drown my sorrows in a thousand calories of fat."

Her brother proved he was a patient man by staying silent while she made her way through the container. Her preference would be to finish this pint off, then hide in her room to cry the day away. That he'd let her get away with that, she knew better than to expect.

Logan had been her protector from as far back as she could remember. He'd kept her safe from Lovey Dovey's obvious resentment of her daughter, kept her out of the hands of men who'd turned unwanted attentions on her.

She'd once asked him why their mother hated her. "Because you're prettier than her," he'd said.

It had taken her years to understand, but eventually she had and it had been just another heartbreak in what appeared to be her destiny. The only person in her twenty-four years who'd never hurt her was Logan, the brother who wouldn't let her leave the kitchen without telling him why she'd been crying.

Stuffed, she sighed and pushed the empty container away. If she told him everything Jake had said to her . . . well, she didn't want to even imagine the consequences. "He said it wouldn't work between us." She managed to tell him that much without her voice betraying just how much she hurt, but she swallowed hard before she admitted her worst fear. "I think I acted too much like Lovey Dovey. You know, like a slut." Crap. Under the table, she pinched her wrist in an effort to keep the tears away.

"Did he say that?"

The tone in his voice held a death threat. "No," she hurriedly said. "It's just what I think."

Unable to meet her brother's eyes, she pulled the container back and peered into it to see if she'd missed any bits of brownie. They'd both hated their mother, although Logan's hatred had been far stronger than hers. Until now. That she'd acted like the whore her mother was brought on a rage for the woman Maria had never felt before. Until the day Lovey Dovey died, she'd always held on to the hope that the time would come when her mother would look at her with something that resembled love.

"And you think that because?"

He was starting to piss her off, and she loved him for it because he enabled her to get a handle on her raging emotions. "There are some things in my life I'll just not discuss with you, brother of mine."

Pushing her chair back from the table, she stood and kissed his cheek. "I love you." She left before he could grill her any further. The humiliating way she'd come apart in Jake's arms wasn't open for discussion. Not to mention if she told Logan that she and Jake had had wild sex and then repeated Jake's parting words, her brother would kill him for sure. If anyone was going to kill Jake, it was going to be her.

"You're not like Lovey Dovey. Don't ever think you are."

Logan's parting call didn't reassure her any. She was her mother's daughter, and it only made sense that some of Lovey Dovey's bad blood had contaminated hers. The way she saw it, she could go all out and turn whore like her mother or join a nunnery.

———— ❧ ————

Whatever.

Christ, he really hated that word. Jake threw back the sheet and reached down to remove the condom. It was weightless, too weightless for how hard he'd come inside Maria. He held it up and watched the last few drops of semen fall onto his knee from the tear in the prophylactic.

"Shit." He threw it across the tent, watched as it splatted on the canvas where it stuck, mocking him with all he'd lost.

What if he'd gotten her pregnant?

Falling back onto the air mattress, he pressed an arm over his eyes. Was there no end to the lives he screwed up? There was nothing he could do to return Tennessee to the living, but he didn't know how to deal with the guilt and the mistakes he'd made.

If only he'd stepped onto the plane when he was supposed to. Yet, if he had it to do over, knowing Maria was in danger, he'd do the same thing again. So, where did that leave him? The only safe thing would have been to return to his old life, the one where nothing but the job mattered. There had been no risk of anyone or anything diverting his attention from a mission.

And now?

Peeking under his elbow, he stared at the condom as it slid down the tent's wall. If they'd made a baby, that changed everything. His child would have a father. After his parting words, he doubted she wanted anything to do with him anymore. Because of his crudeness toward her, he didn't blame her. If he'd realized the condom had torn, he'd have handled it differently, but at the time, he'd done it for her. He'd wanted to make her hate him, thinking it would be easier for her that way.

If she was pregnant, he'd have a truckload of groveling to do, but he deserved that and more. Should she point to the ground and order him to beg on his knees, he'd do it. For Maria, he'd do anything she asked.

The thought that they had possibly created a child settled in his heart, surprising him by how much he wanted it. And if they hadn't? Then she was free to find happiness with someone who deserved her. His hands clinched with the need to grind whoever that man was to nothing but pulp.

It would be at least a month before he knew, so the question was, what would he do with his time until then? What should he do about Maria? Leave her alone until he knew if she was pregnant, or apologize and try to make things right just in case?

What if she was, but didn't tell him? Or worse, what if he'd made her hate him enough that she couldn't bear the thought of having his kid and got rid of it? Would she do that? Somehow, he didn't believe she would have an abortion without telling him, but he should go talk to her immediately. Make sure she understood that if she was pregnant, he had a right to know.

———— ❧ ————

Jake sat up, not sure what had awakened him. That he'd fallen asleep after Maria left just went to show how damn tired he was. Of everything. He reached for a pair of shorts and slipped them on. The tent flap flew open and two hundred pounds of muscles with a badass attitude tackled him to the ground.

"You son of a bitch. I warned you."

Jake's first instinct was to fight back, and he got in a good hit to Kincaid's gut, grinning in satisfaction when an *Oomph*, rasped in the air between them. Then he dropped his arms to his sides and opened himself up to the assault. He had this coming and wouldn't fight Maria's brother.

"Damn you, you fucking shit. Fight me."

Jake looked into eyes turned black by rage and shook his head. "Not gonna."

Straddled above him, Kincaid grunted his displeasure just before he reared back his arm and swung a fisted hand right at Jake's jaw—one he saw coming a mile away and did nothing to stop.

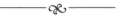

Someone was talking to him, but the fuzzy state surrounding Jake was just too comfortable for him to respond. A hard slap across his face had him rearing up and sputtering. "What the hell?"

"Get up you piece of shit."

Jake blinked his eyes in an attempt to focus. As his vision cleared, he saw the boss crouched on the end of the air mattress, his arms braced on his knees.

"Feel better?" Jake asked and swiped his hand across his face. When he saw blood on his hand, he ran a finger around his teeth to make sure they were all still there. A ray of bright sunshine fell on his eyes through the open flap of the tent and he squinted. How long had he been out?

Kincaid grunted. "Not yet, but I will when you make things right with Maria. Which you're gonna do today. When she cries, I'm not happy."

He'd made her cry? Well, of course he had. What had he expected, that he could use her, then turn nasty and mean without hurting her? That she'd understand he was doing it for her?

"I did what I thought was best for her," he said. Saying it aloud made it sound stupid. He'd have to think about that when his head cleared and he could think again.

"You're an ass. Get up. Let's go swimming."

Oh, Christ, Kincaid was going to lure him into the Gulf and drown him. Jake narrowed his eyes. "Why?"

"Cause I'm hoping a shark'll come along and eat you. C'mon, get your lazy ass up."

The thirty-minute swim did the job of clearing the cobwebs Maria's brother had planted in his head. Now, as he jogged down the beach alongside the boss, Jake began to feel like he was back in SEAL training.

Since he hadn't been devoured by a great white, maybe Kincaid planned Jake's demise by exhaustion. The man hadn't said a word since they'd walked into the water. Unfortunately, it had given Jake plenty of time to think. Could be that had been the plan all along.

What if Maria was pregnant? What if she wasn't? Did it make a difference? Either way, he loved her and, bottom line, nothing else mattered.

"Do you love her?"

Startled from his thoughts by the sudden break in silence, Jake stopped and braced his hands on his knees as he tried to catch his breath. Was the boss a mind reader now? That was one hell of a scary thought.

"Your answer better be yes, or I really will kill you. And why are you breathing so hard? Christ, you're a wuss," Kincaid said. He turned, jogging back toward the campground.

"Asshole," Jake called after him, straightening up and forcing his legs to start moving.

"Pussy."

Jake gathered the last of his energy and put on a burst of speed, tackling Kincaid around his knees. "Those're fighting words," he rasped as they wrestled in the sand. He held his own until the boss called it a draw and Jake grinned. Damn, he'd needed a good fight to knock some sense back into his head.

"You're grinning like an idiot, Tiger Toes. It better be because you love my sister and you finally realize how stupid you're acting." Playing dirty, he twisted up and dug a knee into Jake's stomach.

"Uncle," Jake gasped.

"I'll interpret that as a yes to both, so you get to live another day." Kincaid stood and offered a hand.

Jake gave the hand a wary eye before accepting help up. "I just knew you were going to do that," he muttered when he was flipped through the air, landing belly down. Levering himself up, he brushed sand off his face.

"That detective called me last night. Fortunada wants to see her."

What? "No. No way. He's put her through enough already." Kincaid obviously wasn't any happier about this than he was, so why did it sound like he was considering it?

"It's not our decision to make. She doesn't know yet, and I don't know how she'll react when she does. Hopefully, she'll tell him to go to hell."

Jake wasn't so sure. He'd seen the longing in her eyes when she'd talked about finding her father. If nothing else, she'd want to eliminate the bastard as a possibility.

"When you going to tell her?" He really should have killed the son of a bitch.

"As soon as you pack things up here and follow me home."

He kicked a broken shell, sending it tumbling ahead of them. "That was my plan before you let that little bomb drop. I need to see her. Try to explain." If that was possible. Preferably, he'd never have to talk about what happened in Egypt, but he had to tell her or she'd never understand why he'd been such as ass.

Kincaid lifted his head and watched a line of pelicans fly over. "It's not easy to live with losing a man on your watch, but it's too damn easy to blame yourself. The guilt's a bitch."

"I'll be okay." If he kept saying it, he might believe it.

CHAPTER TWENTY-FIVE

——— ∽ ———

Maria hosed the suds off Sally, glancing up when Logan's car turned into the driveway. She lifted her hand to wave, then dropped it when Jake pulled in behind him. Her first thought was to run inside and hide, but she'd never been a coward and wouldn't start now. Besides, her Mustang still had soap on it and at the moment, she was fonder of it than Jake.

Why would her brother bring him here, anyway? If they had a meeting, Logan should've gone to K2. She went to the other side of her car, away from the sidewalk, and kept her gaze on Sally—or would have if her eyes had been kind enough to obey. Against her will, they insisted on peeking at Jake.

The way her heart pounded against her chest physically hurt. "Stupid heart," she muttered. He'd go inside and be out of sight in a minute, and then maybe she could breathe again. *Don't let him see you're even aware he's here.* Right, there was still some soap on the wheel and she'd look at that. She stared so hard at the chrome her eyes almost crossed.

"Chiquita?"

His voice sounded right behind her and she spun, hose in hand.

"Well, I was in need of a bath," he said as water sprayed over him.

"Ha ha."

He deserved that and more so she kept the hose aimed at him. Water dripped down his beautiful face and if his eyes appeared sad, she didn't care. Really, she didn't. He just stood there in his wet T-shirt, board shorts, and flip-flops as if waiting for her to say something. Turning away, she twisted the nozzle to "Off" and grabbed a soft rag to dry Sally.

When he took another rag from the pile and joined her, she said not a word. They worked in silence, him at the front and her at the back. It didn't take long for it to occur to her that they'd meet in the middle eventually, and she'd be close enough to smell him, to feel his body heat. Even if he was in need of a bath, she'd probably still drool. She was so freaking pathetic.

Stupid tears burned her eyes, but she refused to let him see her cry. Dropping the rag, she walked away. With no destination in mind, she ended up at the path leading to the beach. Halfway down it, Jake called her name. She kept going.

"Maria," he said again, closer.

The sand was hot on her bare feet, but she hardly noticed. Not caring that she wore cutoffs and a T-shirt, she walked into the Gulf, leaned against the breaking waves, and when she was past them, started swimming. Maybe she'd swim to Key West, adopt some of the six-toed descendants of Hemingway's cats and screw every beach bum that crossed her path. Okay, probably not that last part. That'd be too much like Lovey Dovey.

The salt burned her eyes, a perfect excuse for the tears she couldn't hold back. The water next to her rippled and Jake swam up beside her. She changed direction and he moved with her as if they had practiced a synchronized swimming routine. No way she could outpace a SEAL, so she turned for the beach, her unwelcome shadow at her side.

Furious that he wouldn't leave her alone, she spun to face him. "You're an idiot, Jake Buchanan. You're in love with me, but you're as stubborn as a donkey and won't admit it, even to yourself. There's going to come a day when you'll want to poke your eyes out for not seeing it. And if you're really, really lucky, it won't be too late. In the meantime, there's a gallon of double chocolate fudge brownie ice cream calling my name. Who knows, I might get brain freeze and forget you even exist."

There was the barest twitch of his lips. "I freely admit that I'm a donkey, stubborn or otherwise."

"That's not what I meant, and you know it. But that works too." The hint of a smile on his face, though, gave her hope that he was ready to talk. She turned to leave, praying he would stop her.

"Chiquita, please. Don't go."

It seemed sometimes prayers were answered. At the edge of the surf, she sat and stared at the horizon as the waves pushed sand into her cutoffs, not at all surprised when Jake settled next to her. As the silence stretched between them, she had to bite her bottom lip to keep from speaking. If she opened her mouth, she'd likely make a fool of herself by begging him to love her.

"The way I treated you was unforgivable," he finally said.

There was a sad truth. A sand crab scurried to bury itself before the next wave and she kept her attention on it. If Jake wanted her to speak, he needed to say a lot more than that.

"I want . . . no, I need to tell you what happened in Egypt. I mean, I know you already know what happened, but I want you to understand . . . shit, I don't even understand half of it." He punched his heel into the sand as if he were furious with that particular spot.

"I'm listening." She'd known losing Rick was eating at him, but he'd used his grief and guilt to build a wall between them. She could have lived with that for a while, but not with the way he'd treated her and the things he had said.

If he couldn't share his heartaches with her, along with his joys, there was no future for them as a couple. That he sat with her now, willingly ready to talk, gave her hope. As he spoke, she drew a heart in the sand at her side where he couldn't see, then watched as a wave washed it away.

"Tennessee panicked. I knew he was on the edge of losing it, so I put him at the end of the hall where I thought he'd be safest. He would have been safe if one idiot bad guy hadn't needed to take a piss."

Taking a deep breath, he continued. "All Tennessee had to do was slip around the corner and we'd never have been noticed. I guess something snapped inside him. He started screaming like some kind of wild man . . . firing his gun . . . just screaming over and over. Christ, I still hear him every time I close my eyes."

"Go on," she said softly and slipped her hand into his.

He brought their joined hands up and stared at them. "Between the yelling and the gunfire, the other two Tangos woke up. No surprise they had guns. Stewart and I managed to kill them, but Bayne was also shot. I ordered Stewart to get the kid out of the house and . . . and . . ."

"And what?" She didn't even try to stop the tears running freely down her face.

"I-I held Tennessee in my arms. He begged me not to let him die, so I promised I wouldn't even though I knew . . . God, I knew I was lying to him. The last thing he said was, 'I don't blame you.' But I looked in his ey-eyes . . ." He cleared his throat. "I looked in his eyes and saw the truth. He did blame me. If he didn't, he'd have never said that. And he was right. I should have called the operation off or at least left him behind at the safe house. He was coming apart and I knew it."

"Now you're afraid to sleep because you'll see him in your dreams?" When his eyes widened as if surprised she could know this, she shrugged. "When Logan got home after Evan was killed, he would cry out in his sleep."

Jake picked up a small piece of driftwood and sent it flying over the tops of the waves. "Yeah. I'm kind of screwed up right now, but I'm trying to work my way through it."

"Oh, Jake." His eyes brimmed with tears, and she straddled his lap and held him close.

Pulling her tight against him, he pressed his lips to the top of her head. "I need you, Maria. I don't deserve you, but I can't let you go."

She leaned her head away and peered at him. "That's what all this has been all about? You pushed me away because you don't believe you deserve me?"

"I know I don't. God knows, I tried to give you up, leave you to find a better man than me."

"And I thought I was stupid," she muttered.

"Hey, now. You calling me stupid?"

"If the boots are the right size, you should put them on."

He gave a rusty-sounding little laugh. "Don't you mean if the shoe fits?"

"Whatever." Maria hid her smile, pleased she'd gotten him to laugh. She lifted her face, hoping to see a hint of light back in his eyes.

He glanced away, out over the water. "Yeah, whatever. That about sums it up."

"We all make mistakes of one kind or another. Yes, this one had the worst of consequences. Thing is, you can't undo it. That leaves you two choices. You can let it ruin your life . . . wallow in your misery because you think that's what you deserve. Or, not only can you learn from it, but you can find a way to honor Rick's life."

An idea occurred to her then, something that just might help him. She'd need to make a phone call, set everything up.

A muscle twitched in his jaw. "The *thing is,* the next time I'm about to step on a plane and find out you're in danger, I'll do exactly what I did before. I'll come for you. That makes me a danger to my team."

"Do you really believe Logan wouldn't have done the same if it had been Dani? Do you think he's a danger to the team?" She could tell he didn't want to answer. If he did, he'd prove her point. Gah, men were so stubborn.

Finally, "Okay, I concede your point. Happy?"

"Deliriously. Your mistake wasn't in not leaving when you were supposed to. You gave them their instructions, and you caught up with them in plenty of time. What you didn't do was heed your instincts where Rick was concerned. I'll bet you everything I own you'll never make that kind of mistake again."

When he didn't agree, she tried again. "Rick had to know better than even you and Logan that he wasn't ready to go on an operation, yet he kept his mouth shut about it. I suppose he was trying to prove otherwise, to the team and himself. You know, not able to admit such a thing to all you macho, 'I eat nails for breakfast' dudes. But we're responsible for ourselves first and foremost. He should never have put you in that position. That's what I think, anyway."

At his silence, she stabbed a finger against his chest. "Am I wrong, Tiger Toes?"

"Next time you poke at me be prepared for the consequences."

"Whatever," she said just before his mouth came down on hers.

Jake hadn't dared to believe she would ever let him kiss her again. Not after the way he'd treated her. When he'd walked up

Kincaid's driveway and seen her in the sexy red top that didn't quite reach the waist of her little denim shorts—when did she start wearing a belly ring?—with the fringe hanging down her long, tanned legs, he'd lost any hope of uttering words.

All the things he'd thought to say when seeing her had joined the blood flowing south to below his waist. Wet from washing her car, her perky nipples had poked through her shirt and he'd just stood there, like an idiot gone even dumber, and stared. He'd heard and dismissed Kincaid's "That's my sister you're wanting to bang" before the boss went into his house, slamming the door behind him.

So he'd tried to show Maria he loved her by helping her dry her beloved car. When she'd walked away, he'd almost left with his tail between his legs like a kicked dog. Instead, his feet decided they should follow her. Then his mouth and brain decided they should team up and speak his shame.

He was so messed up, but he was kissing her, and she was letting him, and there was someone tapping on his shoulder.

"Hey, take it somewhere else. My kids aren't old enough for a birds and bees talk, but they are old enough to be fascinated by what's going on here."

Jake glanced over his shoulder to see a boy and girl staring at him and Maria. Something to remember—Maria had the ability to make him forget his surroundings. He'd been mere seconds away from laying her down in the surf and proving to her that she belonged to him.

"Sorry," he said. "I just told her I loved her and things got a little out of hand."

The man's eyes flicked to Maria with more appreciation than Jake cared for. "Can't say I blame you. The wife, she made me come over, but seriously, man, from what I've seen, a room's in order."

"I'm so embarrassed," Maria whispered from where she had her nose buried close to his ear. "Did you just say you loved me?"

Well, he had, but it wasn't how he'd wanted to. There were supposed to be flowers, an expensive dinner, maybe a two-hundred-dollar bottle of wine, and a moonlight stroll.

He tugged her face away from his neck so she'd look at him. "You weren't meant to hear that."

"You don't love me?"

The hurt in her eyes tore at him and he almost caved. But dammit, he had something special planned. "I didn't say that." He stood and pulled her up. "I want to ask you out on a date. Saturday night. If you want to find out if I love you, you only have to say yes." This was it. She'd either agree or tell him to go to hell.

"That's four days away."

Her impatience made him smile. "I know, but I promise it'll be worth waiting for." First, there was something else she had to decide before he talked about love and marriage, not to mention the possibility of a baby.

"Doesn't sound like I have a choice." After giving him an irritated little scowl, she turned to leave.

"You have lots of choices, Chiquita," he said, catching up with her. Like the one she'd need to make in a few minutes. He took her hand and led them up the path. "Right now, we need to go talk to your brother. Although I wish otherwise, there's something you need to know."

CHAPTER TWENTY-SIX

———— ❧ ————

Maria made a quick call when Jake excused himself to go to the bathroom. Once everything was set up, she only wondered how to get him there and how to get him to agree. Then she went outside and took a seat across from Logan and Dani, Jake joining them a minute later. By the darted glances between the three of them, they knew something she didn't.

"No," she said after Logan told her Fortunada wanted to see her. Standing, she glared at them. "I can't. I won't." Three pairs of eyes watched her pace across the back deck, and the only pair that appeared pleased with her announcement was Logan's. "You two don't agree?" she asked, flicking her gaze between Dani and Jake.

"I don't want you anywhere near him," Jake said. "But can you walk away never knowing if he's your father? You don't owe him a damn thing, so if you want to tell him to go to hell, that's your choice. I just think you should take a few days to think about it."

She never wanted to see Fortunada again, yet several times a day she thought of him and wondered. What she'd really like was for him to agree to a DNA test and for it to come back negative. Then she could walk away and never think of him again. In fact, the whole idea of finding her father had lost its appeal.

She turned to Dani. "And you?"

Her sister-in-law shrugged. "What Jake said."

"If I decide to go, will you go with me?"

"Yes," Logan and Jake said in unison.

Dani rolled her eyes on a sigh and stood. "She wasn't talking to you, sweetie. Let's you and me go watch our son sleep."

"Come here," Jake said when they were alone.

He'd moved to a chaise and she crawled between his legs, resting her back against his chest. They still had some talking to do, but she no longer considered him a jerk. Which was good because she'd hate being in love with a jerk. Pushing her hair aside, he pressed his mouth to her neck.

"I've got sand in my panties." Dumb words were coming out of her mouth, but she couldn't think straight after Logan's announcement.

His lips curved in a smile against her skin. "Can I see?"

She slapped his hand away when he tried to sneak his fingers under the hem of her shorts. "Stop that. Do you think I should agree to see Fortunada?"

"Not my decision, Chiquita." He circled his arms around her waist and leaned back. "I just keep remembering your saying how you couldn't stop thinking about the names in that book. What about the one in San Diego, what was his name? Garcia something?"

"Miguel Garcia. No, I'm done with it. I tried once and look where it got me. My father could just as easily be the one who's dead. It's not like I'm a little girl anymore and need a daddy." She didn't. Her life was perfectly fine without one.

It was a pipe dream without a happy ending. The little stabs of regret would disappear soon enough, she was sure of it. It wasn't like she'd dreamed all her life she would someday find her dad.

Damn Lovey Dovey and her stupid stud book. Even gone, it seemed her mother still found ways to mock her.

"I don't want to see Fortunada. He's trying to pull my strings, and I'm not going to play his game." She fiddled with a soft ring on Jake's finger.

"Good. I was hoping that's what you'd decide."

"What's this?" she asked holding up his hand for a closer view. When he didn't answer, she craned her neck to look at him. His face had gone blank, which only increased her curiosity. She peered at his finger again and frowned. Was he wearing another woman's hair braided into a ring?

"Who's hair is this?" she asked, dreading to hear there'd been someone in his past he cared enough about to wear a part of her. Why hadn't she noticed it before?

"Yours."

His answer stole her breath. She twisted around and knelt in front of him. "Mine? I never gave you any of my hair."

Two spots of red colored his cheeks. "I . . . ah, I took some. When you came to the tent. While you were asleep."

The rat thief had stolen her hair and made a ring out of it? The smile on her face felt so lopsided she was sure she was grinning like a fool. A man didn't do something like that if he wasn't in love, did he?

She leaned closer to him. "I want to kiss you."

"Hell, yeah," he said.

Jake had a way of taking over without seeming to take over, something she loved about him. He guided her, set the pace, and made her want to prove she could keep up with him, all the while understanding he took nothing from her she didn't want to give.

Kissing him was one of her favorite things to do, and she closed her eyes, shutting out everything but the feel of his lips on hers and how his hands felt gliding over her thighs. The hard press of his erection low on her stomach sent fire racing through her bloodstream.

He rocked his hips, rubbing against her. "Maria."

"Jake."

"Jesus."

Logan's voice penetrated her haze, and she lifted her gaze to her brother. "Go away, Logan."

Jake ignored the intrusion, not taking his eyes off her. "You tell 'em, Chiquita."

His grin reminded her of a mischievous boy caught with his hand in the cookie jar. She grinned back. "Let's just ignore him and hope he goes away."

"You left your phone on the kitchen counter." Logan handed her the cell. "It rang." He gave her a disgruntled glare before striding back into the house.

As if she hadn't caught him kissing Dani more times than she could count. The call could be the one she was waiting for. "Just a sec." She punched in her code and listened.

Jake slipped his hand under her T-shirt and walked his fingers up her stomach to the laced edge of her bra. "Hang up the phone, Chiquita."

"Sure." She flipped it closed and hopped off the chaise. "Go home and take a shower. I'll pick you up in an hour."

"Because?"

"Because we have somewhere to go. See you in an hour." The way his eyes devoured her as his gaze traveled from her bare legs to her breasts made her toes curl. If he didn't stop looking at her like that, she'd melt into a messy puddle at his feet. She left before she decided they should get it on in broad daylight on the back deck of her brother's house.

———— ✺ ————

Maria pulled Sally into a parking space at the boys' club. Jake hadn't said much since getting in the car, had just mostly stared out the window as she drove. As she'd suspected, his brief show of happiness back at Logan's house had been mostly an act.

He scowled at the building. "Why are we here?"

Finally, curiosity . . . of a sort. She twisted in her seat and took one of his hands, entwining their fingers. "I need you to keep an open mind and listen. Did you know Rick volunteered here during his free time?"

The barest of interest sparked in his eyes, and he glanced out the window. "No, but what's that got to do with me?"

"I'm hoping you'll take his place." When he swiveled his head back with a look on his face that said she'd lost her mind, she rushed on before he could flat-out refuse. Please, God, let her say the right words.

"It's the best way there is to honor Rick's memory. He loved these boys and made an amazing difference in their lives. To know that you picked up where he left off . . . well, it would have meant everything to him. But it's not just that, although that's a biggie. You need to do this for yourself. I don't agree, but you hold yourself responsible for Rick's death and, for you, this would be an act of atonement." She caressed the skin between his thumb and index finger. "Who knows, you might even find you like it."

"I wouldn't have a clue what to do with a gaggle of boys."

"They mostly play sports. You've played pickup games with Logan and the guys. You were on the baseball team a few summers ago. If there's a football game on TV, you're right there, glued to the screen, so I know you can play that sport." A tiny—so slight she almost missed it—twitch of his lips said she had his attention.

"How do you know so much about me, Chiquita?"

She rolled her eyes. "You think I haven't been paying attention to you all these years? I studied on you as hard as I studied on any of my law classes. Will you consider it if for no other reason than to honor Rick's memory?"

Sadness clouded his eyes. "I'd be an ass to say no when you put it that way, wouldn't I?"

"Totally." She leaned into him and planted a kiss on his lips. Let him think he was doing this for Rick. "Come on, let's go in."

"Now?"

"Yes, now. I called, told them we were coming so they're expecting us." If she had to, she'd drag him inside, kicking and screaming. If stepping into Rick's shoes and working with the kids didn't help him, she didn't know what would. This had to work, it just had to.

Jake didn't want to walk inside that door. He turned to Maria, about to refuse, but the hope in her eyes stopped him. For her, he would agree to this one visit, but nothing would come of it. Those boys belonged to Tennessee. What right did he have to them? None.

A kid raced past the car, and Jake followed his progress until he disappeared inside the building. "Let's get this over with." He opened the door, exited the car, and strode up the sidewalk, leaving her to catch up.

Hell, he was acting like an ass. Stamping down his irritation, he stopped and waited for her. "Do you know what we're supposed to do when we get in there?" He wasn't in much of a mood to stand around watching a bunch of boys staring at him.

"The director, Larry Palmer, he's expecting us. He'll show us around, answer any of your questions."

This shouldn't take long then; he didn't have any questions. He opened the door and let Maria pass before following her inside. A man about his age came hurrying over, hand outstretched. Jake slid his gaze to the group of kids too busy picking sides to be paying any attention to him. He held out his hand to the man he assumed was Mr. Palmer.

"You must be Mr. Buchanan." He gave Jake's hand a hearty shake.

"Jake will do."

"Larry Palmer."

The fond smile he turned on Maria just added to Jake's irritation. Slipping his hands into his back pockets, Jake turned his attention to the boys and tried to ignore the friendly conversation going on between Maria and the director. The kids had finished choosing their teams and were starting their game. It didn't take long to realize a few of them were talented athletes.

The boy with the ball dribbled it to the sideline near where they were standing. "Yo, Mr. Palmer, you gonna play or ya just gonna hang there, jabber'n all day?"

"I am going to play, Rudy. I thank you for asking." Palmer enunciated clearly, making a point—Jake was certain—about Rudy's street talk. "I'm just taking a minute to recruit another player."

"Oh, no. Not me. You go on ahead. I won't take up any more of your time. Nice meeting you." This wasn't for him. He had no clue how to talk to a teen, no desire to learn. As for being some kind of role model to these kids, that was a joke. What Maria had tried to do for him, he understood, but there was no way a bunch of gangly, pimply faced boys could help him fight his demons. He was outta here.

Which was why, two hours later—after a game of pickup basketball, a tour of the facilities, and answering a dozen questions from the kids—he was surprised to find himself agreeing to return. It was the despair in Maria's eyes when he'd tried to leave that had done him in.

It was the light in the kids' eyes when they found out he was Mr. Bayne's friend that had made it impossible to say no when they'd asked if he'd come play with them again. Later, as he listened while they'd shared their memories of Tennessee, the strangest thing happened. His. Damn. Heart. Didn't hurt as much as it had before he'd followed Maria inside. These adolescents—naive in their belief he was a hero just like their friend had been—needed him.

Shit.

They'd held a ceremony for Mr. Bayne after they were told he had died. They had showed Jake the tree they'd planted in Tennessee's memory. Jake had lost it then. Embarrassed, he'd tried to leave. Again.

Rudy scrambled after him. "Mr. Buchanan, none of us has much. We come here 'cause we got no reason to stay home."

Jake stilled, not wanting to listen but unable not to. He turned and faced the kid. "And?"

"And . . . these kids," the boy shifted his gaze to take in the group huddled together, watching them. "Well, coming here keeps them off the street. If they weren't here, they would be standing on some street corner selling drugs."

The little conniver was speaking perfect English now. Amused in spite of himself, Jake raised a brow. "Your point is?"

The boy lifted his chin in a gesture of pride, one of the best Jake had ever witnessed. "My point is, *sir*, I know where I'm going. Most of them don't. Mr. Bayne was helping them, but he's gone now. What are you going to do about that?"

Buying time to answer, he said, "Satisfy my curiosity, Rudy. Exactly where are you going?"

"I'm going to be a SEAL, just like Mr. Bayne. You have a problem with that, sir?"

Jake searched for the right thing to say. This kid didn't have a clue what it took to be a SEAL, but who was he to steal a dream? "Can't say I have a problem with it. Just not sure what you want from me."

The boy stared at his shuffling feet. "Thing is, sir, I don't know how to swim. Mr. Bayne was going to teach me, but now he can't. Will you?"

Double shit. "What're you doing Saturday after next, kid?"

CHAPTER TWENTY-SEVEN

It's like deja vu all over again," Maria grumbled.

Logan smirked. "I think Yogi Berra beat you to that one, brat."

"Whatever. Where is he?"

"Who, Yogi Berra?"

She glared at her brother. "Don't be stupid, Logan." The question was getting old. Jake had disappeared, *again*, without a word. Not one word, note, text, or call. Should she be worried? When she'd dropped him off after going to the boys' club, he hadn't invited her in, claiming he needed to make some calls. Thinking he just wanted some time alone, she hadn't pushed him. Logan smirked in a way that said he knew things she didn't. Gah, she just hated that.

"I already told you, he's doing something for me."

"What? I know you wouldn't send him on an operation without telling me." She narrowed her eyes. "Would you?"

Leaning against the doorway to her office, his arms crossed over his chest, he gave her a loud, manly sigh. "No, and he wouldn't take off on one without telling you."

Well, she knew that, or was pretty sure she did. "So why all the secrecy?"

"Give it a rest, Maria. He'll be here in time for your date Saturday night. Insisted he had to be back by then."

That was encouraging, but it still didn't give her a clue where he'd gone. "Go away. I don't want to talk to you anymore."

When he laughed and turned to walk away, she threw a pen at his back. She'd settled into a routine of work during the day and helping with baby Evan and Regan at night, trying to give her brother and sister-in-law some alone time.

Work was turning out to be as satisfying as she'd hoped. One thing she'd worried about was Logan being willing to turn over the business side of the company when she came on board full-time as they'd discussed when she'd first entered law school. Turned out, he was more than happy to dump all the accounting, payroll, supply ordering, and other miscellaneous responsibilities in her lap. As she worked on setting up the accounting records to her satisfaction, she decided it was a good thing she'd minored in economics.

Their long-term plan for K2 was to branch out into international law as soon as she passed the bar, advising and consulting with companies wanting to expand their overseas business. Once she had the financial side of the business set up the way she wanted, she'd hire a manager to oversee it and then turn her attention to what she loved best—the law.

She would be the happiest girl in the world if someone would just tell her where Jake was. As for the little tug of regret she felt in her heart that she hadn't found her father after all, she did her best to ignore it. Some things just weren't meant to be.

Her stomach rumbled as she leaned back in her chair and stretched her aching shoulders. "No wonder I'm hungry," she muttered when she glanced at the clock to see it was coming up on one.

Jamie walked by her office door. He'd do. "Jamie."

He backed up and stuck his head inside. "Yeah?"

"Let's go get some lunch." Actually, a good idea. Maybe she could get some answers from him.

"I already ate."

She grabbed her purse and stood. "Then you can watch me eat."

"Would it do any good if I said I'm busy right now?"

"Nope." Ignoring his sigh, she walked past him. Men really loved sighing. Why was that? "C'mon, I'll let you drive Sally." He loved driving her souped-up Mustang, so it was a good bribe.

Over a smothered burrito, Maria grilled Jamie. "I didn't get a chance to ask Jake where he was off to before he left. Where'd he go?"

"Don't know," he said between bites of the small appetizer of nachos he'd ordered.

"I'm not buying that. Jake wouldn't just take off without telling you where he was going, considering you're second in command until he returns."

Leaning back, he stretched his arms over the back of the booth. "If the boss or Jake wanted you to know, they'd have told you." He rolled his eyes. "You can give me that pouty look all day, Maria, but it won't work."

"I really hate not knowing something, which has been happening a lot recently." She stuffed a forkful of burrito into her mouth. These ex-SEALs were tight-lipped when it came to their secrets, and even if she tortured him—right now, an appealing thought—she'd get nothing from him.

"Listen," he said and leaned toward her. "What you want to know, it's not my place to tell you, but everything will be all right, I promise."

He did know something. She pushed her empty plate to the side. "You don't have to tell me what he's doing, just where he is."

"No can do. You done? I need to get back."

"Okay, but I'm driving." She had a little detour in mind.

⸺ ❧ ⸺

When there was no answer to her knock on Jake's door, she turned to Jamie. "It was worth a try."

"If you'd asked, I coulda told you he wasn't here."

"No, you would've just said, 'I know nothing and that's the story I'm sticking to.' Am I wrong?" His answer was a shrug.

The door of the next condo opened. "Well, hey. You looking for Jake?"

"Hi, Sugar. Yeah, seen him lately?"

"A day or two ago." Her gaze slid past Maria and her eyes lit up. "Well, hello handsome. Are you a SEAL like Jake? I mean, with all those sexy muscles, you must be."

"Ex-SEAL," Jamie said, an edge to his voice.

Well, that was interesting. Maria would've thought Sugar was the kind of woman a man would trip over his feet to get to know better.

"I'm Sugar Darling. Pleased to meet you."

Her gaze was locked on Jamie and when he didn't offer his name, Maria decided to be helpful. "This is Jamie Turner. Saint, to his friends."

"Really?" Sugar eyed him from head to toe and back up. "Please tell me it's one of those opposite things. You know, they call him Saint 'cause he's anything but."

"Sorry, he really is a saint."

"Now that's just too damn bad."

Jamie snorted. "If her name's really Sugar Darling, I'll eat my combat boots."

Whoa, what was with him? Jamie was usually a role model for how a man should treat a woman. Always polite, considerate, and seemingly interested in whatever they had to say, although that didn't seem to be the case with Sugar.

Sugar grinned, her eyes sparkling with mischief. "Guess you're gonna have to eat those boots, lover boy. Name really is Sugar. Says so right on my birth certificate. Wanna see it?"

"Don't call me 'lover boy,' and no, I don't want to see your birth certificate. Let's go, Maria."

"I think he likes me," Sugar said after Jamie walked away.

Maria thought he did, too, but also that he'd let someone pull his fingernails out with pliers before he'd admit it.

The girl sighed. "Does he have a girlfriend?"

"Not at the moment." Maria groped in her purse for her cell phone, pulled it out, and clicked on contacts. "What's your number? Maybe I'll try to arrange something."

"I hope so. I'd really like to see him again."

"You owe me big time," Jamie said when she slid into the driver's seat.

"Crapola." She reached over and squeezed the muscled arm Sugar had drooled over. "Admit it, you were intrigued."

Jamie snorted. "Not even."

"Liar."

As she backed the car out of the parking space, she glanced at Jake's door. *Where are you, Jake?*

CHAPTER TWENTY-EIGHT

───── ❧ ─────

Jake tugged at his collar for what seemed like the hundredth time in the last hour as he watched Maria eat her dessert. And for the same number of times, he thanked his lucky stars he had a job where he didn't have to wear a tie. He was nervous as hell for a lot of reasons.

Planning dates wasn't his forte, and special ones? Never done it. There was so much riding on this night and how Maria would react, but that part was for later. He'd chosen an upscale Italian restaurant, a place where they could dress up, and she would like the food.

At the moment, she was licking the last of the chocolate gelato off her spoon, and if she didn't stop moaning and put that pink tongue back in her mouth, he was going to take her on top of the table, audience be damned.

He subtly readjusted himself, then tugged on his shirt collar again. The two dozen roses he'd held out when she'd answered the door had delighted her. The lasagna had disappeared from her plate, and the gelato had been devoured to sounds that had him hard and aching. A success so far, but there was still a big surprise to come and he wasn't sure what her reaction would be.

She set her spoon down. "That was delicious."

"You're delicious. And beautiful." Her almost-black hair hung down her back and over her shoulders, looking soft and glossy. The red silk dress hugged her curves, and he'd already glared at two men who'd eyed her in appreciation.

"Thank you," she said with a smile that was both sweet and sexy. "You're not so bad yourself, Tiger. You wear a suit very well."

"You don't think I'm handsome in jeans and a T-shirt?" he asked, teasing her.

"I think you're hot no matter what you're wearing . . . or not wearing."

That did it. "Check," he called when the waiter passed. If he didn't get them out of the place, he really would do something to embarrass her.

"So where were you?"

He grinned. "You're persistent, I'll give you that. What did I say the last ten times you asked?"

"That you'd tell me when it's time."

Her lips formed an adorable little pout, drawing his attention to them. "I need to kiss you."

"Will that get me a bigger tip?"

When had the waiter appeared? Maria burst into laughter, and pressed her napkin against her mouth. "Funny," he said, keeping a straight face.

"I thought so," the waiter quipped, giving Maria a wink.

Jake tsked. "Winking at my woman? There went any hope of a tip." After signing the check, and leaving a generous tip, he walked Maria out, his hand possessively at her back.

At his car, he pressed her against the door and braced his arms on either side of her head. "I really do need to kiss you." He lowered his mouth and brushed his lips over hers, a soft teasing touch. Then a little nibble at one corner of her mouth before moving to the other side. What he wanted was to thrust his tongue into her mouth and see if she tasted like wine and gelato, but he resisted, or tried to, until her lips parted.

God, yes, she did taste like dessert. He'd been gone for four days and all he'd thought about was coming home to her. And kissing her. And making love to her. And waking up in the mornings and making love to her again.

She rubbed against his erection, and he reluctantly broke the kiss. There were still things on his list he had to do before he could claim her once and for all. The evening had been planned out in his mind from the moment he'd visualized it, and as he drove to the beach, he listened to her sing along to the love songs playing on the radio. She had a surprisingly good voice, one that reminded him a little of Stevie Nicks, all throaty and sexy as hell.

That was something he hadn't known about her, or that she would know the words to every song that came on. How much more about her was there to discover? She was a gift, one he wanted to tear the wrapping from in a frenzy and, at the same time, slowly peel the layers back, building the anticipation of discovering the surprise inside.

Her fingers danced over his thigh to the beat of the music as she sang along with Foreigner. Although he hadn't realized it, he had been waiting for a girl like her all his life. Even though he'd fought it, some part of him had always known she was the one.

His skin rippled under the press of her palm on his leg. The urge to grab her hand and press it over his cock, aching for her touch, almost had him doing it. But that would be kind of crude, and he wanted tonight to be romantic and special. As if reading his mind, her fingers brushed over his erection and he jerked against the confines of his briefs.

"You're killing me, Maria." The smile she gave him was seductive and knowing. The little witch knew exactly the effect she had on him.

"I hope so."

At the beach, he pulled into a public parking space. "Take off your shoes." He removed his coat, tie, and socks, then rolled up his pant legs. Opening her door for her, he offered his hand to help her out.

"I used to run around barefoot as a kid and not even notice little stones," she said as she gingerly walked over the pavement.

"We all did, I think." He sighed in pleasure when his feet stepped onto still-warm, sugary sand. The moon was two or three days from full and cast a ribbon of yellow light across the Gulf. The waves were gentle, a rhythmic splash over the shore, and the breeze was soft against his face.

A perfect night for telling a woman he loved her.

Slipping his hand around hers, he listened to the sound of the surf as they strolled along the hard-packed, wet sand. She seemed content with the silence between them, but he wasn't fooled. The question she'd asked almost a dozen times already was on the tip of her tongue, and he could sense the tension in her body.

Both he and Kincaid had made his trip such a secret that she couldn't help but wonder what they were hiding from her. Each time she'd asked, he had said he would tell her when the time was right, and he was pretty sure she suspected he'd brought her to the beach to tell her something she wouldn't like. Whether or not she would like it remained to be seen, but he thought—hoped—she would.

"You're stalling," she said. "Are you going on another danger-ous mission? Is that what all the secrecy's about? I finally decided you went to Washington to get briefed on something so top secret that they'd cut both your tongues out if either of you talked about it. Either that, or you've been in Tallahassee dealing with some-thing to do with Fortunada, and you didn't want to upset me by telling me."

Jake grinned. Did he know his woman or what? Stopping, he turned to face her, cradling her face with his palms. "Wrong to both, Chiquita." He kissed her then, and when she went all soft against him and circled his neck with her arms, he groaned and deepened the kiss.

This was different from the other times they'd kissed. Whether it was because he wanted her to feel his love for her, he didn't know—just knew this was the woman he would always want in his arms. The only one.

Lifting his head, he stared down at her a moment. The time had come, and he wished his heart would stop trying to pound its way out of his chest. His lungs felt like bellows, and he was afraid the words would get tangled up with the air he was trying to breathe and nothing would come out of his mouth.

Do it and do it right, Buchanan. He dropped to his knees and pressed one of her hands between his. Tilting his head, he looked up at her.

"I love you, Maria Kincaid. Will you marry me?"

Amazing. He hadn't even stuttered over the words. He had a moment of panic when she didn't immediately answer. Then she fell to her knees in front of him, tears streaming down her face, and plastered herself against him.

"Yes, oh, yes, I'll marry you, Jake Buchanan." She leaned away and looked at him, and he felt as if she were peering into his soul, so intense was her gaze. "I thought I'd lost you after you came home. It hurt so bad." She thumped her heart with her fist. "Here."

When her tears turned to sobs, Jake held the woman he loved, the one who owned his heart, body, and soul, and made a promise. "I'm sorry, baby. I'll never treat you like that again. I thought . . . It doesn't matter what I thought, I was wrong."

"Yeah, you were," she said, and rubbed her face over the sleeve of his shirt.

Well, now he knew it was love because he didn't mind at all that she'd wiped her nose on his clothes. He found her mouth and tasted the salt from her tears as he kissed her. "Forgive me?" he asked when they finally came up for air.

"This time. Next time you won't be so lucky."

"There won't be a next time, I promise." A wave crashed over their legs. "You're going to ruin your dress."

"I don't care."

"That's all fine and good, but do you love me?" She'd told him before, but that seemed a hundred years ago, and he needed to hear her say the words again.

"I love you. I do. I love who you are and everything you stand for. I love your hair; your eyebrows; your beautiful eyes; the muscles that flex in your arms, making me drool; your toes; your—"

"I get the picture," he said, laughing from pure joy. "Are you sure you don't care if you ruin your dress?"

"This dress is up for anything tonight. Why?"

"This is why." He put his arms around her waist and turned her with him onto the sand. As they lay on their backs staring up at a sky lit up with millions of stars twinkling like diamonds on black velvet, he entwined his fingers with hers and brought her hand up, placing a kiss on each of her knuckles.

For so long, he'd gone along thinking he was happy with his life, with the numerous women he'd taken to his bed, refusing to acknowledge there was something missing. He'd thought he could never settle on one woman, would never be able to make that kind of commitment. Never had he been so glad to learn he'd been wrong.

If there wasn't one more thing he had to tell her, he'd cover her with his body and make love to her as the waves rolled over them. But there was, and any loving would have to wait. He lifted onto his elbow and picked up a strand of her hair, now damp from the wet sand.

"Cold?" he asked as he wound the curl around his finger.

"No, but now that you love me, I'm thinking you should tell me where you went."

Damn, if she didn't make him want to grin like a lovesick puppy. "I was wondering how long it would take you to ask again. How would you like to honeymoon in San Diego?"

"Don't tell me you were scouting out honeymoon locations."

Her feet were flat on the sand, her knees up, the bottom of the silky red dress draped around her upper thighs. Dark brown hair was spread out over the sand, and the moon hanging overhead was reflected in her eyes. She looked like a goddess come to earth, and he wanted to bury himself inside her, grounding her to this plane so she'd never leave.

"You're so beautiful, Maria. If we could arrange for food delivery, I think I could spend my life right here just looking at you."

"And I'd look right back at you, but what's this about honeymooning in San Diego? Why there?"

"You have a one-track mind, Chiquita, but to answer your question, we should honeymoon there so you can meet your father."

Maria ceased to feel the chill she'd lied to Jake about. Being cold, ruining an expensive new dress, and getting sand into various crevices meant nothing when the man she loved had asked her to marry him. This, she hadn't expected.

"What?" She sat up. "What did you just say?"

"I found your father . . . I should probably say I'm ninety-nine percent sure I did."

"That's where you've been? Why? How do you know for certain? Is it Miguel Garcia? He's the one who lives in San Diego. What did—"

He put his finger over her lips. "Easy, Chiquita. Did you know Chiquita means baby? I didn't until a few days ago. I just called you that because I liked the sound of it, but now it has meaning. Are you mad? I'd hoped—"

"Stop it, Jake. You're rambling like Professor Lumaris, and I always found him annoying. No, I'm not mad." She pressed her hand against her chest. "I swear, my heart's beating faster than a racehorse at the end of a race. Start at the beginning and tell me what possessed you to take off to San Diego and why you believe Garcia's my father."

He lowered his head and seemed to gather himself, then lifted his gaze to hers. "I don't know if it's occurred to you that you'll have to testify against Fortunada when he goes to trial."

It wasn't something they'd talked about, but for sure it was something she'd thought about, although she'd been unwilling to share with him or Logan the sick feeling it gave her. If she had, she wouldn't have put it past either one of them to find a way to make it appear her maybe-father had twisted his sheets into a rope and then hung himself. She could not—and would not—put that burden on either of them.

"Go on," she said, refusing to reveal what she'd thought.

"It was something I couldn't stop thinking about. If there was a chance you could take that witness stand and look the bastard in the eye, knowing he wasn't your father, and put him away for good, then I was determined to make that happen."

Only a few minutes ago, he'd told her he loved her. But those words hadn't come as close to proving it as what he'd taken it upon himself to do. The hope of knowing her father, that she'd decided to banish, blossomed against her will. She didn't want to be disappointed again, didn't want to resurrect an impossible dream.

"If you're wrong, I don't know—"

"I don't think I'm wrong." He traced the outline of her lips with a finger. "You have his mouth . . . and the same eyes."

"You met him?"

"Yes. I also met his daughter. She's three years younger than you, and she could be your twin, Maria."

Could it be true? She tried to speak, but no words would come. There were so many questions she should be asking, but she couldn't think of a one. If Miguel Garcia really was her father, that meant Fortunada wasn't. It was too much to hope for, and if it turned out Garcia wasn't, the disappointment would be too much to bear. She'd managed to quash the dream and now here it was, wanting to come back.

"There must be a thousand things going through your mind right now."

She nodded.

"While you work on taking it all in, I'll tell you what I know so far. He agreed to a DNA test, and it's already been sent to one of K2's contacts, marked high priority."

Didn't they need something from her to compare it to?

"You're wondering if you need to donate blood or something?"

She nodded.

His smile was sheepish. "Yeah, about that. The hair I took from you, I plucked some of it out and as long as they have the roots, that's all they need."

"And Logan knew all this? Knew where you were?" Her voice sounded shaky to her ears, but at least she was over the shock enough to talk.

"Yes, but we didn't want to get your hopes up until we were as sure as we could be and until I'd met him. You know, to make sure he was open to having a daughter. Well, another daughter, one he didn't know about."

"Is he?" She squeezed her eyes shut, afraid of the answer.

"Very much so, Chiquita. In fact, he's waiting by the phone for you to call him. If you want to. He would have come back with me if his daughter's baby wasn't due any day."

"I have a half sister," she whispered, hardly able to take it all in.

"You do. Her name's Elena, and like I said, she's the spitting image of you. It was kind of scary, actually, seeing another you."

Tears mixed with her laughter. "You better not get us mixed up."

"Never." He pulled her onto his lap so that she straddled him. "Are you happy?"

CHAPTER TWENTY-NINE

———— ❧ ————

When Maria burst into tears again while furiously nodding, Jake spread his fingers over her nape and pressed her face against his neck. These were happy tears, at least. He slid his other hand up a silky-smooth leg to her bare ass, cradling a soft but firm cheek. That she cried wasn't much of a surprise considering all he'd hit her with. That she wore no underwear definitely was.

"Chiquita," he growled into her ear. "You've been naked all night under this dress made for sinning and you didn't think it was something you should tell me?"

She giggled, and her lips trembled against his skin. "I thought it was something you'd enjoy discovering for yourself."

Couldn't argue with that. He glanced around to make sure the beach was still deserted. "A few minutes ago, you listed all the things you loved about me, but you forgot something, maybe one of the most important things." He took her hand and pressed it over his hard cock.

"I didn't forget. I was just saving the best for last." She fingered the hook on his pants, slipping it apart, then unzipped him.

His breath hitched when she took him in hand and began to stroke him. Although she was fairly new at sex play, she learned damn fast. She leaned away and watched as she toyed with him. He braced his hands behind him, half reclining, and let her have at him for a few minutes. Jesus, she excited him like no other.

"Lift up your dress and touch yourself, Maria." He brushed her hand away and wrapped his fingers around himself. She gave him an uncertain look. "Do it. Make yourself wet for me."

Fisting the skirt, she held his gaze as she tentatively slid her middle finger through her folds. "Does this turn you on?"

"Hell yes, it turns me on. Can you make yourself come?"

"If you'd close your eyes and not watch, maybe."

Was she kidding? "Not a chance." He stroked his hand up his shaft, pleased when her gaze followed his motions. Whether she realized it or not, she began to mimic him, pushing her finger inside her when his hand reached the base of his cock, then playing with her clit when he moved up to the head. It was the most erotic thing he'd ever experienced, and he imprinted this moment in his mind so he'd never forget how she looked pleasuring herself in the moonlight.

"Jake."

He heard her need and reached up, lightly pinching her clit between his finger and thumb. Her eyes closed, her body gave a great shudder, and she fell onto him. The beat of her heart thumped, thumped against his chest, and he wrapped his arms around her back and held her close.

Mine, his heart screamed, and the whole of him was in complete agreement. Always and forever, she would be his. When she quieted, he pulled his wallet out of his back pocket.

"If you're reaching for a condom, we don't need one."

He stilled. What was she saying? With everything else they'd needed to talk about, he hadn't gotten to the part about the broken condom. If she was pregnant, he would be joyously happy but if not, a little time together before any babies would be nice.

"I'm on the pill . . . never went off them after Jonathan. Even then, he always used a condom and I've not been with anyone else since. So I'm healthy, you're healthy, and we don't need that."

"Then you're not pregnant?"

"No, why would you think so?"

"No reason." He lowered his mouth and nuzzled her neck, a little surprised he was disappointed she wasn't pregnant. "How do you know I'm healthy?"

"I know everything. You had a company physical right before you left for Egypt and it came back clean."

"And you know this how?"

She gave a little snort. "Seriously? Along with accounting, payroll, and all the other stuff, I'm also in charge of human resources. I saw the report from the doctor."

It was something he'd never thought to wonder about, where those reports from the doctor went. K2 required an annual physical, so he went and then forgot about it. He stuck the wallet back into his pocket.

Smiling, she rocked against him. "Love me, Jake."

"My heart's desire," he answered and slid into her. Sweet Jesus, he never could have imagined how good it would feel without a rubbery barrier between them.

Jake squirmed on the car seat. His pants were soaked through, his ass was wet, and his skin gritty with sand. Maria hadn't fared much better. Her dress was probably ruined, but she didn't seem to care as she talked to her brother on the phone, assuring him she was happy they'd contacted Miguel Garcia.

"Oh, and I'm engaged." She glanced at him and winked. "And we're going to San Diego on our honeymoon so I can meet my father."

The closeness of the two had always been obvious. Jake was glad because without her brother, God knew what her life would be like today. The one thing he did know was that he'd have never met her and now, he couldn't imagine his life without her in it.

He turned the car onto his driveway. "Hang up, Maria. Tell him we'll come by in the morning and you can talk his ear off."

Maria told Logan she'd see him the next day, then handed Jake his phone back. She'd wanted to call her father—it still astounded her she could say that—as soon as they returned to the car, but Jake had convinced her she should wait until they got home.

She was still trying to take everything in. Jake had said he loved her, asked her to marry him, then told her he'd found her father. Her mind was so scrambled by the thrill of it all, she didn't know what to do with herself.

"I know you're dying to call your father," Jake said when they walked inside his condo . . . their condo? "Let's get you in the shower first so you're not picking at pieces of sand stuck to your legs while you're talking to him."

The next thirty minutes, she was treated like a princess as he bathed her, washed her hair, dried her, and wrapped her into a fluffy white robe that still had a tag on it, explaining his mom had given it to him one Christmas. Obviously, he'd never worn it and just as obviously—and pleasing—no other woman had.

When he leaned back and looked her over as if approving his work, she put her hands on his shoulders, lifted up on her toes, and kissed him. "I love you," she said as her lips brushed over his. He made a little growling noise and clasped her bottom with his hands, pulling her against him. Their tongues tangled for a few moments before he gave her bottom a little slap.

"Go make that call. I have plans for you the minute you hang up."

"He really wants to talk to me?"

Jake flicked a finger under her chin. "Yes, he really does. His number's on the coffee table. Go on." He gave her a little push.

"Aren't you coming with me?" She needed him beside her for moral support.

"No, I need to throw some clothes on, then check my e-mail."

He was purposely giving her privacy, but she wanted him with her. "I'll wait. Besides, I like watching you get dressed, especially the part where you remove the towel."

Hazel eyes instantly heated. "Then we'll never get around to your making that call. Go. I'll be there in a few minutes."

The number was on the coffee table where he'd said it would be, and she stared at Miguel Garcia's name. What should she call him? Could she ask him questions now, or should she wait until they met? Did he remember Lovey Dovey? Probably not. Had he ever wondered if he had another child somewhere in the world?

"I thought you'd be talking to him by now," Jake said, setting two glasses of wine and a box of tissues on the table.

"I'm scared." She was petrified to be honest. This was something she wanted too much and if she sensed Mr. Garcia—Miguel?— wasn't particularly thrilled about learning of her existence, she'd be devastated. "I don't even know what to call him."

Without a word, Jake picked up the phone and dialed, then handed it to her. "Just say, hello, this is Maria."

"Put it on speaker," she said, surprised she could talk while her heart was in her throat.

It rang twice, then a man's voice. "Is this Maria?"

No words came out of her mouth and she turned to Jake, panic welling up inside her.

He smiled and leaned toward the phone. "Miguel, this is Jake. Maria's here, but she's feeling a little shy. I think she's worried you won't like her."

Maria punched him.

"Understandable," a voice she liked very much said. "Jake said you look just like my second daughter, so how could I not like you?"

"You have another daughter? Jake only told me about Elena." Thank God, she could speak after all.

An amused chuckle sounded from the phone. "Since you're older, that would make you my first daughter, Maria."

Oh. Oh. She'd not dared to hope he would think of her that way, at least not until someday down the road after he got to know her. "Thank you," she whispered before her throat completely closed up and she really couldn't utter a word.

"I'm only sorry I didn't know about you sooner. Jake promised you'd send me some pictures of you. He also said you might come here soon and we'd get to meet. You probably have a lot of questions."

Jake handed her a tissue and she swiped at her eyes. "He asked me to marry him tonight, Mr. . . . I don't know what to call you."

"What would you like to call me?"

"I don't know." That wasn't true, she wanted to call him Dad but couldn't bring herself to tell him.

"Elena calls me Papa, but if that's too uncomfortable for you, maybe we can work up to it. How about Miguel for now?"

Papa. She liked how that sounded. "Okay. What I was going to say is, Jake asked me to marry him tonight, and we'd like to come to San Diego for our honeymoon. If that's okay with you."

"I'll look forward to it."

They chatted for a few more minutes before agreeing to talk again in a few days. When they said good-bye, she could no longer hold back her tears. He'd hinted that he'd like to attend her wedding and that someday, he'd like her to call him Papa.

She looked at Jake through her tears and shrugged. "All I've done tonight is cry."

And the man she loved wrapped his arms around her and held her while she cried because there was so much joy in her heart it couldn't be contained.

"Can you take the rest of the day off?"

Maria glanced up from the Excel spreadsheet to see Jake leaning in the doorway, looking just as hot in his K2 uniform of cargo pants and an olive-green T-shirt as he'd been in a suit and tie Saturday night. Maybe even hotter. It was hard to decide.

She might as well take the day off as she'd been pretty useless, unable to concentrate on anything for more than a few minutes. It had been such an emotional weekend and she was still riding on the high of all that had happened.

Tapping her pen on her lips, she sat back in her chair. "What's the boss going to do if I leave? Fire me?"

A grin spread across his face. "I could kidnap you. Carry you out against your will."

"You wouldn't dare." As soon as she said the words, she realized her mistake. His face went blank—warrior mode, she called it—but the little crinkles of amusement at the corners of his eyes gave him away.

"I'm on a mission and you're my objective."

"Jake, no!" she cried when he scooped her up.

"Maria, yes."

When he walked past the K2 staff with her in his arms, they clapped and cheered. Just as she started to bury her face against Jake's neck, she caught sight of Logan. When their gazes met, he mouthed three words, winked at her, and slipped back into his office.

Love you, brat.

Tears burned her eyes. Her brother had just given his approval, was letting her go. He'd been her friend, her protector, her mother, and father from the day she was born. She chided herself for being silly. It wasn't like she would never see him again, yet she understood he'd just turned her care over to Jake. Not that she couldn't take care of herself, but these K2 men liked protecting their women, considered it their duty.

"Why are you crying, Chiquita?"

"I'm not." She pressed her face harder against his skin, willing the tears to stop. It seemed like all she'd done the past three days was cry.

"Are too. My neck's wet."

He walked out of the building, stopped at his car, and set her down on the hood. Leaning back, he studied her. "Tell me."

"I'm happy."

"So they're happy tears?"

"I'm sad."

"I see." He pinched the bridge of his nose with his fingers. "No, I don't see."

Not that he could ever understand, but she tried to explain. "Logan just gave me to you. It made me happy and sad."

"He did? How did I miss that?"

"You were too busy playing caveman and abducting me. It was just something I knew by the way he winked at me when you were carrying me out."

"To say that pleases me is an understatement considering his previous threat to kill me if I came near you." Tilting his head, he studied her. "He's always been there for you, protecting you, and now he's passing the mantle so to speak."

"Yeah, I guess he is. Is it possible to feel sad and happy at the same time?"

He chuckled. "So it appears. Bet I can help with the sad part."

Maria spread her legs and tugged on the belt loops at his sides. "You think so, Tiger?" she said when he stepped against her.

"I'm pretty certain of it." Cradling her face with his hands, he lowered his head and kissed her.

God yes, he could make her forget her own name. His tongue found hers and she laughed into his mouth when their duel for dominance began, a game she loved playing with him.

He leaned back and raised an arrogant eyebrow. "Mmm? You find kissing me funny?"

That set her off, and she really didn't know why she was laughing so hard except that she was just so damn happy. His mouth went from mock insulted, to a smile, then a wide grin, and then he was laughing with her.

"Time to go," he said when they finally caught their breath.

She hopped down from the hood. "Where to?"

"Not telling you. It's a surprise."

A few minutes after making love to his future wife, Jake sprawled on the sofa, Maria between his legs, her head on his chest, neither of them paying attention to the ball game on TV. Instead, they admired the new diamond engagement ring on the finger she held up in front of them.

She turned her hand this way and that, catching the light. "It's so beautiful."

"Almost as beautiful as you." The little pink camisole he'd left on her when he'd stripped her of all her other clothes was sexy as all hell. He especially liked how it stopped just above her belly button, showing off the little silver ring. "Nice," he whispered, tugging on it.

He was going to have to do something, however, about the throw pillow she'd tried oh so covertly to cover her naked lap with. How she could still be shy after the wild makeup sex they'd just had, he couldn't comprehend.

They'd had their first fight as a newly engaged couple. Two disagreements to be precise. She'd balked at the size of the diamond he'd wanted to put on her finger. His man-self had wanted something so big that no other male could miss seeing she was taken.

Not wanting to spend money she didn't think he had, she'd picked out a ring that required a magnifying glass to see the stone. Finally, the jeweler had taken him aside and asked his budget, then had taken it from there. The result was an engagement ring closer to what he'd had in mind.

The next balk was on his part. She'd wanted them to pick out matching wedding bands. He didn't want to give up the ring he'd braided from her hair. To him, it held more meaning than any circle of metal ever could. They'd finally compromised, agreeing he would move the hair ring to his other hand when it came time to put a wedding band on his finger. Still, he felt a little sad about that.

"What're you thinking?" she asked, her voice drowsy.

He combed his fingers through her hair. "I'm trying to list all the reasons why I love you, but I'm having trouble coming up with any." That got her attention, and he swallowed a grin when her head jerked up.

"What do you mean?"

"Well, let's see. You can't cook, so that's not one. Tomorrow, you're bringing that creature you call a pet to live with us. That's a big strike against you. Can you clean house?"

She turned her head to the right, then the left, surveying the mess they'd made of the living room. "I could try."

"Hmmm." He stroked his fingers along the back of a thigh up to her ass. "You need to do better than that. A good little wife keeps her man's house neat as a pin, has his dinner on the table at precisely six, and always dresses pretty as a picture for him."

Her eyes narrowed. "Whatever."

He gave a burst of laughter. "Ah, Chiquita. I don't need a reason to love you. I just do."

"Do you mean it?"

The camisole's strap slipped down her shoulder, catching his attention. His cock took notice of the pert little nipples clearly outlined by the silk. "I mean it. Now come here."

She grinned and crawled up his body until her face was inches from his. "I love you, Tiger Toes."

Jake wrapped his arms around his whatever girl and silently vowed she'd never be sorry for loving him. All that mattered was that they were together.

At last.

Acknowledgments

There is nothing that authors love more than to know people are reading their books. Without you, dear reader, we might as well shut down our computers, throw away all the yellow sticky notes plastered all over the place, and go do something else like clean the house or start the laundry that has piled up while on deadline. So above all else, I want to thank you for reading books, whether they are mine or others. (And if you're reading this right now, then it's my book in your hands and I love you for it.) To those readers who take the extra time to leave a review, you have my heartfelt gratitude.

I am blessed to have a supporting cast of family and friends who believe in me and cheer me on. Jenny Holiday, Erika Olbricht, Nancy Goodman, and Lindsey Ross, my world would be sorely lacking without each of you in it. Thank you for everything (and y'all know what everything is). To my sister Embracing Romance authors, I'm honored to be one of you. Also, I would be remiss if I didn't thank my Golden Heart®, Lucky 13 sisters for all their support and cheerleading!

Just when you think you've written, revised, then revised some more until you have the perfect book, it goes to your editor. Ah, turns out it wasn't quite perfect after all. I have an awesome team of editors at Montlake Romance, but the one I work the closest with is Melody Guy, my developmental editor. This acknowledgment wouldn't be complete without profusely thanking Melody for showing me how to take my story to the next level. I just hope you're my forever editor. Maria, Thom, Jessica, Kelli, and Scott, I heart each one of you.

Always there to hold my hand through the process of writing my books is my agent, Courtney Miller-Callihan, of Sanford J. Greenburger Associates. Courtney, all I have to say is, you rock!

About the Author

JCP 2013

A native of Florida, Sandra Owens once managed a Harley-Davidson dealership before switching from a bike to an RV for roaming the open road (though she's also chased thrills from skydiving to upside-down stunt plane flying). In addition to *Crazy For Her*—a 2013 Golden Heart® Finalist for Romantic Suspense— her works include the Regency Romance novels *The Letter*, winner of the 2014 Golden Quill for published authors award, and *The Training of a Marquess*, winner of the 2013 Golden Claddagh Award. A member of Romance Writers of America, and potential cat owner, she lives with her husband in Asheville, North Carolina.

Connect with Sandra on Facebook at: www.facebook.com/SandraOwensAuthor

Twitter: twitter.com/SandyOwens1 (@SandyOwens1)

Website: www.sandra-owens.com/